Spinster
EVER
After

Also by

Rebecca Connolly

The Arrangements:

An Arrangement of Sorts

Married to the Marquess

Secrets of a Spinster

The Dangers of Doing Good

The Burdens of a Bachelor

A Bride Worth Taking

A Wager Worth Making

A Gerrard Family Christmas

The Spinster Chronicles:

The Merry Lives of Spinsters

The Spinster and I

Spinster and Spice

My Fair Spinster

God Rest Ye Merry Spinster

What a Spinster Wants

Spinster
EVER
After

REBECCA CONNOLLY

Phase Publishing, LLC

Seattle

Cover art by Tugboat Design
http://www.tugboatdesign.net

Phase Publishing, LLC first paperback edition
November 2020

ISBN 978-1-952103-17-9
Library of Congress Control Number 2020920155

Cataloging-in-Publication Data on file.

Acknowledgements

For Carly, who is growing into a beautiful, intelligent, independent, and creative young woman. I am so proud of you and can't wait to see the magic you work on the world. Carve your place and own your space! And keep fostering your love of books, from one dedicated bookworm to another.

And to chocolate chips. You make everything better. Everything.

Thanks to the Phase Publishing team for letting me toss in a random series about spinsters in my publishing lineup and for loving them as much as I do.

Thanks to Deborah at Tugboat Design for knowing exactly what I want before I know it, and whose artistry gave the Spinsters life. Thanks to Heather and Jen for being my sounding boards, even though I kind of held you hostage about it.

Thanks to the readers, who love these ladies and their adventures, and have made this so worthwhile.

Special thanks to the Spinsters themselves. That day in the Cheesecake Factory when you all sprang into my mind and demanded your own series was one of the greatest days in my career. Thank you for the ride. It's been very sweet.

Want to hear about future releases and upcoming events for Rebecca Connolly?

Sign up for the monthly Wit and Whimsy at:

www.rebeccaconnolly.com

Prologue
London, 1815

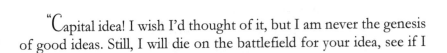

"Capital idea! I wish I'd thought of it, but I am never the genesis of good ideas. Still, I will die on the battlefield for your idea, see if I don't."

"I don't imagine we will be facing any battlefields in this…"

Charlotte Wright looked at her friend Georgiana Allen as though the girl were a simpleton, which she might actually have been. Could she really not see that, in doing this, they would be waging a war?

"What do you think a ballroom is but a battlefield?" Charlotte sputtered, reaching for the fresh cup of tea that sweet Isabella Lambert had made for her. "Do we not gird ourselves with armor before we go in?"

Izzy wrinkled up her nose as she handed Georgie her tea. "I've never considered silk or muslin to be armor myself."

Georgie snickered a laugh while Charlotte gave the best soul in the room a dark look. "No, because you are the nicest creature in any ballroom at any given time, so why would you? Everyone is good and kind and has the very best intentions. You don't need armor, Izzy, you're immortal."

"Impervious, too, apparently."

Charlotte ignored this comment and returned her attention to the more fallible of the two. "I can assure you that Society as a whole will rise up in arms against us. Spinsters not particularly caring that they are so? And speaking about it? It will upset the entire balance. I cannot wait to begin."

Georgie looked troubled for the first time. "I don't mean for us to incite a rebellion or to recruit followers…"

"We are hardly Jacobins," Charlotte retorted without shame. "Don't look so scandalized. I only mean that it will be quite a noise we create, and it will make such a difference to the other young ladies of Society."

"That is what we hope for," Izzy assured her, her relief evident. "After what poor Elizabeth Daniels suffered…"

Charlotte waved a dismissive hand, cutting her friend off. "Elizabeth was a fool, and that is a rather common predicament. We most certainly have something to say about that, do we not?" She quirked her brows, taking a long and silent sip of her tea. "Now, what does Emma have to say about this, hmm?"

Emma Asheley was Georgie's other half, in many respects, though the same could have been said for Izzy, as her cousin, and it was generally known that Emma and Georgie were approaching the actual spinsterdom shelf. Society had written them off despite the lack of an actual discriminating age. Apparently, it was behavior more than a number with regards to their marriageable state. Izzy, on the other hand, was the sweetest creature Charlotte had ever met, but it was clear she would follow in the same course as the other two. Already spinsters and not yet decrepit or faded, Society said. It was not fair, but it was the truth where those three ladies were concerned.

They were also some of Charlotte's oldest friends.

Charlotte was, of course, of a similar age with the lot of them, but there was one particular difference that kept her from the same harsh categorization.

She was an heiress.

Money erased all sorts of sins. But Charlotte did not care about the money apart from what opportunities it afforded her, and the protection it gave her. She wanted a love match. All girls did, she presumed, but she was one of the rare few who could actually insist upon it.

And insist she would.

"Emma is unsettled," Georgie admitted, wrinkling her nose a little, "but she is for it. She thinks writing some articles would be useful, but she suggests we do not put our names to them."

Charlotte raised a brow at her. "Anonymous? Interesting idea.

She fears being labeled?"

Izzy cleared her throat softly. "She believes it could spare all of us the worst of things if we would refrain from attaching ourselves to anything."

That was certainly a thought, but it would not spare everything.

"They'll know who we are," Charlotte warned. "Even if they don't know who writes which article. They'll still know it's us."

"But with enough blame to spread around," Georgie said, "pointing fingers would be impossible."

A slow smile spread across Charlotte's face, and she settled into her chair more comfortably. "Then I declare the first meeting of the Spinster Chronicles authors to be open."

"We'll never get married after this," Izzy warned with a laugh. "Everyone will say so, no matter what our charms. Or our fortunes," she added, nodding to Charlotte.

Charlotte barked a hard laugh. "Balderdash! I say I will marry, if and only if I can find a love that pales all other loves to persuade me out of what is sure to be a most glorious spinsterhood."

Chapter One
London, 1820

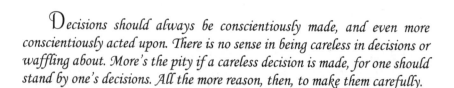

Decisions should always be conscientiously made, and even more conscientiously acted upon. There is no sense in being careless in decisions or waffling about. More's the pity if a careless decision is made, for one should stand by one's decisions. All the more reason, then, to make them carefully.

-The Spinster Chronicles, 24 November 1815

Marriage was not a foreign concept to Charlotte Wright.

She doubted it was a foreign concept to any person of the female gender in England. It would surprise a great many people to know that she did not consider it a foreign concept, however. She could hardly blame them, considering she was a spinster, and a Spinster with a capital S, as well. Which of those sins was the greater evil, no one could say, nor did they dare. Charlotte was one of the most respected and most popular heiresses in London. She did not suffer under any delusion that people felt any less about her involvement in the Spinster Chronicles than they had with her friends. She had no doubt she was reviled behind closed doors in some circles and hailed behind others.

She was not married. By definition, spinster was an entirely appropriate description and category. Most particularly because Charlotte had been given ample opportunities to marry. To date, she had received fourteen offers of marriage from ten different men, none of which had been revoked despite her refusals. Kind, respectful, but adamant refusals.

Somehow, she was less of a spinster for being wealthy and refusing proposals.

Her mother wanted her to accept a proposal. Her father wanted her to accept a proposal. Her brother wanted her to accept a proposal. She had no doubt all of Society wanted her to accept a proposal.

But Charlotte had not wanted to accept any of those proposals, and so she had not. Her family had not pressed her, and for that she was grateful. She was well aware of her good fortune in that regard, as several other ladies, including some of her friends, were very much pressured by family into marriages. Even forced into some.

It was not that she hated marriage, or despaired of it, or found great satisfaction in her life as a spinster. Not even putting a capital S on the thing could take away the sting of such a label. Yet she had not despaired of being a spinster, either. She had found the greatest friends in being so and meaning in her life beyond being a pretty fixture at Society events with a sizeable fortune behind her name.

All anybody talked about in Society was the marriage status of various members. It was the most social topic by far, and there was no use in denying it. Charlotte had known this from before her very first Season, and nothing about the conversation, or the marriage state, had particularly surprised or interested her.

No, marriage was not a foreign concept by any means. It had simply never been an avenue of interest.

Until now.

How did one go about marrying? She knew the conventional process, of course; she had dallied with the thing for ages. But she had grown so accustomed to engaging in attention from eligible men while politely refusing their offers of marriage that she wasn't entirely sure how to adjust things appropriately.

And she still clung to the one thing she had always said would be her reason for marriage: she would only marry for love. Sweeping, dizzying, fall to one's knees for the pain of it love. Nothing more and nothing less. No marriage of convenience, for nothing about marriage would be convenient for her. No marriage of comfort, for what comfort could be greater than she already knew? No marriage in name, for what in the world would be the point of that? It would be a love match or nothing at all for Charlotte Wright. It had always been that way, but now…

Well, now she felt rather abandoned.

The last five glorious years had been spent reveling in her unmarried state, embracing it publicly just as she had done privately. And she had not done so alone. The Spinster Chronicles had exceeded anybody's expectations, becoming one of the most popular news sheets around town, if one could call it a news sheet. It was really more of a Society commentary, but the fervor might as well have been newsworthy. Izzy's cousin Frank, their benevolent publisher, had never been more pleased in his life, they had been told, and there was some question of increasing the output of the page.

Considering they already published at least once a week, if not more, that could hardly be accomplished.

And then there was the matter of the Spinsters with a capital S no longer containing many spinsters of the lower-case S variety. Of the original members, only Charlotte remained unmarried. She did not mind being unmarried; she only minded that nobody else was.

Perhaps she was not so very independent after all.

Sitting here in her personal parlor, Charlotte glumly stared out of the window, the downpour outside matching all too perfectly the dismal nature of her mood. What else could she be but dismal at a time like this? Every single one of her friends had cried off on gathering today, leaving her to sit here alone with no one to talk to, no ideas on what to write for the Chronicles, and no one to confide her terrifying plan to.

Unless she brought in her brother.

Charlotte shuddered at the thought. Charles would never behave in the way that Charlotte would need him to, whatever that was, and the plan would not stay secret for longer than it took him to exit the room and find a body to talk to, be they servant, corpse, or monarch.

There were no secrets in the Wright family.

Neither was there creativity or originality, as evidenced by the names chosen for the children, but that was neither here nor there. Lottie wasn't Charlotte's favorite pet name, but it did lessen the confusion in the household, and her brother adamantly refused to be called Brutus.

That did not stop Charlotte from referring to him as such, but she was the younger sister. It was expected of her.

Either way, she would not bring the man into her confidence in this matter. She was not so desperate as that. After all, she had only come to her decision a few weeks ago, and only out of boredom with no one but Lieutenant Henshaw for company.

Their mutual wager on each other's marital status was made in good humor, but there was a thread of pressure running through it. The first to wed would win a hundred pounds from the other, as well as have their name bestowed on the other's firstborn child. It had been a silly idea born from boredom, though that did not change the stakes. Henshaw would win, there was no doubt about that. Unless one were blind as well as obtuse, it was impossible not to know precisely where his affections lay.

The only challenge he would face would be the lady herself, as she was shy, modest, and perfectly unreadable as to her emotions. Without guile and in every way ideal. There was no way for the poor man, or anyone else, to have complete confidence in her own affections or her answer.

Charlotte knew, of course, as she always knew everything. She also knew that if Hensh would be a little less insecure and a little more romantic, he would have an easy time of it. He'd be best suited to a proper and dedicated courting of the lass. There was nothing like pointed attention to bring the heart aflutter. A quiet, sweet courtship that Society barely noticed. That's what they needed. It was assuredly the best way for them to proceed.

Now that she had determined how to get Hensh married, surely her own efforts would come easily enough. But alas, matchmaking for one's self was never so simple.

Hensh would never ask Charlotte's opinion on how to proceed in romantic affairs. He knew as well as anybody that, for all her collection of would-be suitors, Charlotte had no real experience in the thing.

She had never, ever been courted.

How in the world any man truly expected Charlotte to accept his hand in marriage without proper courtship was beyond her. Some poor lads were convinced that merely spending time in her company amounted to such a thing, and they were sadly disappointed.

Now, looking back on it all, it was Charlotte who was most disappointed of all. How could she not have gained a single worthy admirer in all the years she had been out? For heaven's sake, she was an heiress! A beautiful one at that, and she had several sources to testify to the fact! How could every one of her professed lovers be lacking? What in the world had she been doing all these years?

Of course, she knew the answer.

She had been enjoying the life of a spinster, in which there was no harm or sin, but now she had nothing but the fortune and beauty she had been born with to show for it.

She had her friends, of course, but her friends were not here. Which brought her back to the situation at hand.

Charlotte groaned and turned away from the window, glowering at the empty parlor. This was how her thoughts had been of late; always going round and round until they came right back to the same problem, the same defenses, the same process of consideration. She had not gotten anywhere, and her lack of intelligence in this area was more maddening than the situation itself.

Surely there was someone who could give her some insight.

Georgie was tending her son, who had managed to come down with a cold. Prue was in her confinement. Izzy was unwell, which likely meant she, too, would have a blessed announcement shortly. Grace was taking tea with her mother, which undoubtedly could have been pushed off. Edith was in Scotland with her new husband, most assuredly reveling in bliss. And Elinor...

Charlotte shuddered, rubbing at her brow. Elinor was spending time with her husband, she had said. That was undoubtedly the worst possible excuse of them all, considering the identity of the aforementioned husband.

Idiotic girl.

She could have invited Kitty Morton, she supposed, but Kitty, bless her, was not much for company on her own.

Where was Michael when she needed him?

She pursed her lips, calculating quickly. He ought to be back in London by now; if she sent for him, it may prove fruitful. He had been gone far too long, leaving her to resort to keeping more company with Hensh. It was not good for a lady to spend much time in the company of a single man she has no intention of marrying.

Or so she had been told.

Hensh was like a brother to her, and Michael was, too. More so, even, for Michael had been her friend since they were children. And he scolded her like a brother, as if there needed to be more discipline in her life.

Not that her own brother had scolded her, for Charles was far too obtuse and obsessed with his own entertainment to care about her antics. Unless they interfered with his wishes, and then they would have a perfectly frightful row until he gave in and stormed off.

They were due for another soon.

But yes, she could send for Michael. If nothing else, she could regale him with tales of all that he missed while he was away. He wasn't as dedicated to Society as she was, but he was just as informed. His opinions on the recent actions they had taken for Edith, for example, would be most interesting to hear. He had been away for their attempts to show her off in Society, for their escape to Lord Radcliffe's country estate, and for the dramatic manner in which Edith had finally been freed from her lascivious cousin by marriage. It seemed impossible that he could have missed so much, or that he could have stayed away so long, and yet…

Settling it in her mind, Charlotte rose and moved to the door of her parlor.

"Annie! Annie, are you still out there?"

"Yes, Miss Wright!" came the distant reply. Footsteps soon echoed in the corridor.

"No, don't come to me," Charlotte called back. "Will you see that Mr. Sandford is sent for, please?"

"Yes, Miss Wright!"

"Charlotte, must you bellow?" her mother moaned from somewhere nearby in the house.

Charlotte grinned, eyeing the massive ancestral portraits hanging on the walls above her as though her mother were among them. "You bellowed too, Mama!"

"Lottie, leave Mother alone," her father's voice echoed, his amusement evident.

"Sorry, Papa!" Charlotte snorted a laugh, covering her mouth.

"You are all mad!" Charles hollered, no humor to be heard in his voice.

Rolling her eyes, Charlotte ducked back into her parlor and flopped onto a divan. There were not as many benefits to having a fine house if they all stayed in rooms close enough to hear each other. It was trouble enough to manage privacy with their ingrained level of curiosity, but to be cloistered in such proximity?

She adored London, but one must surely go to the country to find any space to breathe.

Her eyes widened. She must truly be bored beyond reason if she was wishing herself at Brancombe Park. The place was expansive, sprawling even, but it was also in the middle of Oxfordshire with nothing at all to amuse anybody for ten miles around it.

Unless one enjoyed quaint villages, busybodies, and hordes of local children that seemed to increase in number at an exponential rate. Her annual visits with the family had long given Charlotte the opinion that the village of Cambryn was in desperate need of a gamekeeper to control the number of locals. And perhaps to stock some strapping men of a certain attractiveness to work at the blacksmith's or stride out in regimentals or farm the lands.

She'd never marry one of them, but at least the drive through Cambryn would be more appealing.

It was not long after her note had been sent that Michael was announced, and Charlotte picked up a book to hide her grin and her state of utter boredom.

"What are we reading today?" Michael asked, striding into the room with his usual easy lope.

Charlotte pointedly turned a page. "Shh. This is the best part."

"I'm sure it is. And if I actually thought you were reading, I'd ask you to read it aloud so that we both might enjoy it. But since you were not actually reading, and your eyes are not actively moving across the page, I'll thank you to lower the book and tell me what I'm doing here."

Slowly, Charlotte lowered the book, scowling darkly at her oldest friend. "You are distinctly less entertaining than when you left, Michael."

Michael's clear blue eyes surveyed her without rancor, his mouth quirked in the slight smile he was never without. "I've never been known for my entertainment value."

"No surprises there." Charlotte tilted her head at him, smiling in earnest now. He had been gone several months, and it was remarkable how pleased she felt at seeing him now.

He, at least, wasn't married. There was that.

"How was the country?" Charlotte asked, softening even in her pretense of cynicism and indignation. "And your family?"

If Michael noticed anything, he kept his opinions to himself. He only smiled at her question. "Perfectly quaint, if you must know. My sisters much prefer the country to London, and I think my brother may turn out to be a great sportsman." He chuckled and shook his head. "He's already a better shot than me."

Charlotte smirked. "Good for Peter. Did your mother try to convince you to stay again?"

He nodded, still looking almost whimsical. "Of course. And took me to several events in the surrounding area, introducing me to any young woman over the age of sixteen."

"It's fortunate she is not desperate," Charlotte muttered dryly, a feeling of disgust welling up. "One might do something drastic otherwise."

Michael snorted a laugh. "Quite. But, alas, none of the young ladies were to my liking. Pleasant enough, but..." He shrugged, unconcerned by his apparent failure.

The irony between his lot and Charlotte's was not lost on her.

"How many young ladies of adequate fortune and breeding are there in Oxfordshire?" Charlotte lifted a dubious brow. "And how many of those possess fair enough looks to be really considered?"

"You'd be surprised," Michael assured her. "I was. Pleasantly."

She frowned. "Not pleasantly enough, evidently. Was she very cross that you returned to London?"

He shook his head, drumming his fingers on the arm of his chair absently. "Not at all. It is during the Season, after all, and she expects that. I promised to return to them in the autumn, so I have no doubt she will run me through my paces again."

"She'll have you married by Christmas."

"Very likely."

They shared a bemused look, knowing that it wouldn't happen, no matter what his mother said or did. Michael had no inclination to marry, had never courted anybody, and, as far as Charlotte knew, had never even considered such a thing.

Other than the one time.

But that was ages ago.

"Charlotte…" Michael said slowly, his voice both teasing and prodding.

She pursed her lips, only answering with a questioning look.

His expression was all too knowing, and his eternal patience was in full force. "What's wrong?"

Closing her eyes, Charlotte exhaled, feeling a strange tension begin to whirl in her chest. "Nothing at all."

"Try again."

Her eyes squeezed more tightly shut, willing the emotion she'd hidden to stay as such. "No."

"Charlotte."

How did he do that? How did he see through her fortress of defenses and through her deferrals into the truth of her feelings? He'd been able to do so for years, with such accuracy that she was convinced that, at times, he was the only one who could see her.

She had plenty of friends, the best of which were like sisters.

But Michael was different. He always had been.

"I'm not married," Charlotte admitted in a whisper.

The silence in the room was almost deafening.

"Are you supposed to be?" Michael asked slowly.

She glanced over at him, managing to smile at the sight of his abject confusion. "No. And yes. All of the Spinsters are now, and…" she bit her lip, shrugging, "I've been left behind."

Michael's brow furrowed, and he straightened in his chair before leaning forward. "I don't think they've done so on purpose. It's natural to bind themselves to their husbands."

"I know that." She flicked her hand in a quick gesture. "What's more, I like their husbands. I understand why they've done it, and I encouraged it. It's just… I don't know. I feel the strangest sense of loss, Michael."

"But you haven't lost anyone," he pointed out. "You still see your friends all the time, don't you?"

Charlotte nodded. "I do. And we still write the Chronicles, but everything is different now. We can no longer be the same friends as we have been. Everything has changed."

She shook her head, looking down at her fingers now resting in her lap. "They have husbands who need them, and children, in some cases. The freedom to do as we please whenever we please is gone. I am not among the first in their thoughts."

Pausing, Charlotte scoffed to herself. "Not me, you understand. Not alone, but us... We. The collective Spinsters. Of a truth, Michael, I have never minded being a spinster, especially not when I had such friends around me in the same straits. But now I find that I alone remain, and I wonder if I wasn't grossly mistaken in finding satisfaction as I was, for now I feel so terribly alone."

Her voice broke very slightly at the end, and she clenched her fingers together, as though it could somehow strengthen her.

"I'm sorry, Charlotte," Michael murmured, his voice low and soothing. "I never thought... Never considered that you'd feel like this."

She shook her head, forcing a lightness back into her tone. "Nor did I. I'm an heiress, it does not particularly matter if I marry or not. I've always known this. Ironically, if I hadn't made friends with the other girls and grown so close, I'd likely not care that they had gotten married off. Everybody does, after all."

"Not everybody," Michael insisted. He raised a dark brow at her. "You know that."

"Clearly." She rolled her eyes and huffed. "Most everybody does, and it's hardly a surprise that they do so. But it never quite occurred to me that the Spinsters would."

He grunted once. "Did it not?

"Even Elinor got a husband! *Elinor*, Michael!" She shook her head, sputtering. "If you can call that a husband."

Michael exhaled noisily, not nearly as upset about the thing as he ought to have been. "So what are you going to do, Charlotte? I'm assuming you already have some sort of plan to recover yourself."

Charlotte lifted her chin, smiling with a calm she did not feel as she prepared to speak her plan aloud. "I have."

"And?"

"I'm getting a husband."

Chapter Two

Far be it from this author to tell anyone how to behave, but it seems that one's reaction to surprising news ought to be restrained and words carefully chosen, lest offense be given. Privately, however, one may hold any number of opinions on the subject, in word and expression.

-*The Spinster Chronicles, 17 October 1816*

"Explain it to me again."

"It's simple enough."

"Yes, but I need to hear it again."

"I'm getting a husband."

Michael Sandford blinked, blinked again, then shook his head. "Right, that's not getting any clearer." He exhaled roughly, wondering if Charlotte had truly lost her mind this time.

She was getting a husband? How? Where?

"Who?" he asked, his voice dipping as something sharp lanced through his chest.

Charlotte's brow furrowed, shielding her dark eyes slightly from view. "Well, I'm not sure yet."

"You're..." The tension eased slightly, but Michael stared at his oldest friend without any actual comprehension. "Charlotte, you aren't making any sense, and normally that doesn't bother me, but this is really too much."

She sneered at him, then sobered. "What's so complicated about it? I've simply decided that it is time I marry, and I am determined to do so. I'm not set on a man, given I haven't seen many worth considering since I've made my decision, but I will make a concentrated effort from this moment on to find a husband."

Michael could only shake his head, bringing a hand to his brow. "Haven't you been absolutely avoiding that? You turned down fourteen proposals, after all."

"Fifteen."

He looked over at her in surprise. He was positive he knew every one of them, she'd kept him very well informed over the years.

Charlotte blushed slightly but met his eyes. "I still count yours."

Nothing could have prepared him for that. After all these years, they had never once discussed that day. He'd never forgotten his folly, but she had never reminded him of it.

She counted it? Why would she tell him that? Why now? Why ever?

"Serious proposals, Charlotte," he recovered with a snort he hoped would hide his shock. "Legitimate ones."

She held up her hands, smiling at some private joke. "Fair enough." But she quickly sobered and became markedly interested in the nails of her fingers. "It may not make sense to anyone else, Michael, including you, but I've made the decision to do this. Edith said something to me some time ago, and it has haunted me ever since."

"Edith did?" Michael repeated. "I find that hard to believe."

Charlotte immediately shook her head. "It wasn't cruel, that isn't in Edith's nature. It was simple candor, and I can neither forget it, nor deny it."

Michael blinked at that, the raw honesty in Charlotte's voice, without the amusement or fire so in her nature, taking him as off guard as her suggestion had. "What was it?"

A sad smile appeared on her full lips. "She told me that she did not think I had really tried all that hard to find a husband."

The words hung in the air between them, and Michael scrambled within himself for the correct response to the statement. He wanted to tell her it wasn't true, that Edith was mistaken in her well-meaning words, that he had seen Charlotte entertaining suitors and the like. But Michael had never lied to Charlotte, and he wouldn't start now.

"I can see that," he said after a moment, careful not to look at

Charlotte as he did so. "She's not wrong."

"I know."

He glanced at her then, unable to resist. "You do?"

Charlotte nodded, the dark falls of her half-bound hair concealing most of her face as she continued her study of the tip of each finger. "I have entertained suitors, it is true, and an outsider would think these my efforts, and perhaps they would seem sufficient. Despite my wit, intelligence, and influence, I could not give you half of the names of those who have admired me over the years. I barely remember their faces."

"You never were very good at that," Michael admitted with a rueful chuckle. "That was one of the reasons I lingered at the edges of your circle."

"Yes, you were vastly helpful there." She lifted her chin, and Michael caught a glimpse of a whimsical smile. "Entertained would be the best word to describe what I have been and what I have done with my time. I have been entertained, and I have entertained. I'm an heiress, so what need had I to give effort?"

There were no words for any of this in Michael's view. Charlotte had clarity of vision where her life and behavior were concerned, and always had, but this? This was an unburdening of the deepest secrets, and the overturning of every stone within the fortress of her soul.

And for what? Out of loneliness? Envy? Regret? None of those things would have suited Charlotte Wright, and he knew it well. It had to be something else. Something stronger than them altogether.

"Why didn't I even look?" Charlotte whispered harshly, and he thought for a moment there might have been tears in her voice, though he'd never be sure. "What if he was there all along and I wasn't seeing him?"

The irony in that statement would have made him laugh had it not chilled him.

"Charlotte..." He paused, wetting his lips, willing the tingling in his fingers to subside. "Are you afraid?"

Slowly, she looked over at him, her eyes wide. "Don't tell," she rasped, looking and sounding very young.

He rose and was to her in an instant, crouching before her and taking her hands. "Of course not!" He gave her what he hoped was a consoling smile. "Who would I have to tell, anyway?"

Charlotte giggled softly. "True. I am your only friend."

That wasn't exactly accurate, but it might as well have been. He'd devoted enough of himself to her to make it so.

"I thought," he began, returning to the subject with as much tenderness and tact as he could, "that you were looking for love. A great, sweeping love that sent you to your knees."

"I am," she replied with a firm nod.

He shrugged as if that should have been her answer.

She frowned at his gesture. "I'm afraid that I missed it, Michael."

"I don't think that sort of thing is easily missed," he retorted, scrunching up his face for effect. "You'd have to be really thick to miss the lightning bolts and singing angels and feelings of imminent death."

A sharp thump across his chest nearly set him off balance, but he recovered swiftly enough, pushing to his feet and moving back a safe distance.

Charlotte skewered him with a dark look. "You are hopelessly unromantic."

"I've heard." He smiled blandly and folded his arms.

She watched him for a long moment, then slumped on a resigned sigh. "I wanted love to find me, Michael. I don't need marriage, not in the way others do, but that doesn't mean I wanted to be alone with my money."

It sounded so cold when she put it that way, but the reality was that she'd summed it up neatly there. Unpleasantly, but neatly.

"It wasn't supposed to be like this," she went on. "Love was supposed to happen to me, not be hunted for. Did I miss it?"

"No," he said before he could stop himself. "No, you didn't miss it."

She didn't reply, but her attention was on him still. As though he hadn't finished. As though he had more of an answer or explanation.

He could have. He had answers aplenty, and he'd waited years to give them. He could end all of this right now, end it for them both. He wasn't a man of speeches, but he'd do his damnedest to be one now.

It was time. It had to be.

He stared back at her, willing the words to come.

"It might be that you're meant to be the huntress, Charlotte, rather than the hunted."

Michael blinked at the words, wondering what idiot was saying them at a moment like this. And why they were said in his exact way of speaking and tone of voice.

Oh. His voice.

Idiot.

Charlotte stared at him as though she were thinking the very same thing, though Michael knew full well she was not. She already knew he was an idiot; there was no need to hash it out again. This was not directed at him at all. It was a realization too late and feeling ridiculous for that fact.

"Bloody hell, Michael," Charlotte hissed, her gaze turning to the window as she shook her head. "Why didn't you say this before?"

"I don't tend to consider the reasons for your lack of marital state on the regular, you know," he told her with as much indignation as he could muster. "You never said much bemoaning the subject, so why would it even occur to me?"

She didn't seem to hear him, her brow furrowing as she considered his words. "A huntress. You think so?"

She was going to torture him again and again if he didn't somehow put an end to this conversation. Telling her to look for love? Knowing she would never look where he wanted her to?

Michael watched her for a long moment, making the decision he told himself he never would, and soaking in the sight of her as though he would never see her again in his life.

"You said so yourself," he answered, surprised his voice was as clear as it was. "You're an heiress. Marriage would actually hinder your independence, factually speaking, so if it is something you want in spite of the logic there, you are going to have to do the work to find it."

"A marriage of love is what I want," she replied, still not looking at him, "not a marriage for the sake of it."

The words lashed across his heart, and he inhaled sharply, but silently. "Then find it, Charlotte. If you want it, go and get it."

As though he had spoken to a soldier before battle, Charlotte rose to her feet, her brow clear and her expression set. "Yes. I intend to." She nodded and began to stride from the room, pausing as she passed him to look in his eyes and smile with all the warmth she had ever done. "What would I do without you, Michael?"

With a quick stretching of her smile, she continued out of the room, her fingers briefly grazing his hand as she did so.

His skin burned fiercely at the contact, and the feel of it was all the more poignant for the silence in the now empty room.

"We're about to find out," he murmured in reply, though there was no one around to hear it.

He ran a hand over his face, exhaling heavily, and sank into the closest chair with the weight of the last few minutes pressing him further into it.

He wouldn't stand by and watch while Charlotte actually conceded herself to someone else, no matter how worthy the man might be. He wanted her happiness, it was true, but at what cost to himself would that happiness come? Years of lingering at the edges of her circle, practically the one who tended her flock and shooed the strays away from her, and for what? He hadn't found amusement in it but for her own wit, and all he could say he had done was furthered her own interests of absolutely nothing useful.

He'd never encouraged her behavior, but it wasn't as though he had done anything about it. She had never behaved badly, though she was a novelty when compared with other young ladies in Society. He'd spent years ignoring his own life for the sake of remaining in hers.

It was time to end that. End this. If she would begin searching for love in earnest, then so would he. He would not hover at the edges of her courtship as a spectator.

He could not.

"Sandford, why is my sister whistling and skipping down the corridor?"

Of course she was.

Michael groaned, not bothering to remove his hand from its position, pressing as it was against his brow. "You would think after all these years, you would stop asking any questions at all about your sister's behavior."

"Skipping, Sandford. And whistling." A rustle of clothing was heard, and the tread of footsteps approached. "Either she has just bested you in something, or she has an idea. Kindly relieve my curiosity."

Michael's hand dropped, and he stared up into the speculative face of Charlotte's brother, so like her in coloring, but with the hard angles in features of their father. While Charlotte's glower was powerful and impressive, her brother had the firm countenance that demanded submission without a word. Where Charles had inherited the height of his maternal relatives, Charlotte had to fight for every inch of her stature.

Repeated exposure to both Wright children over the years had given Michael some insight into each of them, and while he wouldn't have said Charles was among his more intimate friends, he shared a near-familial bond that didn't exactly set him outside of that circle.

"Charlotte has decided she is going to marry," Michael said flatly. "Husband to be determined."

Charles blinked at the announcement, folding his arms after a moment. "I'd say it's about time, though I'm more inclined to say I'll believe it when I see it. What the devil does she have in mind?"

Michael shrugged and began drumming his fingers on the armrest. "I believe she is going on a hunt for love."

Charles snorted. "Where in the world did she get that idiotic notion?"

A wince flashed across Michael's features. "I may have given it to her."

The long moment of silence might as well have been a gong against his head in punishment.

"I know," Michael said before he could be scolded, waving his hand. "I know."

"You're a bloody idiot, Sandford," Charles told him as if it were helpful. "I've thought so for years, but this trumps everything else. How many times have I told you to leave this madness? You had to know it was pointless once she refused you; she never goes back on her word. Yet you stayed. Never understood why, it had to be torture if you had feelings for her. But this? From a lapdog to a romantic advisor, what the hell have you done to your manhood?"

He had endured ribbing and teasing from Charles over the years, and usually brushed it off with a laugh, but this…

He was wondering the same thing himself. How had he let himself waste so much time in his life on the smallest hope?

Not that time spent in Charlotte's company had been a waste, for her friendship had been the most important in his life. From the moment he'd met her, swinging as she had been on the low-hanging branches of a willow over a flooded pond, he'd been drawn to her side like no connection he'd ever known. There was no friend like Charlotte Wright anywhere in the world. He'd loved her within three years and had never stopped.

And that was a waste.

"I don't know," Michael admitted for the first time in his life. "But enough is enough. I'm finished."

Charles became almost startled in a single blink. "You agree?"

"About my being an idiot? Absolutely." He nodded for emphasis. "Very much so."

There was no response as Charles processed that. "You have never agreed with me. You usually change topics or tell me to shove off. What's changed?"

Michael snorted a soft laugh, anything actually resembling humor nowhere in sight. "Opening my eyes. It's over." He pushed to his feet and met the derisive look of his companion. "I've nailed my own coffin shut, and I have to find a way out."

Charles winced with some sympathy. "To be fair, I tried to tell you that…"

"I wouldn't have believed you before," Michael admitted, smiling ruefully. "I know better now. She'll never see me that way, I've simply been denying it naïvely. But I'm not going to be one of her Spinster friends in this. They can speculate and laugh about suitors all they like, but I will not hear a word of it."

"Does my sister know?" Charles asked, his brow lowering slowly.

Michael shook his head. "Of course not, don't get so protective." He gave him a scolding look, then went on. "I don't intend to abandon her entirely from this moment. I will gradually ease away and find a natural reason for doing so. Trust me, she'll hardly notice."

For a moment, he thought Charles would express further concern, disdain, or some other brotherly emotion that belied his affection for and bond with his sister.

But Charles only nodded and uttered a low laugh before clapping Michael on the shoulder. "Well, it's about time you walked away from her and lived your own life. Good man. Billiards?"

Michael shook his head, feeling no satisfaction in the praise. "Thank you, no. I've got business to attend to. I was on my way there when Charlotte commandeered me."

Charles chuckled ruefully as he gestured for them both to leave the room. "No doubt it will be a pleasant change to have that end for you, eh?"

Somehow Michael's silence was acknowledgement enough, though he didn't agree. Pleasant it would not be, but a necessary change it was. It would be vital to his survival.

And his sanity.

Chapter Three

———— ⟨∞ ∞⟩ ————

One can always count on one's true friends to be honest, supportive, and loyal, even when one's idea is an unconventional one.

-The Spinster Chronicles, 1 May 1818

"Thank you for coming here today. I know you're all wondering why I've asked you here."

"Not really, no."

Charlotte glared at Elinor Sterling, who was smiling back at her with the sort of impudence that was maddening in its inconvenience. "That was not a question that required an answer, Elinor."

Elinor raised a pale brow. "It wasn't a question at all, and I didn't answer. Only commented."

"She's going to throttle you," Georgie informed her as she calmly sipped her tea.

"Eagerly," Charlotte added with a menacing hiss.

Elinor only shrugged. "Well, it was a beautiful life while I had it. Kindly tell Hugh what happened to me, and that I adored him to my last breath."

Grace, Lady Ingram, rolled her eyes dramatically as she sat on the sofa in a flurry of elegant skirts. "Oh, please, Elinor. You've been married nearly six months; it is high time the glow of the thing faded."

"And yet…" Elinor smiled to herself as she brought her tea to her lips.

Charlotte shook her head and looked around the room. "I don't understand at all how she can be so desperately in love with a villain while the rest of you simply tolerate your grand husbands."

"Tolerate?" Izzy Morton echoed with a laugh.

"Villain?" Elinor replied with her usual sharpness.

"Yes, Tony is rather grand," Georgie allowed with a bemused smile. "I shall endeavor to amend my ways to be more glowing about him, as Grace would say."

The tension in the room broke as laughter sounded from them all, even Charlotte.

Tony was the first of the truly admirable Spinster husbands, and he'd seemed to set the precedent for the rest of them. They had all met and matched the quality with each subsequent husband, growing their influence and enviable states markedly.

Apart from Hugh Sterling.

Charlotte glanced at Elinor, who was sitting with her eyes lowered to her lap.

For the first time in the six months of her marriage, Charlotte felt something crack in her heart as she saw the effect her opinions had on Elinor. It was easy enough to combat her roaring indignation about the thing, given her own temperament bordered on the fiery. She had yet to see Elinor anything but angry over her opinions. It hadn't exactly occurred to Charlotte that such things might hurt her friend.

Elinor had hated Hugh as much as Charlotte had before all this. She'd been even more vocal about it, and more violent in her threats. It had been almost a betrayal in Charlotte's eyes when she had suddenly announced her engagement to the man.

Surely it had been manipulation and delusion, Charlotte had been convinced of it. Surely Elinor had been naïve and accepted lies under the influence of charm and attention. Surely she had fallen victim to the same ploys they had spent ages warning other young ladies of.

No one could love a villain like Hugh Sterling, and no villain of such a caliber could repent enough to truly be redeemed.

And yet...

As though she could hear Charlotte's thoughts, Elinor looked up, her attention going directly to Charlotte.

Hurt shone through her pale eyes, and the glimpse into such a raw, vulnerable feeling in someone as bold as Elinor was disconcerting. Charlotte couldn't leave well enough alone. Not this time.

"Elinor…" Charlotte said softly, smiling with some hesitation.

"He's not a villain," Elinor murmured, her gaze direct, even if her tone was not. "I of all of us should know. And yes, I do love him." Her eyes turned almost misty, but there was no quiver in her voice or her chin. "I know there have been comments as to why he has not come around or tried to become part of our group. He's not avoiding you because of shame or superiority. He just doesn't want anyone to feel uncomfortable about being seen with him."

Charlotte stared at her in silence, her mind struggling to spin on the thought.

Georgie sighed softly. "I was wondering why he wouldn't come to our dinner party last week."

Elinor nodded, though continued to keep her focus on Charlotte. "He's finally accepted that his family supports him and wants him among their number, but if there are others, he will not venture out. He doesn't want it to affect my friends and my reputation, and I've told him I don't care, but he is determined."

"Poor man," Izzy remarked in an almost choked voice. "I have a reserved husband, as you know, and he often chooses to politely decline invitations, but not for anything like this."

"Why do you think Hugh did nothing for Edith?" Elinor asked the room in general. "He was terribly concerned for her, wanted to know everything about the situation and privately advised Tony and Francis, but he did not think it would help Edith for him to be seen as involved. Not when Society still sees him as the man he was rather than the man he has become." She lifted her chin slightly, her eyes shining somehow brighter for the tension in her jaw. "And especially not when my friends do."

Charlotte fought for a swallow, a strange lump having formed in her throat.

"I didn't know that," Georgie murmured to no one in particular. "Why did Tony not tell me?"

Elinor managed a small, bitter smile. "Hugh wasn't sure where your opinions lay, so he begged Tony to keep it secret."

Georgie shook her head, returning the smile. "I wouldn't have cared, dear. Please, please tell him so. Come to supper tomorrow. Tonight. Any time, we'll be delighted."

"Steady on, Georgie," Grace told her with wide eyes, smiling mischievously. "She didn't say Hugh was desperate, either. The poor man doesn't want to be fawned over in so obvious a fashion. He might suspect you're making up for something."

"Aren't we?" Georgie shot back without concern.

Izzy made a face and looked at Elinor with sympathy. "I'm afraid you will have several invitations arriving this evening. I'll wait and send mine next week, if you don't mind."

Elinor didn't seem to hear, still watching Charlotte.

Charlotte wished she wouldn't. Being so neatly called out without having her name said was unbearable; she was guilty of prejudice where Hugh was concerned, just as Society was. She could not offer a defense, as no real accusation had been made of her. And she had not laid eyes on Hugh Sterling in a full year now, let alone conversed with him, so she had no proof that he still was the man she had always known him to be.

Ignorant assumptions, and arrogant in those ignorant assumptions. It was no wonder she was a spinster. What man of quality would want a wife like that?

Why would her friends wish to continue to be such? She hadn't meant to hurt anyone, would never wish to, but hurt had been felt, and she had done nothing to stop it.

Finally managing a swallow, Charlotte then cleared her throat. "If you and your husband would come to dine with my family on Thursday, we would be much obliged."

Elinor's brows rose slowly. "What?"

Charlotte nodded, the idea taking on more merit and a greater hold the longer it lingered in her mind. "Yes. Please, if you like." She continued to nod, the speed of her thought picking up. "Hugh would likely detest having to endure supper without any perceived allies. I must be the devil in petticoats." She immediately turned to Georgie, smiling. "Would you and Tony come? I'll invite Francis, Janet, and Alice, too. What about Hensh? Do you think Hensh would make Hugh comfortable?"

"Can I interrupt this sudden excursion into invitation

27

generosity?" Grace interjected, laughing once. "When did we start calling him Hensh? I missed that announcement, and it sounds like the noise one makes on a sneeze."

Snickers rippled around the room, and Charlotte, feeling slightly lighter at seeing Elinor join in, scowled playfully at Grace. "It is a sign of affection, Grace, which I think Lieutenant Henshaw deserves, and if I could shorten Aubrey's name without seeming unfashionably intimate, I daresay I would."

Grace made a face and put a hand to her cheek. "Please don't say 'unfashionably intimate' when talking about my husband ever again."

The snickers turned to full blown laughter, and Charlotte was relieved to be able to join in. She hadn't felt much like laughing of late, though laughter tended to be a habitual reaction even when there was no amusement to be found. She could laugh about anything and everything, had made a practice of doing so for the benefit of those around her for years, but to actually feel the desire to laugh... That hadn't been with her in some time.

"Shortening names can be very sweet," Izzy reminded them when the laughter faded. "Molly Hastings, Edith's lovely new ward, calls her uncle, Lord Radcliffe, 'Gray' rather than his given name of Graham, which I find charming."

Charlotte nodded, then cocked her head. "Is it odd, though, that he is not Uncle Radcliffe? Or Uncle Graham, at least. I wouldn't dream of addressing any of my aunts or uncle without their formal family connection. It's so peculiar."

"But your Uncle Herbert did not bring you up from the time you could barely speak a full sentence," Grace reminded her, smiling fondly. "Radcliffe is raising that sweet girl, and no doubt, he will be the only father she remembers. She could hardly call him 'Papa', so why not a fond name of equal affection?"

"I'm not judging them, Grace," Charlotte insisted with a wave of her hands. "Heavens, you forget that I called my grandfather Pumpernickel before he died, much to the chagrin of my parents. And Uncle Herbert, come to think."

Grace simpered, clasping her hands before her heart. "Did you? That's precious."

Charlotte only snorted before returning her attention to Elinor. "I do mean the invitation, Elinor. And everything it says that we aren't saying in so many words."

Elinor smiled in response, her cheeks coloring as a testament that she was more pleased than she would admit.

And just like that, the friendships were as pristine as ever.

Fortunate, as Charlotte had a very great need for them just now.

She cleared her throat again, sitting up and barely avoiding the temptation to bite her lip. "Elinor, do you still have your records of the eligible bachelors in Society?"

Elinor lowered her teacup, swallowing as her brow furrowed. "Of course I do. Your column on London's best bachelors was our most popular issue, so I've continued on for when you start to run it annually. Perhaps at the start of the Season, say?"

"What a brilliant thought!" Izzy exclaimed, clapping her hands in delight. "It would be such a lovely tradition of sorts, don't you think, Charlotte?"

Charlotte smiled with a thrill of satisfaction, not for the idea of an annual review of preferable bachelors, though the idea had more than enough merit to dwell upon later, but for the availability of the resources.

Most capital.

"I will need the collection of them as soon as possible," Charlotte said without directly answering Izzy.

"Whatever for?" asked Elinor with a laugh. "The Season is practically over now, and it would undoubtedly do nothing for anyone."

Charlotte lifted a brow, her smile curving further still. "It would do a great deal for me, seeing as I'm obtaining a husband."

The room stilled with the power of a thunderclap and the somberness of a funeral. Every eye was fixed upon her, and every eye was round in shock.

It was perfectly comical, and Charlotte could have burst for laughing.

"I beg your pardon," Georgie eventually said with a wry, almost stiff giggle. "I thought you said you were obtaining a husband."

"I thought she said that, as well," Grace replied without any hint of laughter, her lips barely moving. "Extraordinary sensation."

Elinor gaped freely at Charlotte. "That's because she *did* say it. Charlotte Wright, are you ill?"

"Not at all." Charlotte folded her hands calmly in her lap. "Why shouldn't I? The rest of you have husbands, and it is no longer fashionable to be a spinster and write for the Spinster Chronicles. One does not wish to stand out so conspicuously."

"That's not a good enough reason to marry," Georgie snapped, any hint of amusement gone. "Who in the world have you decided to wed?"

This wasn't going according to plan at all, not that she'd specifically ironed anything out into specifics. That was what she had hoped they would do here, but clearly, she'd have to explain herself first. Provided she could explain herself without baring her soul. They might persuade her out of it if she did that.

"No one in particular," she replied with a shrug. "Hence my need for Elinor's information. I need to know who my options are, and which man would be best to pursue."

Her friends looked around at each other in disbelief, then looked at her again.

"I already hate this plan," Grace muttered. She sat back roughly on the sofa, her posture slouched and entirely inappropriate for a lady of her station. "The phrase 'obtaining a husband' is not intended to be an orderly process of selection as though we are fetching something from the grocer."

"Why not?" Charlotte shot back. "I'm an agreeable person, and my charms are not inconsiderable. I'm willing to fall in love now, so why should it not be a straightforward process?"

Georgie put a hand over her face and exhaled with a groan, which seemed entirely unnecessary. "It's as though you learned nothing from what the rest of us went through. Charlotte, you cannot plan such things!"

"I disagree." Charlotte shook her head emphatically. "I am determined to marry, and to marry for love, and when I want something, I get it."

None of them had a rebuttal for her there, likely because they knew it was true. Charlotte was many things, but she had never in her life lacked determination, will, or commitment. Fate itself would make way for Charlotte Wright when she was on her mettle.

With an almost smug lift of her shoulders, Charlotte grinned around at her friends. "So, how should I do it? Pick a date for my wedding and will it into existence?"

Izzy's mouth popped open in shock. "Why in the world would you do that?"

"Why would you think that would work?" Elinor sputtered in derision.

Georgie's hand dropped from her face as she gave Charlotte a hard look. "Nobody has ever said 'Oh, I think I'll get married on October the second,' and then miraculously found their true love on a schedule! If you want to marry John Brown from Kent and have no care for affection, that might work, but if you want something emotionally substantial, that's just a load of tosh and nonsense."

"How would you know?" Charlotte asked, folding her arms as she considered Georgie. "You didn't try it."

Her friend scoffed softly. "I have a modicum of sense, Charlotte, which is apparently more than you have."

Charlotte sniffed and looked over at Grace, who had yet to say anything. The beautiful woman stared at nothing in particular, but in Charlotte's general direction. Her expression was thoughtful, but not troubled.

She would take that as a good sign.

"Grace?" she prodded. "What do you think?"

Grace blinked, her expression clearing as her eyes focused on Charlotte. Her lips curved into a smile that didn't say much at all. "I think you'll have a difficult time forcing love into a schedule or picking it out of a file of options. I presume you don't want to marry for comfort?"

Charlotte shuddered and made a face. "No, indeed. I've always said I wanted a love match, and I will marry for nothing less. I have independent wealth and connections, so matrimony only makes sense if it is for love. And I refuse to surrender myself for the sake of something as paltry as comfort as Emma did." She bit her lip and glanced at Elinor in apprehension. "Apologies if you…"

Elinor shook her head, holding up a hand. "No need. Mr.

Partlowe was not my choice for my sister, nor did she love him, but I believe they have a warm relationship now. And Mr. Partlowe has been quite kind to Hugh since our marriage." She smiled, looking more like herself than she had all afternoon. "If you want to find love, Charlotte, you can't command it into being. Believe me, if it happened that way, my husband would not be Hugh Sterling."

"A great pity, then," Charlotte commented, smiling for effect, relieved when it was returned. "No, I don't intend to command love and order it to exist between myself and the man of my choosing. I ask for the information so that I know where to look."

Izzy sat forward, her brow puckering in confusion. "What about your usual circle? Surely you know enough of them to start encouraging…"

Charlotte silenced her with a look. "Izzy, have you seen my circle? I wouldn't invite a single one of them to take my dog for a walk, let alone to court me in truth."

Elinor snorted a laugh and pinched the bridge of her nose. "Oh, Charlotte, that is too perfect. What have you been doing all these years if they were all so stupid?"

"Believe me, I've been asking myself the same thing for some time now," Charlotte muttered. She reached forward to snatch a teacake from the platter, choosing not to bother with a plate or any real show of manners. "A complete waste of energy."

"I would give anything to have Prue and Cam in London for this…" Grace laughed, clapping her hands. "We have to write them."

Charlotte chewed quickly, then swallowed. "Oh, I've done that already. I suspect Cam will have a great deal to say shortly, provided the impending arrival of Miss Vale hasn't got him entirely distracted."

"So sure it's a girl, are you?" Georgie hummed in consideration, laughing to herself. "You'll be very disappointed when it's a boy."

"Not as disappointed as Cam, to be sure." Charlotte looked over at an empty chair, sighing. "I do wish Edith was here, though. She's got a head full of sense, and I daresay I could use it."

"Her head is full of love at the moment, so I'm not sure it would help." Izzy shrugged, rubbing her hands together. "Are you sure about this, Charlotte? You really want to find someone you can love and marry?"

Charlotte smiled at Izzy, undoubtedly her sweetest friend. "I've always wanted to do this, Izzy. From the very beginning, this was what I wanted. I just didn't let myself do anything about it until now." Her smile grew, and she sat back in her chair more comfortably. "I fully intend to do something about it now. So help me get on with it, will you?"

Chapter Four

———— ⌒∞⌒ ————

*When starting out on a new adventure or journey, one should ensure
that they have the appropriate allies to accompany them. Without allies, one
would not get very far, and what sort of journey would that be?*

-The Spinster Chronicles, 7 July 1819

Michael Sandford had no friends.

That wasn't true, he had plenty of friends; fellows he'd met at
school, gentlemen of Society he'd associated with at events, and
various other individuals that years in London had brought into his
circle. The problem was that none of those friends were here.

Not a one.

What did it say about a man that he sat at a table at his club alone
without anything to fill his time? More than once, Michael had looked
around for a friendly face, and while many were familiar, none were
his friends in truth. Just associates. Friends of Charlotte's.

Not of his. Never his.

Wasn't this just a delightful way to start his new way of life?

He stared moodily at the drink before him, one he'd hardly
touched and had minimal interest in. What in the world was he even
doing here? How was this going to help him?

The short answer was, of course, it wasn't. But it always seemed
that when a gentleman had nothing better to do, he went to his club.
Michael had never been much of a club-goer, so he wasn't entirely
sure what one did there. Aside from sit, read, and gossip, that is.

Rather like a meeting of the Spinsters might have been.

Michael looked down at his hands as a bout of near-hysterical laughter threatened to rise and roll out of him. That would certainly get him thrown out of Brooks's, and he couldn't have that right now. His club was all he had.

The image of the Spinsters with a capital S gathering in a gentleman's club and fitting right in, however, was something he was not going to forget for some time. He couldn't wait to tell Charlotte.

He frowned at the habitual thought. It was things like this impulse that he needed to adjust, or he would never find a life away from her. He'd be the fool adjusting the lace on her bonnet on her wedding day, watching her walk down the aisle of the church to marry some classically handsome prat she thought good enough to give up her independence for. He'd be godfather to at least one of her children, and always be invited to her family events, which would eventually irritate her husband and cause some deeply seated resentment and thinly veiled threats.

Good heavens, that was where his life was headed. He could see it clearly before him, and it was pathetic. Completely and utterly pathetic.

He returned his attention to his drink, wondering if he should down the whole thing at once, or behave like the gentleman he was supposed to be in this club.

"What, may I ask, did your drink do to deserve such a scowl?"

Michael looked up at the sound of the almost familiar voice, his mind scrambling to place it. Nothing could have surprised him more than to see Hugh Sterling standing there, looking far more kempt than Michael had seen him in years. He was thinner, yet more robust, his clothing fine without any sense of opulence, and his smile was hesitant.

Had he not known it was Hugh Sterling, he would not have recognized him as Hugh Sterling. He'd heard about the change in him but had yet to see it.

Now he had.

Michael managed to smile back. "It failed to give me adequate answers."

Hugh winced playfully. "I have yet to find a drink that appropriately answers anything, and I've tried my share of them." He gestured to the seat opposite Michael. "May I?"

"Please," Michael replied with a nod.

It was pleasantly disconcerting, if such a thing existed, to have a changed Hugh Sterling at the table. They had never been friends, though they had certainly been acquainted, but Michael had certainly heard enough from Charlotte on the subject of Hugh. He knew every perceived sin the man had committed against the Spinsters, against his family, and against any member of Society.

He also knew that Elinor had softened enough towards the man to actually fall in love with him. Given where the girl had come from in her opinions of him, that had been no small thing, and well worth considering when the subject of Hugh came up. As far as Michael was aware, Society as a whole had yet to pass judgment on the change, or even on the couple, as they still kept to themselves more often than not.

Even seeing Hugh here in the club was something unexpected, though Michael could very well say the same for himself. Perhaps there was some significance in that for them both.

"I haven't seen you in here for some time," Hugh remarked as he leaned back in his chair, surveying Michael with some interest.

Michael lifted a corner of his mouth. "I was just thinking the same of you."

Hugh shrugged with a nonchalance that bore no superiority. "I haven't any friends remaining with my change of perspective. You?"

"I haven't any friends that are not Charlotte Wright." Michael offered a bland smile as an accompaniment to his words.

"Ah."

The simple word held an entire existence in its syllable.

It conveyed that Hugh understood the weight of the statement. That he saw the reason behind its utterance. That he saw Michael in his well-established role and could infer the necessary details without further explanation. Perhaps he believed that either Michael was more pathetic than he'd originally thought, or Elinor Sterling had confided a certain announcement to her husband.

Perhaps both.

Yet Hugh said nothing further, which bore witness to his increase in wisdom. The version of Hugh Sterling that Michael had

36

previously known would have begun to berate Charlotte, if not Michael's behavior, in an attempt to form some show of solidarity. It would have failed miserably, but he had never been one to keep his opinion from the ears of others.

Now he was the opposite.

Oddly enough, Michael found himself actually wanting to discuss Charlotte and his present situation. He might not have considered Hugh a potential candidate for a listening ear originally, but opportunity made for strange adjustments.

"Your wife told you," Michael stated without inflection.

Hugh tilted his head ever so slightly. "Told me what?"

He rolled his eyes. "Marvelous. Now you both have learned the value of reserve?"

That earned him a rueful smile. "It's a wonder, is it not? Marriage has matured both of us."

"I doubt marriage is the reason for it," Michael muttered. He took a quick sip of his beverage. "Has Elinor told you what Charlotte has decided?"

"Oh, that?" Hugh's smile remained, and he nodded once. "Yes. Took me by surprise, but Charlotte usually does."

Michael snorted in derision, opting to keep further remarks to himself.

"It must have been quite a shock for you."

Michael's nod was slow, and it was also a blessed relief. "Yes. She'd never said anything about actively pursuing marriage, though it was always possible, and after all this time…"

Hugh grunted softly. "Is she in earnest? She loves a laugh, you know."

"Oh, she's in earnest," Michael assured him, "and when Charlotte sets her mind to something, she'll make it come to pass. I have no doubt she'll be wed by Michaelmas."

Saying the words aloud made the whole fearful scenario real, and Michael swallowed with some difficulty.

Charlotte being wed.

He'd had nightmares about this, but he'd always been able to comfort himself that the dreams had not been real. There was no comfort now.

"And this is a problem for you." Hugh offered a sympathetic look. "I take it you have feelings for her."

Michael laughed limply. "Feelings would describe it well. I was the first to propose to Charlotte Wright, Sterling."

Hugh's expression did not change. "I knew that."

"You knew that?" Michael blinked, his mind struggling to process a single thought. "How did you know that?"

The sympathetic smile turned almost pitying. "Everybody knows that, Sandford. It's the most well-known secret about you that exists."

Responding to such a revelation was almost impossible.

Almost.

"Do people know that I meant it?" Michael countered in disbelief.

Hugh's eyes widened, and, while his lips remained pressed together, his jaw clearly went slack.

Michael nodded once. "I'll take that as a no. Good."

"I don't know that we are close enough friends to have this discussion," Hugh managed, scratching at the back of his head, averting his eyes.

"I haven't had any quality male friends in ages." Michael sat up and folded his hands across the tabletop. "None that come to mind, as it happens."

Hugh fully gaped at Michael now. "What the devil have you been doing when you aren't with Charlotte?"

Michael's hands parted just enough to feign a shrug. "That would be the question I wrestle with now. Had I the answer to that, I would be much better off." He sighed and barely avoided dropping his head to the table. "I haven't had friends. I haven't had interests. I haven't done anything of note. I don't even know what I enjoy anymore. I've just gone and done things because Charlotte was going and doing them."

"You lost yourself chasing her?"

"So it seems." Michael shook his head, frowning at the thought. "I haven't even been chasing her, Sterling. I've been revolving around her in a near-constant pattern because I didn't want to do anything else. Pathetic, isn't it?"

"Tragic, I think," came the low reply.

Michael only shook his head again. "I've wasted so much time. Time I mean to get back now."

Hugh's brow furrowed. "How's that?"

"You."

A bark of incredulous laughter erupted from his companion, but a plan began to form in Michael's mind that made the situation anything but comical.

His lack of reaction stifled Hugh's laughter creditably.

"You're not serious," Hugh protested, remnants of amusement lingering in his features.

"And yet…" Michael grinned easily, which surprised him to no end.

Hugh sat forward, creases forming in his brow. "I am quite possibly the most unlikely candidate for your efforts, Sandford."

Michael held up a finger, his grin turning crooked. "You *were* the most unlikely candidate. Previously, not presently. You are a changed man, are you not?"

"Well, yes, but…"

"And you do feel that the change is permanent, yes?" Michael went on.

"Of course I do, however…"

"Then I see no reason why you should not be my new friend of the male persuasion while I try to distance myself from Charlotte." He cocked a brow and folded his arms, daring Hugh to find a reason to protest further.

Hugh's eyes narrowed. "I am not saying I will do whatever it is you are thinking about, but I would like to know… What, exactly, are you thinking about?"

Michael parted his hands again. "Think of me as… as a lad fresh out of his education. Imagine that I know absolutely nothing about moving in Society. That I am in need of a mentor to guide me through its navigation so I may be a success."

"Forget being a lad," Hugh muttered, pinching the bridge of his nose. "You're naught but the male illustration of a young miss in her very first Season. Shall I find you a string of beaux as well? Arrange for your first dance to be with the most eligible partner? Purchase new trimmings to display you at your very best for all to see? Or perhaps you might wish to attend every ball, musicale, assembly, and spend every third day at the theater, all to see and be seen, and spread your name about?"

Slowly, heat seeped into Michael's cheeks as the mockery sank heavily into the pit of his stomach.

Every word Hugh said was exactly what Michael needed. Oh, he wasn't so very like a young miss, but as for the rest... It was precisely what Michael would require in order to break off the bindings that years of being Charlotte's lackey had wrapped him in.

The recreation of Michael Sandford. Gads, it was the stuff of nightmares, wasn't it?

"The fact that you look resigned instead of horrified has me scared witless."

"I'm not so comfortable at the moment, either." Michael glanced up at Hugh limply. "I think we may have to do exactly what you said. Though a line of... I'm not sure how I feel about courting."

Hugh blinked once, then cleared his throat, his brow snapping down. "Right... Well, unfortunately, that is the main objective of anyone in Society that isn't independently wealthy, driven to rise among its ranks, or scheming to bring the whole thing down. So despite the lack of general interest, you ought to at least pretend to be pursuing it."

"Why? I don't want to compete with Charlotte for who can get married first." The entire idea was distasteful, and his throat tightened at the thought of someone taking her place in his affections, in his life.

"Because you will undoubtedly be pursued once you become more visible." Hugh flagged down a footman for a drink, which was quickly brought. "And you will find yourself married in spite of yourself when the right one crosses your path."

The idea soured further. The right one had always been Charlotte. How could he ever imagine anyone else?

"There are worse things, you know," Hugh told him softly. "And if you are distancing yourself from Charlotte, who has vowed to marry, you will eventually need to do so yourself."

"I know."

He did know that. He'd known that from the moment Charlotte

had announced her plan. He hadn't admitted it, hadn't exactly thought out each word in turn, but he'd known. But doing something towards that effect seemed wrong, somehow.

"You might as well start practicing for when you are ready for it. What's the harm?"

The harm was that there wasn't any harm. There was absolutely nothing wrong with making it known that he was an eligible bachelor who would be willing to marry the right young lady. It was exactly what he should do, what he was expected to do, and what his mother had begged him to do for years. There wasn't a single iota of harm, danger, or error in the thing at all.

Which meant he should do it.

Which meant he was giving up.

Which meant...

"Fine," he heard himself say. "Consider me an eligible, looking bachelor."

Hugh grunted once. "Marvelous. I'll see what I can do about improving your social schedule."

Michael grimaced at that. "I'm really not very social."

There was no inkling of concern or sympathy on Hugh's face. "Unfortunately, you have to be social to get a wife, even if you are only pretending to find one." He paused, his mouth curving into a rueful smirk. "Unless you get stranded at her estate at Christmas, but that's too far off for your purposes, and the logistics would be a nightmare."

"What?"

Hugh only shook his head and waved a dismissive hand. "Never mind. You just need to be social enough to find someone who interests you. Then your attention can be on her, and the rest of the world can socially go to hell."

That didn't sound too awful. "That's it?" Michael asked warily.

"That's it. If the courtship thrives, so much the better. You can propose. If it does not, so long as no understandings or promises are made, all may part amicably, and the whole charade starts over again." He let that sink in, then tilted his head in invitation. "So, shall we?"

Fearing the insanity of his plan might actually form into being, let alone work, Michael barely managed the nod. "We shall."

Hugh frowned. "Your enthusiasm is overwhelming me. Truly. Do contain yourself."

Michael sneered as though he and Hugh had been friends a great deal longer than fifteen minutes. "Give me time."

His new friend nodded, a hint of a smile quickly flitting before he turned serious once more. "One stipulation."

Already? "All right…" Michael answered in a slow, measured tone.

"My sister." Hugh shook his head with finality. "She cannot be your target, but you may use her as an ally."

Michael's jaw dropped. "What? Why would I…?"

"Alice is beautiful, lively, and brilliant. You'd fall for her if you'd let yourself."

He wasn't about to deny the possibility, but the advanced warning was a little ridiculous. "So why warn me off?" He grinned across the table. "Don't want me in the family?"

The smile was not returned. "Charlotte would bloody kill me, and I've just gotten her to stop spitting venom when I enter a room."

Michael's smile vanished at once, and his gaze lowered to his still mostly full glass. "She won't notice."

"If you think that, you're an idiot."

No, he wasn't an idiot, but he did think it. Charlotte would be so engrossed in finding her heart's desire that Michael's quiet courtship in the background wouldn't even cross her mind. Oh, there would be whispers, but nothing she would seriously concern herself with. After all, Michael was not a candidate for Charlotte's hand. Why would she look in his direction at all?

Hugh sighed heavily. "We're not going to agree on that topic, are we?"

"No, we are not." Michael smiled weakly. "Well, what do gentlemen do in their free time?"

A wince flashed across Hugh's features. "I don't know that I'm a particularly good source for what a proper gentleman does with his free time, but I'm a very good one for what he does not."

Michael laughed once. "That's good enough for me. I think there might need to be more than two of us to consider me a man of friends, though, and isn't that a good sign in a potential husband?"

"Naturally." Hugh's lips twisted, then eased into a smile. "Well, I've got a brother who might give you the time of day, but surrounding yourself with married men might add to your feelings of insecurity. I'll round up a bachelor or two of some breeding and fortune, which should give you some connections worth your time."

"Much appreciated." Michael raised his glass towards Hugh's, the knot in his stomach not easing any less than when he walked in here, but it looked as though his situation was about to improve. "To the recreation of Michael Sandford."

Hugh snorted once and touched their glasses together. "May he have a rather marvelous debut."

Chapter Five

⎯⎯⎯⎯⎯⎯⎯ ⬖⤙⤚⬗ ⎯⎯⎯⎯⎯⎯⎯

Any well-laid plan must be, in fact, well laid before it can commence.

-The Spinster Chronicles, 27 November 1818

"Charlotte, my lamb, what are you about?"

Charlotte glanced up from the list she had been composing, and the last Best Bachelor column she'd written alongside it. "Good morning, Mama. How was your breakfast this morning?"

Her mother did not react to the pleasantry, knowing Charlotte far too well. She pursed her lips and entered the parlor more fully, looking almost regal in her morning gown, her dark but greying hair pulled tightly back, cap in place. There was something majestic about the woman, and always had been.

Yet there was a conniving streak of mischief in her as well, and very few people knew that about Mrs. Arabella Wright, or that Charlotte took after her more than made her father comfortable.

"Tolerable for a tray, but that is not why I'm here, so forgive me if I do not inquire as to yours." She gave her daughter a wry look. "I mean what are you doing there? I've seen you scribbling away, and you haven't been to three events this week. Either you are ill, or you are planning something, and you are never ill."

Charlotte frowned at that, scowling down at the sheets before her. "At the present, I am attempting to identify suitable candidates for marriage. Elinor will bring her reports shortly with the Spinsters, but I would like to think I might have some insight myself before she arrives."

Silence was not the anticipated response, and Charlotte glanced up at her mother in near horror, images of her mother having an apoplexy springing to mind.

But her mother was well and whole, staring at Charlotte with a fully gaping mouth, and blinking unsteadily. "You... You said..." She wet her lips and then cleared her throat. "Marriage, Charlotte. You said marriage."

Charlotte's cheeks colored and she resumed her task. "You needn't be so very shocked. I am not a child; I do know the word exists."

"Yes, but you never use it." Her mother moved to take a nearby seat, clasping her hands in her lap. "Lottie, are you certain?"

"That I want to marry?" Charlotte laughed softly. "No, it would ruin everything. I've always known that. No, marriage is not a sensible course for a woman like me, but I would very much like to find love. And, in good circumstances, marriage should follow love. I'm not accepting a proposal, clearly, but I am opening myself up to the idea." She paused in her writing, then glanced at her mother. "The only thing I am certain of is that I should like to find love, Mama."

There, that was simple enough, and rather succinct. Why had it been so difficult to admit for anyone else? Marriage was not the point. Love was.

Her friends had found love, and here she sat.

Even Emma Asheley, now Mrs. Partlowe, had found some sort of affection in her marriage, though she had done the thing rather backwards, which was what the Spinsters and their Chronicles had been striving to avoid.

But not so for Charlotte Wright.

"Love is all that your father and I would wish for you, Lottie," her mother assured her tenderly. "There would be no cause for you to marry at all without it, not in your circumstances."

"I know, and I understand how fortunate I am." Charlotte grinned at her mother quickly. "Not many girls in England can say they've had no pressure from their parents to marry, so I thank you for that."

Her mother laughed merrily. "Oh, Lottie, my love, you think we have not attempted to pressure you? Or that your father has not longed for you to be married afore now? He's only had a restraining hand from me to keep him from harping on you."

Charlotte sat back, her grin spreading. "I wondered about that. Poor Papa."

"He would have disapproved of any beau you had, at any rate," her mother insisted. "He'd be so very particular, I'm not sure you'd have been married by now had you tried."

The grin faded just a touch as the words sank in. "That's just it, Mama. I'm not altogether sure that I have tried. I've never really come round to the idea of being courted, despite entertaining a great many fellows. Rather far too many, I should think, considering none of them were serious. I'm not altogether sure that I have behaved my age, if you can believe that."

"Darling, you haven't behaved your age since you were three, but it was usually for the better."

There was a wry sort of truth to that, and Charlotte tilted her head in consideration. "Yes, I suppose, but beyond the age of twenty-five, one ought to possess a little more wisdom and severity than I have done."

Her mother scoffed haughtily, shaking her head. "Wisdom, perhaps, but severity I will never agree to. You are a bright woman, and severity would not become you."

Charlotte made a face. "Discretion, then. Surely I could do with more discretion."

The lack of reply was answer enough.

"There, I see I am correct." Charlotte hummed and set her pen down, quirking her brows.

Her mother smiled indulgently. "Who is on your list, then?"

Charlotte handed the document over, twisting her lips. "I'm afraid I'm none too pleased with it. Nobody on that list strikes me as being more interesting in any way than anyone else."

"The point, my love, is that you are to try and find them interesting in spite of your first impression. Your father was a notorious bore before I got to know him, make no mistake."

"Mama!" Charlotte laughed, clapping her hands. "Was he really?"

Her mother shuddered and grinned. "Oh, Lottie, he droned on

and on. I was determined that I would feel nothing for him despite my mother's wishes. But then I got to know his heart, see his mind, and suddenly the things he was saying were more interesting to me, and far more valuable."

"But could you get him to stop the droning?" Charlotte pressed impishly.

"Oh, yes," her mother replied with a nod. "I told him I would enjoy what he said a great deal more if he said a bit less of it. We've been smitten ever since." She winked and rose, rubbing her hands together. "Well, my dear, do enjoy plotting your romantic schemes with the Spinsters. I shan't intervene, I dare say that is the last thing you need."

Charlotte smiled and took her mother's hand as she passed. "Perhaps, but I know now who to come to if I need someone to shut up."

Her mother clicked her tongue and tapped Charlotte's cheek. "Oh, you…" She swept from the room with rather the same air as she had entered.

Charlotte only had a moment to breathe before it was announced that her friends had started to arrive, which was well enough, as her list truly was as pitiful as she had informed her mother. Not one of the Best Bachelors would do for her. Not a single one.

What a perfectly discouraging thought.

Feeling rather sour, Charlotte strode into their usual sitting room, smiling limply at Grace as she entered.

"Good morning, Grace. Lovely shade, suits you nicely."

Grace nodded in greeting. "Thank you, dear. You look a little pale, are you quite well?"

"That's hardly a fair response," Charlotte retorted. "I compliment you, and you nearly insult me? Rubbish."

Her friend rolled her eyes and flicked at her lavender sprigged skirts. "My concern over you outweighed my jealousy of your blue muslin, dear. Apologies for being a true friend. Now, are you well?"

Charlotte managed a smile and sat in her nearest chair. "Well, yes, but I am a trifle disgruntled. Nothing that a good session with the Spinsters will not mend."

Grace's high brow furrowed. "What good would the Spinsters

do for you?"

"Sensible conversation, for one, and a jolly good list of suitors for another." Charlotte widened her eyes in exasperation.

"Ah." Grace sighed heavily and shook her head. "There we are. I wondered if you might have found yourself in a muddle with that."

"A muddle with what?" Georgie asked as she appeared in the doorway, Izzy behind her.

Charlotte winced, hissing loudly. "Finding candidates for my matrimonial prospects. The list is quite depressing."

"Surely not," Izzy protested in her kind way. "There are some lovely men about."

"Lovely men?" Charlotte repeated, indignation raging high. "Where was that opinion just a few years ago? Or has your darling husband influenced your tastes?"

"I know mine has," Elinor chimed in as she entered, smiling with some inner superiority. "Good day, all."

Charlotte groaned with all the necessary dramatics. "Ugh, I cannot bear another blissful bride when my prospects are so dismal. Will one of you please say something truthfully foul about your husband?"

Georgie hummed quickly, then brightened. "Tony bites his fork when he eats. Not all the time, but enough that I feel a chill race up my spine that renders my appetite miniscule."

The other married women in the room shuddered together, and Charlotte frowned at them all as tea was brought in. "There is an air of understanding between the lot of you, and I feel quite left out."

Grace chuckled darkly, reaching forward to pour her tea. "Aubrey snores. Dreadful sound, I could barely sleep when we first wed."

Elinor settled into her seat, grinning to herself. "I am well aware of my husband's faults, thank you. Or his previous ones, at any rate, and I must say it is a vastly amusing time to be married to a reformed man."

Charlotte scowled at her. "Elinor, I've only just got your husband down from his former perch as the devil's representative on earth, I'm not at all prepared to give him a place with the angels in heaven."

"Oh, but he doesn't belong up there, either," Elinor insisted, still smirking in a secret way. "Else he would not deign to marry me."

"On that, we can certainly agree." Charlotte gave her a playful sneer that made the others laugh. Then she turned her gaze to Izzy. "And you, Mrs. Morton? How does your husband irk you?"

Izzy stared back at her, eyes wide, cheeks flushing. Then, after a moment, she smiled sheepishly. "Well…"

When she didn't go on, Charlotte threw up her hands. "Oh, for pity's sake, you can't find a single flaw, can you?"

"He's not perfect," Izzy assured them hastily as laughter made the rounds again. "I don't want any of you to believe he is, it's just that…"

"It's just that nothing he does upsets you," Charlotte finished, rolling her eyes. "You're too good, Izzy, even for Sebastian, and I never thought I'd say that."

Izzy blushed prettily, and looked down at her lap, her fingers wringing together.

Something about the action gave Charlotte pause, and she continued to watch her friend as though she could see into her mind and body with enough effort. Would she, too, have a pleasant announcement to make soon? With two of their group joining the ranks of motherhood, it could not be long before all the rest did so.

All except Charlotte, of course.

Grace sighed, still laughing, and looked at the door. "Is Kitty coming today? I thought she might, it has been a bit."

"She's out with Alice Sterling," Izzy told her, now setting about her own tea. "Alice is keen to become better friends, and I think it would be good for Kitty to have her. Better than being with us constantly, at any rate."

"Because spinsterdom is contagious; everyone knows that." Charlotte made a face and turned her attention to Elinor. "Have you brought everything?"

Elinor straightened up, clearing her throat. "I have, yes. More than that, I've spent the last week making the necessary adjustments. I have no doubt we'll make quick work of this." She pushed out of her chair and fetched a parcel from the hall. Pulling pages out of the parcel, she began to spread them out across the floor in some order she had previously arranged.

"Oh my," Charlotte murmured, turning towards her with some interest. "So finding my one and only love should be quick work, then?"

Pausing, Elinor looked up at her in shock. "Erm... Charlotte, I don't believe we will find the identity of your would-be husband in five minutes. This is not that."

Charlotte blinked at the girl, not comprehending. "What do you mean? Why else are we doing this?"

"Oh, darling," Georgie murmured softly. "It's not as easy as that. You cannot will yourself to love anyone just for the sake of it. It's not an emotion that can be commanded."

"I don't see why not," Charlotte protested, looking around at them all. "I can maintain control of my emotions in every other respect, why not this?"

Grace frowned at her in exasperation. "Charlotte! This was never going to be simple, surely you had to know that."

"I did not," Charlotte protested. "Why should I know that? It seemed fairly straightforward for all of you."

The married spinsters looked around at each other, expressions somewhat mirroring. "I think you will find, Charlotte," Izzy said slowly, "that nothing, absolutely nothing, about any of our courtships was in any way straightforward."

No, that could not be right. Charlotte remembered the course of each and every one of them, having been present for a great portion of all of them. There were bumps and bruises, naturally, but it had always been perfectly clear that they belonged together. Why should it not be so easily arranged for her, simply because she got a head start by finding her match ahead of any actual courtship? Shouldn't it be as obvious to her when the right man came along, now that she would be looking for him?

But their expressions were so settled, so in agreement, that everything Charlotte thought she knew, everything she had planned for this excursion, was in question.

"Then what are we doing?" she cried as she slumped back in her chair. "What is the point of going through the entire scheme?"

"Because I've spent years gathering this information for the exact purpose of guiding young ladies to look for their potential match in a more informed manner, and with candidates actually worth considering," Elinor snapped, pressing her palms against the pages, her brow creasing with many lines.

Charlotte stared at her, eyes beginning to ache with stretching so wide.

Elinor lifted a daring brow. "And unless I am quite mistaken, that is precisely what we intend to do here. So kindly stop trying to dictate the entire process and allow our years of experience to actually do some matchmaking for you. We'll create a grouping, and you can see which of the chaps you get on best with, all right?"

Blinking, Charlotte exhaled roughly. "Well. I see no need for you to take on that tone with me, but if you must have your own way, so be it." She lifted her hands in a show of surrender, feeling more bewildered than irritable.

"Quite right," Grace chimed in, rubbing her hands together. "Who have we got lined up, Elinor?"

Elinor sighed as she finished with the papers, tilting her head in thought. "Well, our first option is Tyrone Demaris. Breeding, looks, five thousand a year, but no real holdings that I'm aware of. He's very thick with Lord Radcliffe, though, so one must allow for that. He ranked one of the best bachelors, and anyone can buy a proper estate with the right fortune." She looked up at Charlotte through narrowed eyes. "Do you want to be tied to the Sterlings, though? He is Lady Sterling's cousin, after all."

Charlotte shook her head, blanching in distaste. "Not if I can help it. He's charming enough, but I cannot imagine it."

"Tyrone and Charlotte," Georgie mused before shaking her head. "If there was ever to be a war to end the world, it would be those two having a row. I will beg that we do not try for that match."

Elinor nodded, eyes wide, and looked at another sheet. "Julian Bruce? Ten thousand a year, on remainder for the earldom of Loukes, and nephew of Lady Fellows."

"Add him to the list," Charlotte instructed, her mind conjuring up the image of the soft spoken, wildly handsome man she'd danced with twice in her life. He was difficult to catch for a word of conversation, let alone anything serious, but could certainly have been worthwhile. "My mother is friends with Lady Fellows, I could have her ensure he comes to events I'm due to attend."

Izzy sipped her tea, then put it down quickly. "I didn't know that. Surely that should have been mentioned by now."

Charlotte looked at her friend with some surprise. "Why? Nobody cared a fig for Julian Bruce before, and he wasn't much to look at when we came out, but now he's grown into himself, I rather like the look of him."

"When you can look at him at all," Grace muttered. "The man might as well be Father Christmas."

"I pray he is," Charlotte shot back, "for then I would have found my perfect match indeed."

Elinor glanced up at her again. "Oh, are we going for Father Christmas, then? That changes everything…"

Charlotte ignored her. This was not getting her anywhere, and a discussion of saintly virtues, or otherwise, would cause more points against Charlotte than as regards any particular gentleman. And if her friends were more inclined to mockery at the present, diversionary tactics might suit the task better.

She quickly scrambled for a proper topic. "Has anyone heard from Prue lately? I wonder how she's getting on in confinement."

Izzy raised her hand in the midst of another sip. "Yes," she said when she was able, "I've a letter here from her." She reached into the folds of her skirt and withdrew the folded paper, opening it quickly. "Let me see… She says she is feeling rather conspicuous, which makes being out of the public eye all the better for her. The doctor says everything is in fine form, and not to be too shocked if the child comes early. He has some concerns about Prue being small, whatever that means, but nothing too dreadful. Erm… Cam is in a right state, constantly fussing over her…"

"Huzzah for his first sensible moment since marrying her," Charlotte praised, looking heavenward. She winked, snickering at the idea of Camden Vale fussing over his expectant wife. It was a comical imagining, but she was quite pleased he was doing so. Prue deserved to be fussed over at a time like this.

"Hmm…" Izzy read over the note, then smiled. "Ah. Prue is also quite pleased to hear that Charlotte wishes to be married, and she hopes that they will be through with her confinement and such in time to come and help."

"Help?" Charlotte repeated, sputtering wildly. "Rushing her convalescing and entry into motherhood to join my own personal melee? Surely not. I will write to Cam the moment we are done here. He may dote upon his wife, but in this, at least, he will agree with me."

Izzy's eyes flicked up to Charlotte's. "Cam has added a postscript of his own for you, Charlotte."

Charlotte paused in the act of bringing her teacup to her lips. "Has he? Why not write me himself? Oh, never mind, I know better than to question the reason behind any man's lack of logic. Go on."

The others chuckled while Izzy resumed her reading. "Cam insists that Charlotte cannot settle on any man until he gives permission. He will be vastly put out otherwise."

Clapping her hands, Charlotte laughed. "Oh, bless him, I'll agree to that. The man I choose must have the blessing of Camden Vale, or it's not blessed."

"The idea of Cam being holy enough to bless anything and have it come to fruition…" Grace shook her head. "Heavens, I think I must pray."

Izzy folded the letter and took up her tea once more. "I cannot wait until Edith sends her thoughts to us. No doubt, Radcliffe will have her down here in a moment."

Charlotte sobered at once and shook her head firmly. "I hope not. I think we all underestimated the feelings of Society where her reputation was concerned."

Georgie tsked. "Oh, Charlotte…"

"No, really," she insisted. "It's good she was swept off to Scotland and married to Radcliffe. Now she's Lady Radcliffe, the fuss will eventually fade, but if you heard what I was hearing just after things…" She hissed, making a face. "Not everyone is as modern thinking as we lot, I can assure you."

"You consider us modern? Goodness." Grace quirked her brows, wisely choosing to say nothing further.

Charlotte wouldn't let them in on what she'd overheard, and what she'd been told before the connection between her and Edith had been brought up to the speaker. Yes, they had spared Edith actual ruin, but she was still damaged in the eyes of so many, tainted by the whole affair. None of it would affect the Spinsters, not with the formidable ties they had among them, and with Lord Radcliffe being of a more reclusive nature, it likely would not affect him, either. But should the couple decide to spend much time in London socially in the near future, they would find quite a shock for themselves.

"Speaking of modern," she said suddenly, pulling herself from bleak thoughts, "shall we get on with my suitor selection? I'd like a decent number of candidates before we truly embark. Who do you have next, Elinor?"

Chapter Six

————⟨∾ ∾⟩————

There is no way around the awkwardness of a first ball, whether it is the first one ever or the first one of the Season. All are awkward and uncomfortable. One might as well get used to it.

-The Spinster Chronicles, 1 June 1818

"I don't know why I let you talk me into this."

"A pity, then, that I didn't. You started this fracas; I merely provided the opportunity to begin. Stop crying about it and thank me. This is the simplest event you will have during this entire venture."

Michael glanced at Hugh with a grimace. "Is it? Why's that?"

Hugh raised a brow at him. "Because it is my brother's house, the guest list is small, and no one here is desperate. Simple event, all things considered, yet it will be enough to get you at the top of the invitation list to a great many more things."

"You see my enthusiasm on display," Michael muttered, gesturing to his face.

Nodding, Hugh's expression remained implacable. "I do see, and I do not care. This was your decision, and you chose me to help you. If you want to stop everything now, so be it, but remember…"

"No," Michael interrupted with a sigh, closing his eyes in resignation. "No, we go forward. I just so hate social occasions."

Hugh made no response to that, which was likely for the best, as there wasn't anything to be done about it now. They were here, at this event, and everything was officially underway.

In a manner of speaking.

"The music has started, and the two of you stand here."

Michael plastered on a smile as their host, Hugh's brother, Lord Sterling, strode over to them, tall and almost grandly arrayed, though without appearing a peacock in any way. "A body has to stand somewhere, don't they?"

Lord Sterling gave him a look. "You can explain that to my wife, Sandford, and see where that gets you. She's the one who sent me over here." He turned to his brother, his expression turning bemused. "And you, brother, have a wife. Why are you not attending to her?"

"She's already dancing," he replied simply, gesturing to the dance floor. "Would you deprive Tyrone of dancing with the most beautiful woman in the room that he cannot have?"

Lord Sterling snorted a laugh. "We're not about to get into another argument about which of our wives is the fairest, Hugh, especially not in front of a guest. Deuced uncomfortable for him to agree with me, as host, when he is starting out a friendship with you." He winced and looked at Michael with sympathy. "He'd probably drag you to the theater during one of the less popular shows, claiming it would be a beneficial excursion as revenge. I couldn't bear to see you suffer so."

Michael grinned in earnest while Hugh protested with some animation. "How very kind, my lord." He inclined his head closer. "I take it Hugh has informed you of my plans."

"He has," Lord Sterling replied. "I'll do what I can, to be sure, but I'll draw the line at matchmaking and gossiping. If you're looking for that, you'll have to call on Janet's services."

Hugh coughed a laugh but said nothing.

Michael only scowled. "That's not what I have in mind at all. Why does everyone seem to think my goal is to marry?"

Lord Sterling reared back, though his mouth pulled in amusement. "You have opted to reinvent yourself because Charlotte has decided to marry. Why wouldn't that imply that you're determined to marry also?"

Was that what he'd said? That wasn't what he'd meant; for pity's sake, he only wanted distance from Charlotte to spare his own feelings while she pursued marriage. He hadn't even considered pursuing the thing himself.

"That isn't what I want," he muttered, averting his eyes from the Sterling brothers to take in the dancing.

"No? Well, better not throw that sort of mood around when you enter a ballroom more crowded than mine. The topic is bound to come up," Lord Sterling warned, his words lacking all sympathy. "I've asked around, and your prospects are quite good. Not only will the eager mamas be thinking marriage, they will be naming your firstborn the moment you dance with their daughter."

Michael closed his eyes again, shaking his head. "And people wonder why I hate Society and social occasions."

"Nobody wonders that," Lord Sterling laughed as he patted Michael's shoulder. "Most of us hate it. If you truly want to avoid all this, take yourself out of London and marry a sweet country girl at your own pace. Since you're avoiding Charlotte and all."

"I am *not...*" Michael began, turning to argue, only to find that Lord Sterling had left them to greet some of his other guests.

How was one supposed to retort anything when the subject departed prematurely? Clearly, Lord Sterling wanted the final word, and had to prove a point.

"I'm not altogether certain I'm particularly fond of your brother," Michael told Hugh as he glowered after their host.

"Yes, well." Hugh shrugged a shoulder. "He tends to have that effect on people. Ah, good. The dance is ending, and Tyrone will deliver my wife to me."

Michael scoffed very softly. "And have you missed her terribly?"

Hugh gave him a sidelong look. "You're not exactly in a position to mock my attentiveness to my wife, Sandford, and we both know it. I need only say the word lapdog, I think."

The word drew in Michael's breath almost at once, his chest seizing with the truth and pain of it. He was right; more than that, Michael could never mock any lovesick man or woman again. Years of only circling Charlotte, lingering at the edges of her attention, praying that she might call on him for a dance to separate herself from the pack. He had been the definition of a desperate man, made pathetic by love, and now that he saw it for what it was, he felt only embarrassment.

"Kindly look less nauseated at the sight of my approaching wife, thank you."

Michael blinked and looked up, forcing his lips to curve upwards, though he wasn't sure how much of a smile it was. Mrs. Sterling, fair-haired beauty she was, grinned brightly on the arm of the darker Mr. Demaris, her eyes fixed on her husband with a single-mindedness that felt too intimate to witness.

Still, Michael nodded in greeting. "Mrs. Sterling, you look remarkably well this evening."

She glanced at him, her smile not wavering. "And as you have remarked, it proves your statement true. Thank you, Mr. Sandford." She tilted her head as she slid her arm from Tyrone's. "And please, call me Elinor. Were we in another setting, you know you would. You've done so before."

Michael smiled, exhaling carefully. "That was before your marriage, Mrs. Sterling, and under far different circumstances."

Elinor chuckled with more warmth than he had ever heard from her. "Michael, you've known me since I was twelve, at least. That's longer than your youngest sister, and you've been calling me Elinor for most of them. Surely you're not going to let a little thing like my marriage create a barrier between us."

He continued to smile, though he blanched mentally. Elinor was thick as thieves with Charlotte and the rest. How could he continue familiarity with her when he was stretching himself further away from Charlotte? Then again, he had all but bound himself to Elinor's husband in pursuit of his new aims, and he could hardly expect Hugh to keep secrets from his wife.

"Of course not, Elinor," Michael eventually assured her, dipping his chin. "So long as your husband doesn't get insanely jealous that I do."

Hugh chortled and took his wife's hand, kissing her glove. "I will fight the impulse to rage and roar and take solace in the knowledge that my wife adores me above all others."

"Too right, she does." Elinor turned his face to hers and planted a firm kiss on his lips.

Michael and Mr. Demaris looked at each other in shock, then looked away quickly.

Elinor giggled and eyed them both. "Apologies, gentlemen. The benefits of a small event in our family's home, we can be as affectionate as we choose, and no one will think us scandalous."

"No, only disturbing," Tyrone commented under his breath.

Michael nodded once in agreement.

Hugh cleared his throat, his color high. "I'll thank you both not to judge."

"Presently, I'm trying to blot it out, so judging anyone isn't exactly at the forefront of my mind." Tyrone widened his eyes and gave Michael a strained look. "Sandford, isn't it?"

Michael nodded, relieved that someone else was as uncomfortable as he. "Yes. Pleased to be remembered, Mr. Demaris."

Tyrone waved that off. "I remember everyone; it's a curse. Not necessarily in your case, especially since I have a strong feeling you and I are going to be saving each other regularly for the foreseeable future. And since there are a great many influential members of the Demaris family, you might as well call me Tyrone." He shrugged and swiped a nearby beverage. "But watch out, you may make Sterling here jealous with familiarity between us."

Elinor cackled a laugh that had Hugh scowling at both her and Tyrone. "Now I understand why Janet despairs of you."

If the statement ruffled any feathers for Tyrone, he gave no sign. He only downed his drink, shrugging yet again. "Better to despair of me than hope for me. Far less chance of disappointment."

"A pity you aren't truly a villain, then," Elinor suggested with a teasing smile. "Then they might wash their hands of you completely."

"I find villainy to be more trouble than it's worth," Tyrone countered with a sage shake of his head. "One does not wish to be rendered irredeemable, after all. No, I am simply not to be counted on, which gives me a remarkable amount of freedom."

Michael found himself smiling at the outspoken man in amusement. "And yet you seem to be one of the most eligible bachelors in London, if the Spinsters are to be believed."

"On that note," Elinor announced loudly, dragging Hugh away before the conversation could move further.

Tyrone scowled in earnest as the two of them departed. "That blasted column. I was perfectly content living in obscurity until then. The only unmarried person who cared a jot about my activities was

Annabelle Wintermere, and I've grown quite adept at avoiding her. Now…" He gestured around the room, which, though hardly crowded or full, boasted at least three young ladies eyeing the pair of them speculatively.

"Good heavens," Michael coughed. "I should stand somewhere else."

"Too late, my friend. I've tainted you. Which, as I understand it, was the goal all along." He quirked an inquiring brow and waited, his mouth curving in a crooked smirk.

Michael met the shorter man's eyes steadily, then looked out at the dancing without much interest. "Yes, I suppose it is. Against my better judgment, I aim to make myself more appealing to the general populace, including, if I must, those of an unmarried disposition."

Tyrone grunted once. "Didn't realize marriage was a disposition. I rather thought it was a state, and one not entirely rising above that of despair."

"You're a cynic," Michael pointed out without venom, actually finding the dark humor more and more entertaining by the minute.

"Of course I am. I'm an English gentleman."

Michael choked on a laugh, which seemed to entertain Tyrone, and left the two of them snickering by themselves as they watched the dancing without any intention of joining it.

"So, you are trying to be popular," Tyrone eventually said in a more normal tone. "Pressure from your family?"

"Always." Michael nodded, exhaling slowly. "Nothing too drastic. I don't need to marry money or a title, we aren't in danger or anything like. She simply thinks I am wasting my time and that matrimony would cure me of it."

Tyrone made a face of consideration. "Interesting. And are you? Wasting your time, that is."

Michael opened his mouth to protest, as he had done so many times before over the years, then, irregularly, found himself closing his mouth without a single syllable escaping. A moment of reflection was needed this time, and some honesty.

"Yes," he heard himself admit. "Yes, I am. Or rather, I was. The realization of the thing has made me wish for a change in my life, and while I'm not intending to seek out a match, I won't precisely oppose one."

Tyrone blinked at him, completely baffled. "Well, well. Aren't you a delightful surprise for the mamas hereabouts?"

Michael would have shrugged himself had Tyrone not filled the evening with the action already. He'd been fully prepared to endure some ribbing from a various number of sources when his opinions and aims were made known, and in gaining some new friends for himself, it was only natural that it should take place. Had he not wasted his time, he might have escaped this, too.

But he could not look back anymore. Only forward. Only ahead.

"I could use your help," Michael murmured to Tyrone as the pair of them took another set of drinks. "Sterling is a good fellow for taking me on, but he is already married, and the nature of his marriage is such…"

"I'll save you from the sentimentality of the thing, never fear," Tyrone overrode. "A lump of sense is worth a pinch of sentimentality." He frowned, then chuckled ruefully. "Isn't that the title of the book that woman wrote? Sense and Sentimentality?"

Michael bit his tongue hard, thinking how Charlotte would have blustered and harrumphed about Miss Austen being referred to as 'that woman' and for one of her titles to be so incorrectly named. She'd have thrown the offender out of the house, whether it was her own or someone else's.

"Something of the sort, I never read them." Michael hid a smile behind a sip of his drink.

Tyrone sighed. "Nor I, and had I any sisters, I am sure that would be a great sin. My female cousins seem to think I lack awareness of the feminine tastes of today, but I don't consider that a failing. If women wished for a man who completely understood them, they'd be marrying a mirror."

At that moment, a young lady passed them, eyeing them both with a boldness that ought to have made Michael squirm. The beauty in her features only made him smile in spite of himself, dipping his chin.

"Well played, madam," Tyrone told her, not bothering to keep his voice down. "Come back with a proper and creative introduction, and I'll engage you for whichever dance you please."

Her eyes widened, as did her smile, and with a flick of a suddenly appearing fan, she sauntered off, presumably to find such an introduction.

Michael reeled at the bizarre interaction. He had spent hours of his life at a time in ballrooms, enough that they likely added up to several weeks, and never had he seen something so blatant that was completely without the accompanying words. There was such a discrepancy between the two that he had to replay the exchange in his head repeatedly.

Charlotte had flirted and teased, undoubtedly danced with the line of propriety, but never once strayed overtly into indecency. The toffs that had crowded her over the years had spouted off flowering words and phrases, creating themselves into buffoons of the utmost caliber, yet seemed to stumble over their excessive politeness. Now and again, there had been a cad of sorts among the group, but somehow Charlotte encouraged decorum in her presence, despite being an imp herself.

She was a paradox and yet more easily understood than what he had just witnessed.

Clearly, he had a great deal to learn.

"What in the world was that?" Michael asked Tyrone with a laugh, wishing he didn't feel like such a dunce at the moment.

Tyrone looked at him in surprise. "What was what?"

Michael gestured. "That interaction with the young lady."

"Flirting?" Tyrone asked slowly, as though Michael were all of twelve years old and had discovered the mystery of growing attraction to a girl. "The unspoken invitation between a man and a woman hidden in the words we do speak?"

There was nothing to do but stare at the man without expression, finding no entertainment in his words whatsoever.

But Tyrone Demaris wasn't going to budge, his face a mask that only just concealed his amusement at Michael's expense. A master at work, and there was no mistaking it. It was obvious he felt that Michael could benefit from his influence; he was absolutely certain of it.

"I'd hardly call that flirting," Michael grumbled, finishing his drink quickly. "I don't know if there's a name for it, but it wouldn't exactly please the matrons at Almack's."

"Then it's a ruddy good thing we're at Sterling House instead, isn't it?" Tyrone nudged him playfully. "Sandford, you've got to play the moments as they come. Not every woman wants you to bow perfectly over hand and kiss the air above her glove. There's an art to wooing, and it requires you to pay attention."

Michael raised a brow in lieu of glowering. "I thought we were not focusing solely on matrimonial prospects. I am quite sure I said so."

Tyrone inclined his head towards the far side of the room, indicating they should walk. "There is a shocking misconception about the word wooing, and of its uses. One must woo everyone in order to be liked, male and female, young and old. I've even tried my hand at wooing Miranda Sterling's bloodhound, but the blasted creature is too thick to take a liking after all my efforts."

The mention of the famed Rufus made Michael smile, trying to picture Tyrone's attempts in persuading the beast to like him. "I've no doubt the animal is a peculiar one, or perhaps he is only a merciless judge of character."

"Don't defend the rascal," Tyrone ordered curtly. "It's all Miranda's doing, and one of these days, I will find a way behind her machinations. At any rate, that is beside the point."

"Is it?"

The musicians struck up a rather bright song with a quick tempo, and Tyrone groaned, weaving behind the line of people closest to the dancing, neatly turning his back to the dancing as he did so.

"Yes," he hissed, his dark brow lowering. "If you want to be liked, you have to be likable, and that requires some very careful, very strategic wooing, especially since you're already established in Society."

"As what?" Michael inquired with a narrowing of his eyes. "What am I established as?"

Tyrone only shook his head. "Doesn't matter. You want to change it, so you've got to change. Wooing, Sandford."

Michael considered that as he sidled up to a nearby wall, leaning without much concern for appearances. "What makes you so knowledgeable in such things? I thought you said you lived in obscurity before your sudden rise to fame?"

"How do you think I managed to maintain my obscurity, despite my family name, my fortune, and my eligibility?" Tyrone demanded with a smug smile. "The art of evasion is rather like the art of wooing, and I learned at a very young age how to do both quite well enough to get what I wanted. I can help you to recreate yourself, Sandford, but you're going to have to decide who you want to be first. And what it is you want."

Who he wanted to be?

Why not himself?

Well, himself had never really been much of a figure, not since his much younger years, so there wasn't all that much to be, in that regard. Yet he had not been entirely without being or personality, he'd simply spent a deal of time considering someone else instead. Nothing wrong in that, per se, but he had somehow managed to completely neglect himself until he hardly existed in truth without Charlotte. Tragic, Hugh had called it. Yes, that was a far better word than pathetic. The tragic loss of Michael Sandford had been occurring for years without anybody noticing.

What did he want?

The image of Charlotte floated into his mind, laughing at something he had said in the many moments they had been alone in her home, unchaperoned because he was Michael.

He was safe. He wasn't a threat. Wasn't an option.

"I see the two of you have made a great deal of progress," Hugh teased as he approached with his brother in tow.

They had, in fact, though not so much that the eye could behold it.

Michael looked at the brothers with a smile. "Lost your wives, I see."

"For the moment," Lord Sterling allowed, returning the smile. "Until they miss us with such abandon, they seek us out, tears flowing and arms outstretched."

Tyrone shook his head. "And to think, you could have been an actor on the stage. Such a pity. Cards, gentlemen? I give us three decent rounds of loo before Janet crowns me over the head for ignoring her female guests and forces me to dance again."

Lord Sterling nodded once. "Four rounds. She's currently in conversation with your mother."

Hugh snickered uncontrollably while Tyrone attempted to find some way to defend his mother without disagreeing, and Michael, feeling rather legless in the face of his newfound realizations, followed the group of them out of the ballroom.

It was time for his transformation to commence.

Chapter Seven

One must never forego an opportunity to revise the impressions of Society. The effort will be well worth it.

-The Spinster Chronicles, 25 July 1815

"It's no good, I simply cannot abide by these deuced new fashions."

"Of course you can. You've managed every other style as it came up from Paris, why should this be any different?"

Charlotte stared at Grace in shock, aghast that she should disagree. "Why? Because the sleeves are barely in existence, my shoulders are very nearly bare, and this bodice is so low that..."

Grace rolled her eyes and gestured for Annette to continue getting Charlotte ready. "Charlotte, the neckline is no lower than any other gown you have worn in the last four years. It only feels amiss due to the other aspects."

"Aha!" Charlotte cried as her shoulders were pulled back to assist in fastening the back of her gown. "So you do concede that there are impossible factors at hand."

"Impossible, no." Grace shook her head, the florets and ribbons in her hair nearly shimmering in the candlelight. "Not in the least. Your figure is magnificent, and you did ask for my recommendations without a proper fitting."

Charlotte scowled, inhaling a near gasp as the fastenings were done. "You are my most fashionable friend. I thought I should be pleased with your tastes, not sacrificed to them." She pressed her hands to her bodice, the intermixed pearls pressing into her palms. "Am I supposed to be rendered breathless without the effect of an attractive man?"

Annette came around to face her, frowning. "You should be able to breathe freely, Miss Charlotte. Your stays are fastened only just past your usual, and the gown is not overly constricting."

"You see?" Grace smirked in a too-superior way and waved a gloved hand at her. "Breathe, Charlotte. Exhale."

"I'll spill out of this contraption if I do that," Charlotte muttered, very gradually releasing air and finding it not impossible to do so.

"You're quite secure," Grace assured her without concern. "We could hang you upside down, and the only scandal would be your drawers."

Charlotte glared at her as Annette pulled her to the toilette and began to pull the papers from her curls. "If I were upside down, the skirts would cover my primary concern, so please do."

Grace ignored her and only watched Annette gather Charlotte's dark tresses into folds, pinning and twisting them in what had to be the most painful manner possible.

Why in the world had Charlotte agreed to this? She had plenty of fashionable gowns and had ever been one of the leaders in fashion in London Society, though she would never have claimed so aloud. She had certainly never been found wanting in any manner of attire, and yet something had possessed her to purchase several new gowns for her new matrimonial scheme.

The gown she wore now had seemed the simplest at first glance, being entirely white and the skirts holding a gently lined pattern along the length of her. Its only real embellishments were the pearls intermingled along her bodice and sleeves and the plaited satin bands at her hemline, though the stomacher and satin ribbon at her waist secured the object of her stays neatly. All told, it was not particularly dramatic unless one took in the expanse of skin upwards of the bodice, across her shoulders, and up into her hair.

But it felt dramatic.

"Should my hair not be pulled higher in the back?" Charlotte queried, catching a glimpse of herself in the looking glass.

"No, miss," Annette replied without looking, continuing her

work effortlessly. "You will see why shortly."

Grace cleared her throat and adjusted her white kid gloves. "Patience, Charlotte, and stop ordering Annette about. She and I have worked tirelessly to perfect this look, and your opinion is not needed."

"Not needed?" Charlotte adjusted her position in the chair, uncomfortable with being rendered voiceless. "Is it not my person we are dressing?"

"Exactly so," Grace shot back. "*We* are dressing you. You are not." Her brows quirked in a defiant show of victory that Charlotte instantly hated.

Well, she could not be expected to be entirely silent while she was turned into a doll of their creation. She was Charlotte Wright, after all.

She picked at her skirts limply. "White," she muttered to nobody in particular. "I haven't worn something so abjectly white since I was sixteen. Am I going as an angel in disguise? Where is my halo? Have I wings, as well?"

"You would need a disguise to be an angel in anyone's eyes," Grace responded simply, her eyes narrowing as she watched the transformation of Charlotte's hair. "We're only making sure we draw attention to you."

"Because that has been such an issue before this." Charlotte nodded sagely, receiving a hard tug on her hair for doing so. "A veritable wallflower am I. No one ever remembers my name."

Grace's eyes flicked down to hers. "Everyone sees you all the time. We must alter what seeing you means. It should bring you an interesting array of new suitors, which is what you would prefer, yes?"

Charlotte made a face, the reality of the situation staring her squarely in the face without mercy. She did need people to see her differently, needed worthy candidates for marriage to see her in earnest, and give them enough interests to pursue something more than idle flirtation in a ballroom. Her fortune was tempting enough, but any fortune hunter would be routed if the requisite affection were not in place.

Michael could help her with thinning the crowd. He knew practically everybody and somehow seemed to know their secrets, too. She hadn't brought him around in recent days, spending much of her time plotting with the Spinsters, but if tonight went as well as she suspected, he would have a great deal to do indeed. He'd see the change in her this evening, and she could explain her plan a bit further than she first had.

Poor man might have thought she'd race off to Gretna Green with the first fellow of substance who could speak the word love and have the marriage done by Friday. He'd admire the plan she'd begun concocting; he was always praising her genius, though he usually called it madness for reasons she had yet to comprehend.

Would Michael be stunned by her appearance tonight? Would he be blinded by her luminescence, expecting his usual chum in her usual splendor? He'd have a witty remark on the subject, whatever his feelings.

New suitors. For some reason, her nerves escalated, bringing dampness to her gloveless palms and heat racing up her neck. She had grown so accustomed to her typical band of admirers and their ways that the idea of originality was unsettling.

She knew the names of several gentlemen that she could consider, but in order for any of this to work, those gentlemen had to show interest in her. At least three would be in attendance, her allies had gotten her that much information, but there was no certainty in their interest, let alone affection.

There was a great deal of work to be done on her side, and she had not exerted effort in a social setting for her own benefit in years.

Perhaps never.

What arrogance surrounded her! What airs and haughtiness, a sickening superiority that would likely have rendered her unappealing to any man worth pursuing. Edith was right; Charlotte had never tried to find the love she'd always claimed she was after. She'd simply expected the thing to fall into her lap like so many of the buffoons that had paid homage to her.

Worthless years, the lot of them. Not in every regard, but in this, there was no other conclusion.

No more.

Tonight, she would begin anew, and she would hunt for love the way she should have done from the beginning. The lone remaining

Spinster with a capital S who was also a spinster of the other variety would soon join the ranks of her peers, and no one would ever claim she had not tried to do so again.

"Yes," Charlotte told Grace, eventually answering the question posed. "New suitors are what I would prefer. The highest quality, if you please."

Grace grinned at the addition. "And who shall be keeper of the candidates, Miss Wright?"

"Why, you, if you've an interest." Charlotte waved a hand regally, a queen in her imagined court. "Send the riffraff away, and only my most valuable options may kneel."

"Marquesses, dukes, and very wealthy earls," Grace announced with a firm nod. "Yes, my lady."

Charlotte would have shrugged had Annette allowed it. "Titles don't mean so very much to me, as it happens. It would be lovely, but I can hardly make that a requirement. Dukes, after all, do not grow on trees. I already have wealth, so what I really need is land."

Grace clapped her hands, laughing merrily. "Oh, but this is perfect! I shall interview each man that wishes to approach. 'Pardon me, sir, but how much property do you own?' And if it be not the finest estate in its county, we shall not accept it!"

"Erm…" Charlotte held up a finger, wincing. "Might we be excused from Northumberland?"

"Northumberland is quite lovely, Miss Charlotte," Annette chimed in with her own slight laugh. "Have you never been?"

Charlotte met the maid's eyes in the looking glass. "When would I have been to Northumberland, Annette? I've nothing against the place, to be sure, it's only the furthest one can get while remaining in England, and that does not interest me in the least."

"What if you catch the eye of a dashing Scotsman?" Grace asked. "Or an Irishman with the voice of a god?"

"That's altogether different," Charlotte insisted, sniffing as she averted her eyes. "If I am to live outside of England, so be it. It can be quite fashionable to be in Scotland or Ireland much of the year. But if I am to be in England, I only ask that it not be so difficult to get to the rest of the country."

Grace snickered and shook her head. "I shall do my best to

render that possible. I do not promise to keep from Northumberland, though. Now you mention it, I think you would be well suited to the county…"

Charlotte scowled at her friend playfully, her head rocking back a little as Annette pulled again. "You'll find my amusement rapidly waning, Lady Ingram."

"Alas, that is when I find mine increases." Grace batted her lashes, baring a would-be innocent smile for her. She sobered and began to nod fervently. "Oh, yes, Annette. Absolutely lovely. A marvelous shade, I think."

Shade? What shade could there be when Charlotte would resemble an adorned snowbank?

Grace moved to stand in front of the looking glass before Charlotte could see, a small smile returning to her face.

Charlotte placed a very deep frown on hers in response. "Grace…"

"Give it a moment, Charlotte," she answered in a voice that held more excitement than her expression or frame allowed. "Trust me in this. Just a few moments more."

Sighing, Charlotte all but slumped back in her chair, and likely would have done were she not in the process of being trussed into the personification of a ray of light. A few moments for what? She was well aware of her appearance, and it wasn't likely to change in a particularly shocking way. What was a new frock and a new style of hair, after all?

Would any of this truly be of benefit to her?

Images of Charlotte standing alone near a wall of the Preston family ballroom filled her mind, the feeling of a full two-meter radius seeming to extend from her imagination to her reality, and she shivered. Were any ideas of gossip columns circulating in the minds of London Society, the sight of her standing so acutely abandoned would certainly be described therein. As it was, the spoken gossip would carry her name in such a reference for weeks.

That would not help her get a husband.

Something cool brushed against the exposed skin of her chest and moved upwards to her throat. Her hand moved to touch it, and the smooth spheres beneath her fingertips surprised her.

71

"Pearls?" she asked the others. "When the gown has pearls already?"

Grace nodded fervently. "Oh, yes. One moment more, and you shall see." She bit her lip very briefly, nearly dancing where she stood.

How in the world could anyone else's dressing up create such joy and anticipation for her? Charlotte would never be good enough in her wildest imaginations to feel so much on someone else's behalf, but this was why she was friends with people like Izzy and Grace. Their influence was undoubtedly responsible for any of the sweetness that Charlotte had developed in her nature, but none of them had managed to bring her into true goodness.

Not yet.

She felt Annette's hands gently press against the sides of her hair and thought that perhaps some sort of conclusion had been reached.

Impossibly, she held her breath.

Grace held out her hands and pulled Charlotte to her feet. "Now, my dear, I think you need to see yourself. Are you ready?"

"I've been ready from the beginning, oh noble jailer," Charlotte muttered, moving to the looking glass Grace had hidden from her.

Her jaw dropped at the sight.

The folds of white and shimmer of pearls rendered her an almost ethereal air, and while the neckline was indeed lower, the expanded view of her skin only added to the charm of it all. Nothing was excessively revealed, and, in fact, seemed somehow more secure than many of the other gowns she had worn a few times over. All about her was white, including the newly purchased kid gloves, though she had several pairs. According to Grace, a special evening was always an occasion for new gloves.

That seemed rather squandering, but in this instance, it was certainly true. The pearls at her neck were the perfect accessory to those interlayered about her gown, and the neat yet lax knot of them just at the base of her throat could not fail to attract attention. Her dark hair held loose ringlets prominently displayed in the front while her hind hair had been dressed low, just as she had felt. What she had not expected was the reason for it.

Several damask roses had been placed at the crown of her head near the back, she would venture a true garland of them, all told.

Scattered about them were pearl hair pins to accentuate the sable darkness of her hair. The gentle rise of color there only heightened the pristine appearance of all else she wore, and the color of her cheeks, naturally rosy, now seemed ready to bloom.

Charlotte Wright could have been a diamond of the first water looking like this, and she had never been that before. She might have been wealthy, might have been lovely, might have had several willing suitors from the beginning, but she had never been the best or brightest or most beautiful in a room.

Tonight, that would change.

"Heavens," Charlotte breathed, looking herself up and down. "I look remarkably tall."

Grace laughed in disbelief and put her hands on Charlotte's arms, meeting her eyes in the mirror. "Is that all you have to say? Charlotte, this is a transformation!"

Charlotte nodded, fighting for the wit she usually had so at hand. It would not be prudent to show overt emotion now, particularly when she was expected to be so very charming and polite later.

"Yes, and now we shall have to carry this on for the rest of the Season at every public appearance," she snapped, though her words lacked the snide edge she had hoped for. "I do hope you will remember that when I become habitually cantankerous with an aching head and a bruised waist."

Grace's eyes narrowed as Charlotte stepped away. "I think you're hiding your true feelings, Charlotte, under a blanket of wit."

"Hmm," Charlotte said simply as she reached for her reticule and fan nearby, winking her thanks to Annette. "Well, you may think that all you like. Why should tonight be any different?"

A huffed exhale escaped Grace as she followed Charlotte out of the room. "Meaning?" she demanded.

Charlotte paused at the top of the stairs. "I always hide my true feelings under a blanket of wit. Surely you know that by now." She winked and descended the stairs without any of the grace a woman in such a gown should have. She couldn't bring herself to care, not with the picture of comportment following her.

Grace could fall down the stairs in a gliding manner and receive praise for doing so. She'd have to avoid her friend the whole evening if she truly wished to get anywhere.

"What was that I heard?" Aubrey, Lord Ingram, asked as he came to the stairs. He smiled a warm, friendly smile at Charlotte and bowed. "Stunning picture, Charlotte. Well done."

Charlotte favored him with a curtsey, a rarity indeed for her more familiar friends. "Many thanks, my lord." She snickered and tapped her fan into her hand. "We were talking of blankets and wit."

Aubrey raised a brow as he moved past her to help his wife down the remaining stairs, though she did not require the assistance. "What in the world for?"

Charlotte ignored the way her heart stumbled as she witnessed the quick but fervent look between her friends, the secrets that only those who shared a heart could know.

Had Aubrey offered his hand to Grace simply to touch her? He was a gentleman to his core, but there was nothing particularly complicated requiring his specific attentiveness to his wife. Was it his way to ensure she was always safe? Did he wish for her to know instinctively that he would always be there? Did he test himself by waiting for her to take his hand, still breathlessly wondering if she would after being married to him this far?

There was a connection she could not understand or translate there, and she was instantly envious. Delighted for her friend, but envious at her own lack. Did that make her ungrateful?

"I am rather fond of both," Charlotte told Aubrey. "Blankets and wit."

His mouth curved in a smile. "Well, it is a rather underrated combination in the evenings, I will allow."

Charlotte looked at Grace with some superiority, and her friend only rolled her eyes at them both.

"Are we the last ones down?" Charlotte asked Aubrey, returning her attention to him. "I am sorry you have had such a wait."

Aubrey waved it off with a quick expression of dismissal. "Not in the least. I am married to Grace, so waiting for the appearance of resplendence is quite a normal thing for me now."

Charlotte sputtered and turned to Grace. "Is he always like that?"

"No," Grace said simply, smiling sweetly at her husband. "He is showing off at present."

"To answer your question," Aubrey went on, ignoring his wife's commentary, "no, you are not the last ones down. Your father kept me company, but when it was clear it would be some time, he retired to his library. Your mother was down but forgot something so went back up. Your brother, I have yet to see."

There was no surprise in anything he had said, and Charlotte could only sigh. "All that fuss and bother, and still Charles takes more time than I do to be presentable for Society. I do not understand it, nor will I. What can he possibly have to prepare?"

"You would be surprised, my dear sister." Charles strode down the stairs, smug expression on his face, her mother on his arm. "There, we are all looking our finest. Would you send for Father?"

"No need, no need," came the sound of their father's voice from further down the corridor. "The sound of your footfall on the stairs echoed into the library, so I felt myself summoned."

Grace snickered and looped her hand through Aubrey's. "Oh, I do love spending time with the Wright family."

"Happy to oblige," Charlotte muttered, moving over to the waiting maids for her cloak. "If nobody minds, I'll ride over with the Ingrams. More room for us all."

"Don't impose, Charlotte!" her mother protested. "And don't invite yourself! Lord Ingram, forgive her…"

Aubrey chuckled with some warmth and bowed. "Mrs. Wright, I can assure you that I rarely see a need to forgive Charlotte for anything. I am well aware of her nature and her antics, and I have no qualms about allowing her to ride with Lady Ingram and myself to the Prestons' home this evening."

"You're a better man than I," Charles informed him as he retrieved his hat for the evening.

Charlotte glared at him. "That was never in question."

Before the siblings could properly spat, they were all ushered out to the carriages and loaded in, and then they were off.

There was not much conversation in the Ingram coach, as Charlotte preferred to look out of the window in anticipation of what the evening could bring. She did not anticipate finding her husband and falling in love in one night, but she hoped that she could make a good start, at the very least. She could not properly set a true plan in motion without these first steps.

She'd accept anything as a beginning. Finding one of the men on her list intriguing. Dancing more than once with him. Flirting mutually. Catching scattered looks throughout the night.

Anything more than the unknown would be of great comfort.

"Do you need me to function in any sort of assisting capacity this evening, Charlotte?" Aubrey offered kindly, as though he could sense her inner nerves and turmoil. "Or protective?"

Charlotte smiled at him, shaking her head. "Only if you see me suffering from boredom or unable to escape someone tiresome. I would be most grateful for a rescue under those circumstances, but I think I should be quite able to manage otherwise."

"Good," he said simply, "because we are here." He quirked his brows and scooted to the edge of his seat, preparing to disembark as the carriage rolled to a stop.

Heavens. Charlotte looked up at the house, nothing too fine by appearances, but certainly lit up enough to be inviting. So why should her pulse begin to race, and her throat dry up?

"Oh, and Charlotte…"

She swallowed. "Aubrey?"

He grinned in his usual mischievous manner. "The Prestons have a son, you know. He is back from the Continent, and apparently very keenly interested in finding a wife." With that, he pushed out of the coach and held out a hand for his wife.

Grace scowled at him, but placed her hand in his, giving Charlotte a meaningful look. "Are you ready, dear?"

Charlotte nodded even as Grace was pulled gently from the coach, then nodded privately to herself. "Yes," she told herself, jumping in near fright as Aubrey's hand reappeared for her.

She cleared her throat and took it. "Yes," she said again, this time for their benefit. "I am ready."

Chapter Eight

———— ❧ ≪≫ ❧ ————

Avoidance is not always cowardly.

-*The Spinster Chronicles, 15 October 1816*

Charlotte was a vision.

It was the worst possible luck.

Michael knew she would attend the Prestons' ball, but the sight of her struck him more powerfully than any sight of her ever had.

She was going to marry someone else, he reminded himself. Anyone else, really. Any eligible man in this ballroom could become her husband one day.

He suddenly hated them all.

It was not fair, seeing her so elegantly arrayed, increasing the effort she put into her appearance and apparel right when he had decided to give her up. But this was never going to be easy nor comfortable, so it might as well be acutely painful from the start.

"Stop glowering, Sandford," Tyrone muttered, shoving a drink in his hand. "That's an obvious sign to anyone in the vicinity, and questions will be asked. If you wish to illustrate a natural distance between the pair of you without anyone questioning an actual rift, you need to master your expressions."

Michael turned away from the entrance to the ballroom, facing Tyrone while trying to adjust his features appropriately. "Why does she look like a goddess, Tyrone? Why? I was prepared for her usual appearance, what I am much accustomed to, but this…?"

Tyrone cut him off, shaking his head and looking almost

disgusted. "If I had any question about why you were doing this, I do not now. Love for Charlotte Wright is your downfall. Can we move past it now? I do not intend to discuss this for the rest of the Season."

"Please," Michael begged. "I would very much enjoy *not* discussing her. Sterling is still tied to her through his wife, so cannot be my true ally, though he may try."

"I thought we were simply finding you a life to live," Tyrone said with a suddenly halting hand. "I am not committing to wage war against Charlotte Wright. I would like to live to see Christmas, if you don't mind."

Of course Michael didn't mean to wage war against Charlotte. Why would he do such a thing? He adored her, still wanted her with an intensity that made his teeth ache, and though she could not see him as any different from the eight-year-old boy who interrupted her tree branch swinging, he had no desire to punish her in any way, shape, or form. Hurting her would kill him.

No, war was not the plan, nor was it the aim.

Feeding his resentment, however…

An odd wave slowly rolled over him, starting from the crown of his head and unfurling down his body. A cool, crisp composure he had never known in his entire life but had seen in the face of every bored gentleman forced to stand in ballrooms and drawing rooms and music rooms for ages of time. A distance that neatly removed him from the present distress ravaging his chest. A perfect, pristine aloofness.

Oh, what blessed relief.

"Of course, not war," he said simply, surprised that the tone of his voice had not changed as well, so different was his present feeling of existence. "Only separation. So find me a string of young ladies to dance with, and let my life begin."

Tyrone snorted once. "Steady on, this isn't some Shakespearean play, and you have no lines. More than that, I am not your nanny."

Sensing his new friend was not at all inclined towards romantic sentiment, Michael nodded and thought it best to move on. "Very well. I will still require your assistance. I haven't been particularly social at a ball in years."

"You don't say," Tyrone replied without concern, the lack of surprise in his tone bordering on the impudent. "How astonishing."

"You needn't make me sound like a bore," Michael muttered as he downed the remnants of his glass and handed the empty vessel to a nearby footman.

Tyrone smirked at him. "You're only a poor git who never got past being a puppy, but never you fear. The Sterlings and I will correct your course."

"How very reassuring." Michael shook his head and looked around the ballroom with some curiosity.

He hadn't really looked about a ballroom before. Likely not ever, unless he was looking for Charlotte. But now, he could freely look and act as he saw fit.

But why would a gentleman without any particular interest dance with any lady? Michael had no interests at present, would need several rounds of introductions before he could dance with anyone worth pursuing, and he wasn't entirely convinced he wanted to pursue anyone at all for now. So what did he do?

Why in the world had he come?

"Gads," he grumbled to himself, wishing the situation were less formal so he might slump against the wall. "This would all be so much easier if Charlotte were ordering me about. She could strategize the way in three minutes without leaving me lost and uncomfortable."

"Oh, stop whining and ask a lady to dance," Tyrone groaned mercilessly. "Or find someone for me to introduce you to. Either way, you decide. I am perfectly content to remain here and do nothing all evening."

That did not sound very promising, and Michael wondered about the wisdom of having Tyrone Demaris as his friend at a time like this. He wasn't sure the man would have stopped him gambling away his fortune, if the opportunity arose.

"Ah, Mr. Sandford!" a young and bright voice chimed in, turning his head.

A tall young woman with hair the color of gold and eyes the shade of rich chocolate approached him, the warm smile on her face almost startling him. He bowed quickly, his mind spinning for her name, though the pure beauty in her countenance was rendering him more than a little befuddled.

"Have you already forgotten that you engaged me for this dance?" She laughed and put her hand on his arm. "How many ladies have begged for your partnership already? Come, I insist on my claim."

No fool to an offered opportunity, Michael went where he was tugged, forcing a smile on his face for the benefit of any watching, given that this woman had taken no trouble to keep her voice down while addressing him.

"I do hope you don't mind a quadrille," his partner said in a lower, much more companionable voice. "Hugh only said to dance with you, and I didn't see a need to wait."

Alice Sterling.

Of course, why hadn't he remembered?

In an instant, he knew that Hugh had been precisely right in warning him away from any intentions where she was concerned. Any man with a working set of kneecaps would have fallen for Alice if left alone and unawares with her for more than ten minutes. Less, if she had an interest herself. Fortunately, Michael was well aware, and thus they were both safe.

In theory.

"I do dance the quadrille, Miss Sterling," Michael assured her as he was finally able to draw a full breath. "Thank you for the rescue."

"Rescue?" She laughed once. "Mr. Sandford, I was just as in need of a partner as you, and any excuse to have one without going through the trouble of waiting to be invited is welcome here."

Michael grinned at her as they took their position on the floor. "I give you the freedom to claim any dance you please with me at any time. No invitation required, no commitment expected."

Alice's smile turned crooked. "I think you might call me Alice for that, Mr. Sandford. Unless it will shock you."

"Not in the least." He inclined his head at the start of the music.

"We're going to be great friends, Mr. Sandford." Alice glanced over at her brother, now joined by Lord Sterling as well. "But I think we had better tell my brothers that we have no intention of starting rumors or being lovers in truth."

Michael chuckled as he began to promenade with her, following the lead couple. "We had better. They would kill me otherwise; I've already been forewarned."

Alice shrugged and parted from him to move to her next position. "At this rate, everyone they know will be forewarned, and I'll be the next generation of the Spinsters with a capital S."

"That would serve them right." Michael smiled at the woman he crossed to, bowing before her and taking her hands as they moved in a circle before retreating back. "Though I must say, I have some sisters myself, and we really cannot help our protective natures."

"So long as I am not protected into a glass box for eternity, I should not mind that." She mirrored his action to the gentleman beside him, turned with him, then returned to her spot.

Crossing to her now, Michael felt himself relaxing more than he had done in some time. "Are you eager to make a match for yourself?"

"Not particularly," she replied, surprising him with the ease of her answer. "I would like to, eventually, but at the moment, I would simply like to enjoy myself."

"That seems reasonable to me." They turned together, and Michael cocked his head. "Now that you mention it, those match my aims as well."

Alice narrowed her dark eyes at him. "Don't agree with me to be agreeable. That's not at all enjoyable."

Michal sighed as they moved in line behind the other couples. "I'm not. No designs, remember? We are friends, and an alliance would see that we both enjoy ourselves for the next few weeks. What say you?"

"I won't pretend that having a gentleman I am not related to and in whose company I'll feel no pressure to behave well would not be a great relief…" She mused, an impish smile appearing. "Very well, I accept. What's more, I'm going to give Hugh a sound bit of advice as to how to best help you make a splash."

"Make a splash?" Michael repeated in some dismay. "I have no intention of…"

"A quiet splash," Alice overrode as they parted, turning about their opposites. "Hardly any noise, barely a drop in the pond."

Michael shook his head, feeling more and more trapped with every new connection he made. "That sounded entirely too much like

Miranda for my liking."

Alice giggled prettily and curtsied as part of the dance, though it seemed she would have done so anyway. "My aunt Miranda and I have grown particularly close in the last few months, and I may say it does me credit."

It was all Michael could do not to run from his partner in terror. Miranda Sterling, lovely though she was, could frighten and intimidate any general, admiral, or monarch into behaving how she thought best. The relationship between her and her stepson Tony, Georgie Sterling's husband, was one of the fondest he'd seen outside of the true maternal bond, but even Tony feared her.

He suddenly had a very clear idea of what exactly Alice might propose to her brothers, and he didn't like it at all.

"Please don't..." he groaned as they continued to dance.

"Oh, it is too late for that," Alice said on a laugh, nearly skipping in the next dance motions. "She heard Hugh tell me to dance with you, so she's already planning something. We're all done for now!"

Michael made a face but managed to finish the dance creditably. He returned Alice to her brothers, neither of whom would meet his eyes, then quickly went in search of Tyrone, possibly the only one who wouldn't feed him to Miranda.

Unless she had gotten to him first.

A laugh he knew too well floated across the heads of the guests and met his ears. An accompanying shiver shot both up and down his spine, scattering in a thousand different pieces about his body.

Someone was amusing Charlotte. It was a true laugh, not a pretended one, and he was one of the few people in the world who could tell the difference.

Who amused her? What had amused her? Had she been amused all evening or just now? Was someone new amusing her or was it one of her regular chaps who wasn't worth a ha'penny?

Why did he bloody well care?

"Michael?"

Mrs. Wright's voice stopped him, forced him to turn, could not be ignored, nor could it be spurned. She had been near as much a mother to him as his own, and whatever he might feel towards Charlotte, he could not extend the same to her mother.

"Mrs. Wright, good evening." He smiled as genuinely as he could, taking her hand and bowing over it. "My, don't you look wonderful."

Her returning smile said far more than he expected, and he was curious how many other people knew more than he expected.

More than Charlotte did, at any rate.

"It is so lovely to see you," she insisted, squeezing his hand tightly. "We haven't seen you at home for a few weeks."

Michael nodded once. "I'm afraid I have taken up my mother's wishes to start establishing a life for myself, Mrs. Wright, and that takes up a good deal of my time. I'm sorry if I... if I have been missed."

"You have been, but all is well." Her smile warmed him as much as it saddened him. "You must certainly look after your own concerns and interests, as you have looked after some of ours for so long." Her smile spread, then she patted his hand and stepped away, moving past him to other parts of the ballroom.

Why did he suddenly feel as though some great farewell had just been made or that he'd been released from a shackling he hadn't been aware of? Whatever it was, however it happened, Michael had to fight to complete a swallow, and, blinking twice, turned to continue his search for Tyrone. Or anyone, really, who might improve his evening from what it presently was.

He caught sight of Tyrone, being oddly social, and headed in that direction.

With perfect timing, Tyrone turned at Michael's approach, grinning in welcome. "Sandford, what a chance. Do you know Miss Lawson and her sister, Miss Anne?"

"By sight, I believe, but not officially." He bowed to the pair of ladies, eerily similar in their fair looks. "How do you do?"

"Tolerably well, Mr. Sandford," Miss Lawson told him with a dip of her chin, though her eyes seemed to not particularly care for what she was taking in. She raised a dubious brow, her expression approaching distaste.

Well, then...

Michael could have smiled, but somehow managed to maintain his polite expression. "And you, Miss Anne?"

Anne Lawson was far less snobbish than her sister, if the way she looked at him was any indication, and she curtseyed with grace. "Well, Mr. Sandford, thank you. Are you finding the ball to your liking?"

"I am, yes," he replied, his smile appearing now.

Tyrone nudged him hard in the side, nearly puncturing a lung with the sharpness, though his expression did not change.

"But," Michael added quickly, "it would be all the better if you would take the next dance with me, Miss Anne."

The eyes of both Lawson sisters widened, and Anne grinned without reserve. "I would be delighted, Mr. Sandford, so long as you do not insist on being the lead couple."

"I would never insist on such a thing, Miss Anne," he assured her.

"My sister does not dance well, you see," Miss Lawson interjected with false sympathy. "Poor thing, such weak ankles, and she has such trouble remembering the steps."

Anne gave her sister a cold look. "I remember well enough to practice with you at your command."

Miss Lawson was not put off. "But confidence is best for the lead couple, is it not? And Anne has no confidence when it comes to dancing."

"Nor do I, Miss Lawson," Michael replied, not bothering to keep with the cool politeness he had begun. "I dance for enjoyment, not attention."

"Thank heavens for that," Tyrone said with a laugh. "Then all the snobs would flock to dance with you instead of refusing." He nodded at Miss Lawson, then at Michael before leaving the group.

Michael turned to Miss Anne as the music commenced. "Shall we?"

Tension ran along Miss Anne's jaw, but she nodded all the same. "Please, Mr. Sandford."

Without a single word to Miss Lawson, the two of them moved out to the dance floor, lining up with other couples.

"I cannot apologize enough, Mr. Sandford," Miss Anne half-whispered, her cheeks red. "My sister..."

"It is entirely unnecessary, Miss Anne," Michael told her,

offering a smile. "If I may say so, I know a bully when I encounter one, and I have yet to find one that I like. I only hope this dance may bring you pleasure enough to be worth her spite."

Anne laughed once, though seemingly without humor. "I doubt it. Roslyn hasn't had anything but spite for me since we were children. Is it horrible to say such a thing about one's sister?"

"Not to me." He bowed over her hand, backing up to his spot. "You're too kind."

The dance began and Michael found his attention drawn to just behind Anne, where Charlotte stood.

Watching him.

If she suspected what he was up to, she gave no indication. At the present, those around her were talking with each other, leaving her without conversation, yet not without company. Her dark eyes were on him, her lips curved in a relaxed, contented smile that was rarely seen in public. Oh, she smiled regularly, always wore a bright expression, and surely thrived upon the energy, but this private moment, this private smile, was not something one saw often outside of her home. Why did the sight of it affect him as much as seeing her arrive had?

Her smile spread just a touch as she caught him watching, and she tilted her head, spreading her hands out just a little. *How do I look?* The question was an obvious one, and he would have given the world not to answer it.

Thankfully, the dance permitted brevity, which she would understand. She needn't know there was nothing more he would want to say.

Michael swallowed once, then nodded once, barely a dip of his chin, but enough to be considered an answer. He saw Charlotte nod in return but did not look long enough to know much else.

He returned his attention to his partner, someone he already liked more than he'd expected after a five-minute acquaintance, and waited for their turn to join in. "Would it help if I laughed during our dance, Miss Anne?"

Anne snickered, her thumbs rubbing against her fists at her side. "Probably not. The last man who laughed during a dance with me found himself shamelessly pursued by Roslyn, all the way into the army."

"Good heavens," Michael coughed in surprise.

"It's all for the best, though," Anne whispered with a quick grin. "He and I still write, and I think he may offer for me when he returns."

Well, there went any potential suit for Anne Lawson, but at least he could enjoy a dance with a reasonable girl.

"So I may consider myself safe from you, then?" he asked, laughing with her. "And you are safe from me?"

"I'm afraid so," Anne said, glancing up the line of dancers before looking at Michael again. "But not, I trust, from Roslyn."

He shuddered. "If the way she looked at me was any indication, she'd rather offer for that footman on the east wall."

Anne looked where he indicated and pretended to consider it. "Well, he is mightily good looking..."

Michael coughed a laugh, then reached for Anne's hand as they finally joined the other couples in the dance.

Chapter Nine

―――――――❦❧❦――――――――

Surprises are a part of life, so one must become adjusted to the unanticipated. Accept the good, adapt to the bad, and move forward in preparation for the next unanticipated event.

-*The Spinster Chronicles, 24 November 1817*

"So how were things at the Preston ball? I'm ever so sorry to have missed it."

Charlotte wrinkled up her nose, picking up her tea. "Well enough. I didn't get on with the Prestons' son, but I got the impression that no one particularly cared. Julian Bruce doesn't talk when he dances, which is not a crime, but it certainly made the whole thing less enjoyable. I met a lovely fellow named Mr. Riley, but only for a moment. If I see him again, I may inquire further." She shrugged, sipping slowly. "It seemed a lot of fuss for precious little results."

"Results that you could see," Grace murmured with a hum. She winked at Kitty Morton, who snickered at it. "The gossips were delightfully unsettled by it."

"They were?" Charlotte sat up and slapped a hand on her arm rest. "What did they say?"

Grace rolled her eyes and set her own tea down. "Let me see if I can recall."

"I think you'll find you can," Charlotte demanded, hating when her friends intentionally put her off for their own enjoyment.

"Give her a moment," Georgie told her without much sympathy.

"It can be very vexing to recall so many details in the days following."

Charlotte threw her a glare. "It has been barely two, and the only reason we did not gather yesterday was because my head ached after the lateness of the hour at which we departed. Or rather, the earliness." She returned her attention to Grace. "What was said, Grace?"

"Oh, the usual shocked fuss," Grace said dismissively, eyeing Charlotte with delight. "What a beauty you were, how marvelous it was that you had come, what a fine catch you'd be, and what a credit you were to your parents."

"They said *what?*" Charlotte clapped her hands together, squealing in delight. "It worked!"

Izzy shook her head in disbelief. "Charlotte, they said the same thing about you three weeks ago. This is what they always say about you."

"Yes, but the occasion is different, don't you see?" Charlotte grinned at her, determined not to lose her enthusiasm in the face of logic. "I will be talked about with new interest! Isn't that so, Grace?"

Suddenly the center of their attention, Grace looked around, her expression not quite so mischievous. "I suppose…"

"It's not going to change in one night," Elinor reminded them all, though Charlotte knew well enough it was meant for her. "It will take repeated exposure to Charlotte as we should now see her in order for her to be taken seriously as a candidate for matrimony."

"I'll do it," Charlotte vowed with determination, nodding firmly. "Every night, I'll put myself through the gamut and become that same beauty they saw."

Georgie snorted softly. "Not every night, surely."

Charlotte ignored that, thinking quickly. "I wish now I hadn't given Edith the lavender silk. It would be beautiful to wear to the Bond family's dinner party. There is sure to be dancing there, and the skirts of that gown move so beautifully."

"I am sure you'll find something," Elinor mumbled, looking at Kitty with exasperation.

"How was the theater, Kitty?" Grace asked as she smiled at her. "Was the music as divine as you hoped it would be?"

Kitty beamed, reaffirming to the entire room what a beautiful girl she was. "Oh, yes! It was breathtaking, and the actors so very talented. I couldn't take my eyes from the stage!"

Izzy giggled to herself, drawing Charlotte's attention while the others went into more detailed questions with her.

"What's so amusing?" Charlotte asked her friend quietly. "Was it dreadful?"

"No, not at all." Izzy shook her head, copper hair dancing as she did so. "No, she's quite right; I thought I had seen all possible renditions of Cinderella by now, and yet Mr. Rossini surprised us all. Delightful show, you should attend."

Charlotte frowned, scooting closer. "I'll tell Mama, but why should that be amusing?"

Izzy bit her lip, snickering softly. "It isn't. Kitty saying she couldn't take her eyes from the stage is quite amusing."

"Because it's incorrect?"

"Because it is utterly correct." Izzy put a hand over her eyes, giggling further still.

Charlotte stared in abject confusion, wondering if her friend had truly lost all sense of herself, or if married life had softened her intelligence. She could only wait for Izzy to recover enough to speak coherently.

There had never been occasion in her life to think those words where Izzy was concerned, but she had learned to never set absolutes in life. They were almost always upset.

She glanced over at the rest and found them still in conversation about the beauty and imagination in *La Cenerentola*. Charlotte had no interest in the discussion, so she returned her focus to Izzy, who by now had put her hand at her throat.

"So Kitty stared at the stage," Charlotte stated. "What of it?"

Izzy's bright eyes met Charlotte's dark ones. "There was someone who happened to be at the theater also. Someone who joined our box, at our invitation. Someone who clearly wanted Kitty's attention to be somewhere other than on the stage."

Charlotte's mouth slowly dropped open, then spread into a wide grin. "Oh dear. How terribly upsetting for him."

Izzy nodded her head slowly. "Indeed. He was terribly disappointed when we left, but by pretending he paid attention to the music, he was at least able to converse with her. Which, I think, was better than nothing."

Now it was Charlotte who giggled uncontrollably. "Oh, I can just imagine his face! The poor man, he must have thought it such a clever scheme!"

"I think he must have, but he underestimated Kitty's love for opera." Izzy pressed the back of her hand to a cheek as though to cool her face. "I cannot wait to see what he attempts next."

"So you and Sebastian know, then," Charlotte said, choosing to avoid naming the man in question, on the chance she was incorrect in her assumptions. And to keep Kitty from hearing a name that might turn her attention to their conversation rather than her own.

Izzy nodded again, this time just once. "Oh, yes. He was rather upfront about it, wanted to be sure there would be no misapprehensions or strain between friends in this. He insisted that both Sebastian and I be present for the conversation, which I said was not necessary, but I think it may have helped his case where my husband was concerned." She smiled ruefully. "There is something to be said for giving honor and respect to the wife of the man whose sister has caused an interest."

"Put that into a Chronicles article," Charlotte suggested dryly. "It will revolutionize the whole nature of courtship."

Glancing over at her sweet but shy sister-in-law, Izzy sighed. "He would be so good for her, Charlotte. Trouble is that she has grown so used to him, so comfortable with having him near, that she cannot see him for what he could be. What he wishes to be. I worry that she never will, and if that should be the case, she will miss out on an utterly perfect match."

Charlotte grunted once and reached for a biscuit, munching it softly. "I wouldn't worry so very much. If I know him, and I daresay that I do, he won't give up. He'll try again and again and again until there is no mistaking him. And Kitty was such a skittish thing when we first met her. It's no wonder he spent so long getting her comfortable with him, it was the only way to be near her. She might have hated or feared him had he spoken before this."

Izzy shook her head again. "He could have spoken in the fall. It would have been perfect timing."

"Don't judge him too severely," Charlotte urged her friend. "He knows very well how he feels, but I think you will find him just as insecure as any woman would be about a man we love. What if she doesn't return the feeling? What if she cannot see him that way? What if he is wrong?"

"Has he said something?" Izzy asked her, eyes wide. "Charlotte…"

Charlotte looked away with a sniff, taking another bite of biscuit. "No, I am sworn to secrecy. Have faith and give him room to maneuver. If she is not engaged to him by Christmas, it will be neither his fault nor my own."

"Are you assisting him?"

"Of course not." Charlotte glanced over at her with a smirk. "But we may have a wager, the pair of us."

Izzy closed her eyes in dismay, slumping back. "Oh, Charlotte…"

That caught the attention of the others. "What?" Georgie demanded. "What have we missed?"

Charlotte settled herself rather cozily in her chair. "Izzy objects to my wagering on matters of the heart."

Georgie blinked, then her brow furrowed. "I object as well, though I daresay I should not be surprised. Are we permitted to know the details of the wager?"

"No," Charlotte replied. "But the first step was the Prestons' ball, and that went rather well." She chewed her lip a moment, then looked at Elinor. "Would you do me a very great favor and look at Mr. Riley as a candidate? I've never met him before, and I liked the look of him."

"Of course." Elinor nodded, stirring her tea. "Do you know his Christian name?"

"Unfortunately, no."

Elinor waved a hand. "No matter. Eugenia Preston will know. I have no doubt she oversaw the invitation list, not her mother." She pursed her lips a moment, then added, "I think Roslyn Lawson may try to outdo you for eligible matches, Charlotte."

Charlotte's eyes narrowed. "What? That venomous cow?"

"Are venomous cows real?" Kitty asked mischievously, playing at some confusion. "Amazing."

Grace scoffed and shared a longsuffering look with the girl. "Charlotte is mistress of all mythological creatures, you know. If she says it, the creature exists."

"Why would Roslyn Lawson compete with me?" Charlotte demanded, her attention still on Elinor. "She has neither my fortune, nor my affability. Nor my looks, if I may be momentarily vain."

"You may," a few of them said together.

She ignored them all.

"I don't know," Elinor admitted. "All I know is what Tyrone Demaris told Hugh, which was that she disapproved of Michael until he offered to dance with Anne. Suddenly, he was far more interesting, and she wished to discredit Anne in his eyes."

Charlotte grumbled incoherently for a moment. "Snide envy between sisters is no cause to alarm me. She is a dreadful snob, which she has no position to be, and the very idea that Roslyn wants what Anne has is laughable. Roslyn would have to sell her soul to amount to Anne's good sense, which would defeat the purpose."

"Did Michael enjoy dancing with Anne?" Kitty asked softly, eyes wide. "She would be a good match for him, if he liked."

Anne? A match for Michael?

"I don't know," Charlotte admitted, staring back at the girl as she realized how long it had been since she had really spoken with her closest friend. "I really don't know."

Michael was not a man prone to profanity, nor was he one to blaspheme or say anything other than what was right, proper, and gentlemanly.

That could all very well change in the next five minutes.

It did not help that this small man stared at him with the same distaste and disappointment that Miss Lawson had a few nights before.

"No," the man said with an almost-but-not-quite-French accent. "I cannot do it."

"I didn't ask if you can. I asked if you would."

Tyrone's question did not make a difference; the man continued to shake his head.

"I cannot work with a country bumpkin. I refuse." To emphasize the point, the man strode away and sat in a chair against the wall, folding his arms and staring at Michael as though he ought to be scolded.

Michael looked down at himself, then at Tyrone. "Country bumpkin?"

Tyrone shrugged. "He's my valet, not my scholar."

"You ought to sack him," Lord Sterling muttered behind Tyrone, sipping Madeira. "That sort of arrogance will end in a revolution in your house."

Tyrone grunted and held his glass out for a refill. "I'll give them the run of the house if they'll give me an occupation that will shut Eden up."

Hugh tutted nearby, looking up from his book. "Your brother pestering you again? I know something of that."

Lord Sterling threw something at his brother, but Michael, standing as he was in the center of the room, arms still outstretched, could not see what it was.

"Apparently, a gentleman bachelor is not an appropriate situation for the brother of Lord Eden." Tyrone scoffed darkly. "I had hoped that Martha would be able to keep him out of my business for a good year or so, but it seems even her charms are not enough to call a halt to his efforts."

Hugh frowned and looked at his brother for a moment. "Does it bother you that I am a gentleman without occupation?"

"No," came the droll reply. "But you have an estate that produces well. Tyrone here…"

"Tyrone has a valet who won't help us," Tyrone announced, changing the subject to Michael and downing his new glass of Madeira. "Which leaves us with few options."

"Wait a moment!"

They all paused at the voice, looking around at each other in dismay.

"Who invited her?" Michael asked darkly, willing to murder any man here for what he was about to be subjected to.

But each man had innocent expressions, which left only an individual not present.

Alice.

Michael glared at the Sterling brothers. "Alice has a cruel sense of humor."

"I've been saying that for years," Hugh insisted.

The last of the steps outside the room stopped, and the door opened to reveal the resplendent Miranda Sterling, silvery blue bonnet in one hand, her gloves in the other. Also in her hand was a lead attached to the drooping form of her beloved hound, Rufus.

"Dear, dear, dear," Miranda said as she looked Michael over. "How is it that we never noticed this before? What a dreadful mess."

"Ah, such vision," the valet praised, rising from his chair and offering it grandly to Miranda, who took it at once, Rufus sitting calmly beside her.

Michael scowled at them both, which was apparently exactly what the valet needed.

"Ooh," he said with some interest, considering Michael as if from a new angle. "Now there is a look I can dress. The brooding gentleman of wealth and consequence is every fair maiden's wish."

Tyrone exhaled a loud groan. "No, Stone, Michael isn't going to be the new Mr. Darcy, thank you."

"Why not?" Stone asked. "Real men never live up to the fictional ones; all of the maids say so."

The men in the room looked around at each other, and Tyrone stared at his valet in amused surprise. "Do they? And who are they saying this to?"

Stone's face became a mask. "I'm sure I do not know, sir. I only hear things."

"I'm sure you do." Tyrone nodded at Miranda and gestured to Michael. "Well?"

Miranda pursed her lips, her fingers absently scratching at the back of Rufus's head. "It would be all very well if this was the country, and I understand that Mr. Sandford has spent a deal of time at his country estate of late. Is that not so?"

"It is," Michael conceded, unsure where Miranda wished to take this line of questioning.

She nodded knowingly. "Such a lovely place, Crestor Grove. You must be so very proud to be master of it."

Michael blinked, knowing full well that Miranda Sterling had never set foot on the property of Crestor Grove in her entire life. "I am, yes. It's done very well since my father's death, despite my failings."

"Such devotion to the family estate and your heritage," Miranda simpered, almost seeming to tear up. "Such tireless efforts to improve life for your mother, your sisters, and your sweet brother Peter. You can hardly think about yourself with all of that weighing on you, can you?"

What in the world was she talking about? Michael had certainly been dedicating much of his energy to improving the estate, but it was not as though his father had left it in ruins. They had been well set up in his death, and his sisters had dowries that were secure. Peter would need a profession one day, but so did most younger sons in England.

And Michael *could* think of himself because he not only had an intelligent and capable estate agent, but a mother who could run the place better than any man he'd ever met, including his father. Michael was barely needed at Crestor Grove, though he was supposed to be lord and master of it.

Before Michael could answer, Miranda looked at Stone with damp eyes. "Such a worthy gentleman deserves the very best, wouldn't you agree, Stone?"

"Yes, my lady," Stone agreed without hesitation.

"He could hardly be expected to maintain London fashions while so dedicated to matters in the country, could he?"

"Of course, my lady."

"We cannot allow him to be pitied and dismissed by Society simply because matters of even greater import than his apparel have consumed his mind, can we?"

"No, my lady."

Miranda placed a hand to her chest, beaming up at Stone. "I knew you would agree, Stone. I knew that you were a man of great principle as well as vision and talent."

Stone blushed like a young girl receiving her first flirtation.

"Well, my lady…"

"Now," Miranda said with a much firmer voice, somehow losing none of her flattery despite the change in tone, "I would ask that you pull the best things from Mr. Demaris' collection and try them on Mr. Sandford. They are of close enough size to give us a fair assessment. Hugh, you will take copious notes of everything Stone and I suggest and hand it over at the end of this gathering. At which time, Michael dear, you and I will be going to Bond Street to have you perfectly fitted and tailored before your next appearance anywhere."

"Miranda," Lord Sterling protested.

"Really, Miranda," Hugh tried.

"I daresay, Miranda," Tyrone blustered.

Michael said nothing, and only stared at Miranda while Stone gleefully obeyed her command.

Miranda raised a brow at him. "Well, Michael?"

"I cannot agree to this," he told her, not caring that the others would hear. "I have stable finances, Mrs. Sterling, but to waste them on this frippery…"

"Personal grooming is not a waste," Miranda overrode with some insistence. "Nor is it frippery. And it does not matter what your finances are, this is my gift to you."

"What?" every gentleman in the room cried in near unison.

She looked around at them all calmly, as though she were merely surveying houseplants. "Hmm. Jealousy mingled with disbelief over here, while this one only has shock. That confirms my decision if nothing else does." She winked at Michael and gestured for him to remove his coat. "Don't argue with me, dear, it will only make things worse. And while I adore the family I have married into, kindly call me Miranda. Neither Georgie nor Elinor would enjoy being confused for me, though I daresay we all appear of an age."

Lord Sterling coughed a laugh that he smothered with further attempts at coughing, which only resulted in choking sounds.

Miranda sniffed once. "Francis, my love, do kindly remember who keeps your mother-in-law from descending upon you more than once a quarter."

Hugh cackled mercilessly from his perch and snapped his book shut. "For that alone, Miranda, I will take notes on anything and everything you wish."

Tyrone poured a glass of Madeira and handed it to Miranda. "I'm not sure if I should be defending Aunt Hetty or applauding the dart, Miranda, so I'll only offer you a drink."

She inclined her head regally. "Very wise, Tyrone. Would you mind terribly if I ask your cook for a dish of water for poor Rufus? And perhaps some sandwiches for myself? The charity gala meeting went on so dreadfully long, and no one thought about luncheon at all."

"What charity gala?" Lord Sterling asked, now fully recovered. "Why don't I know of this?"

"Your wife does, my lamb, and she has assured the committee of your donation." She waved a hand. "That is all you need to know. Janet will inform you where and when your presence is required. Tyrone, dear..."

"Yes, Miranda, of course." Tyrone plucked up her hand and kissed it fondly, scratched Rufus's ear, then stepped from the room to do her bidding.

Michael continued to watch Miranda, wondering what in the world had possessed her to take an interest in him like this, let alone to be so generous. A word from Alice Sterling could not have had this much influence, and it was clear that the Sterling brothers had done nothing to bring this on. Charlotte did not know his plans, even if her mother had shared what he had told her.

So why all this? What prompted the action?

What did she mean by it?

As though she could read his thoughts, Miranda smiled at him in a manner he could only call maternal. "Don't dwell on it overly much, dear. I never had any children myself. And though I adore my stepsons wildly, they were really almost grown when I married their father. They were away at school most of the time, though we had the most glorious fun when they returned. So now, I like to take an interest in worthy parties when I can, and, despite what people think, it can be just as much fun to prepare fashion for a man as it is for a woman."

"I find that hard to believe," he murmured. "Even so... Why me, Miranda?"

Her smile turned from matronly to mischievous in an instant. "Because I have a very good feeling about what may transpire in all this, and I am determined to pay good money to see it."

Chapter Ten

———— ❦ ❦ ————

One can be particularly fortunate or particularly unfortunate in their dinner companions when attending such gatherings. The chances are the same, and it may shape the whole course of the meal.

-*The Spinster Chronicles, 26 February 1817*

"The Bonds have an interesting interpretation of a small dinner."

"Shh! Charles, they will hear you."

Charles looked at Charlotte in wry surprise. "When have you ever cared about what the Bonds think? They are quite good, but hardly the brightest London has to offer."

Charlotte scowled at her brother as they moved into the large drawing room to await the announcement of dinner. "I cannot afford to be particularly stingy about the company I keep at the present, Charles. The Bonds are of sufficiently high station and have excellent connections. If I wish to find a husband among the upper class, I must attend dinners with people like the Bonds."

"Fine," Charles grumbled, no doubt doing his best not to scowl as he gritted his teeth in a show of a smile. "But do not expect me to carry much by way of conversation at the table. I shall be fortunate to use even the smallest portion of my brain."

"That's normally all one can expect of you anyway," Charlotte replied as she slid her hand from his arm, batting her lashes playfully. She turned and nodded indulgently at Mrs. Bond's aunt, Lady Hetty Redgrave, who had long been a friend to the Spinsters, though presently looked as though she had been asked to swallow billiard balls.

Society dinners had never been Lady Hetty's favorite pastime, though it was rather less clear what exactly *was* her favorite pastime. She was more inclined to find disfavor with something rather than to find favor in anything.

"Please don't make me go over there," Charles begged beside her. "She'll make a game out of insulting me."

"I adore that game," Charlotte shot back. "And you needn't stay by my side all night. In fact, I beg you not to. There are plenty of ladies and gentlemen about. Go and socialize."

Charles glared at her darkly. "The only reason there are plenty of gentlemen is because Mary Bond was jilted, and they are desperate for a quick resolution. They only invited ladies to even out the numbers."

Charlotte rolled her eyes and walked away, shaking her head. It wasn't often that her brother accompanied her to events, usually preferring to arrive on his own time and to pretend as though they hardly knew each other, but the rare occasions when they were together reminded her why the occasions were not commonplace. They truly were better apart than together.

The fact that both of them had made it to adulthood was extraordinary.

She continued to smile politely at everyone, walking around as though she were only taking a turn about the room. It was almost aimless, but in truth, she was surveying the gentlemen present. Those that were engaged in conversation, those that were standing alone, and those that, like her, seemed to be examining the guests. The game was an intriguing one, and Charlotte was an expert. She had yet to be outplayed, and she refused to let tonight be a first.

The tall and dashing form of Mr. Riley stood not far from her, and a natural pause in his conversation brought his gaze to her. A shock of sorts raced from the pit of her stomach down the back of both legs, a strange sort of lightning that curled her toes despite never raising them.

Goodness, that was a fun sensation.

Would it have been too much trouble to ask Mr. Riley to look away, then look back at her and see if it happened again? Better yet, what if he smiled?

A composed, possibly habitually stoic man like Mr. Riley would likely need encouragement. But what could she do when they had barely been introduced?

Charlotte paused a step, kept her eyes on him, and lifted a corner of her mouth in a lopsided, bemused smile. History had told her such a smile was one of her best, so why not offer it now?

Mr. Riley saw, and his lips quirked as though he, too, would smile. Yet it never fully formed.

Curiously stubborn fellow.

"Supper is served," Mrs. Bond announced to the gathering. "Shall we go in?"

Charlotte looked away from Mr. Riley, wondering if they would have a formal procession or not. She would be expected to have a gentleman on her arm, and without calling her brother to her side, she would have few comfortable options. Not that her comfort was of utmost importance, but it should have been noted all the same.

Thankfully, it seemed that they would only have the guests enter in an orderly fashion, which would solve a great many problems.

Charlotte moved in the direction of the dining room with the rest, smiling politely at those streaming in alongside her. She knew most of them well enough for passing conversation, though hardly well enough to intentionally seek it out. She could only pray that whomever she was seated next to at dinner would be entertaining enough to enjoy the meal with, and that they would also be wise enough to allow her to eat. It was a dreadful thing to be seated next to someone who did not understand that the primary purpose of a meal was to consume it.

The dining room was simply decorated, though the walls bore some lovely family portraits. If the meal became interminable, Charlotte could always imagine herself striking up a conversation with one of the portrait inhabitants. It could be more entertaining than anything at the table, at any rate.

There was some general murmuring as guests tried to find the place card with their name on it, and a great deal of laughter as each was discovered. Playful waves were sent up and down the table as people began to be seated. Charlotte laughed when she saw her brother being seated next to Mary Bond, who really was a lovely girl, but with her recent disappointment, would be looking for a quick match with excellent connections.

There would be no denying that Charles would fill that position quite nicely, should he be so inclined.

"Ah, Miss Wright, I think you will enjoy the seating arrangement."

Charlotte smiled at Mrs. Bond, who happened to be tottering nearby on the way to her seat. "Shall I? How so?"

Mrs. Bond giggled, the cap on her head bouncing against her mountainous curls of red, her plump cheeks stretching with the laughter. "Why, because I have sat you beside our dear Mr. Sandford, of course. I know how thick the two of you have been since childhood, and I simply could not help myself."

Charlotte looked past the woman at Michael, who stared at Charlotte without much hint of his feelings on the subject. Whatever he was feeling, it was clear joy was not involved. Yet there was no resentment either, as far as she could tell. Then again, Michael had always been quite good about controlling his emotions and never leaving anything on display long enough for observation. The blankness of his expression could simply be due to hunger, after all.

Many a man had been mistaken for angry when it was only hunger he felt.

"Perfect, Mrs. Bond," Charlotte praised with another bright smile. "I may be the most comfortable of your guests this entire dinner."

Mrs. Bond tittered and put a hand on Charlotte's arm. "I do hope so, dear." With a quick pat, the hostess moved to her seat at the head of the table, and Charlotte went to her own chair.

Michael rose from the table to pull it out for her, then saw her quickly settled before taking his own seat.

"Thank you," Charlotte murmured when he did so.

"Of course."

Nothing else.

Charlotte looked down at her plate, then glanced at the person to her left.

Russell Collier, second son of Lord Wittam. Congenial enough, though rather dense. The family fortune was stable for now, though would likely fall sharply when the eldest son inherited. Mr. Russell Collier was in need of a profession and was completely waffling about deciding on one.

Absolutely not worth improving relations with. The fact that he had been invited at all showed a shocking lack of foresight by the Bonds.

Shameful.

"Don't say it."

Charlotte glanced at Michael to her right, who cautiously sipped his water without looking at her. "Say what?"

He shook his head very slightly. "You know very well what. I saw that, and I know you. Don't say it."

A helpless laugh started to well within her chest, and she forced it to remain contained there, biting her lip to ensure it as much as possible. "But you agree."

"It doesn't matter who agrees," he insisted. "Do not say it."

"Say you agree, and I won't."

The corner of Michael's mouth ticked ominously. "Very well, I agree."

Charlotte reached for her water and took a small sip. "What do you agree with?"

Michael grumbled under his breath before admitting, "Mr. Collier is not the ideal candidate for the Bonds to be considering for their daughter."

"For shame," Charlotte scolded in a playful hiss. "To say such things while we sit here. Michael, I am astonished."

"I think you'll survive. Which is more than I can say for my other dinner companion."

As gracefully as possible, Charlotte looked across Michael to identify the lady there, and had to stifle laughter at the sight of a very sullen Roslyn Lawson.

"What seems to be the problem?" Charlotte whispered.

"My fortune is less than twenty thousand pounds," Michael replied in the same tone, "my estate is nowhere near Bath, and I lack a title."

Charlotte exhaled a faux sigh of defeat. "I don't know why I even speak to you. Clearly, I should address Mr. Collier instead."

"Clearly."

Charlotte pressed her teeth into her lip harder, looking away from Michael to find some sort of control. Oh, it felt marvelous to laugh with him like this, and it seemed an age since they had done so. Of course, with her focus on finding matrimonial prospects, she really hadn't cause to send for him for her own amusement. He could have called on his own accord, naturally, but those visits had become less frequent in the last year or so as it was.

It hadn't occurred to her until the other night at the Prestons' ball that there might have been something wrong between them. This wasn't the occasion to discuss such things, but the manner between them at the moment eased her feelings on the subject considerably. They couldn't possibly be on the outs if they could continue to joke as they once did.

Relief swirled within her at the thought. Despite everything, losing her friendship with Michael would have been a disaster. She could gain the world's best match in every respect and still feel a loss if he were no longer in her life. Though marriage would certainly separate them to a degree, she would adamantly refuse to let it part them.

She would not give up Michael.

"Perhaps if you sang for Miss Lawson," Charlotte suggested as the first course of supper was brought out, "she might see you in a more favorable light. After all, it is one of your greatest gifts, and nobody knows about it but me."

Michael gave her a sidelong look, his eyes holding a knowing light she knew well. "I only sing for you, dear."

Warmth hit Charlotte's chest and rose quickly into her lips, prompting a wide smile. His answer was the same as it had been for years, and anything else as a response would have been a disappointment or a shock. As far as she knew, Charlotte was the only one who had heard Michael sing, and while some might have considered that a crime against humanity, given the splendor of his voice, the pair of them had never cared about it. Michael was not one for display, and Charlotte herself did not play, so a duet was never something they had been forced into.

Once or twice, it had occurred to Charlotte to wonder if Michael's mother knew about his abilities, but ultimately, that was neither here nor there. So long as his voice was their particular secret, all was well enough.

"How goes your great plan?" Michael asked after a moment, his attention on his food. "Any success?"

"Not yet," Charlotte told him, swallowing her own bite of food, "but we've only just begun. Grace trussed me up the other night for emphasis... Well, you saw that."

Michael nodded. "I did. Impressive. How much did you hate it?"

She nudged him hard with her elbow. "It was lovely, I'll have you know. I haven't felt that pretty in ages, and though it was a great deal of fuss, I think it helped."

"With what? You've never lacked for attention."

There was something in the tone of those words that Charlotte did not care for at all. Something hard, she would have called it bitter had the speaker been anyone other than Michael. As it *was* him, she could not say what lay behind it.

But she did not like it.

"The right sort of attention," she hissed, focusing on her meal and keeping her table manners in a ladylike fashion, "from the right sort of people. I have been a fixture in Society, which means everyone is used to seeing me everywhere all the time. I am not likely to make any sort of impression now unless I make some drastic changes, which is what we have done."

"Steady on," Michael muttered, smiling for the effect of others around them. "I wasn't insulting your efforts."

She'd have glared at him had they been anywhere else. "Weren't you? I haven't seen you about in ages."

"You haven't sent for me. You could have done."

The flippant words held the same sharp edge his previous words had done, and they rankled just as much. "When have you ever needed an invitation?"

"We aren't sixteen anymore, Charlotte. I cannot just call without a reason and have it pass the gossips unnoticed." He paused in the act of reaching for his drink again, then shook his head and continued. "It wouldn't be right, and it wouldn't be fair."

Charlotte ignored appearances and propriety, staring at Michael blatantly and without shame. "Right and fair? To whom, Michael? Everyone knows we are friends, as evidenced by this seating arrangement. No one would suspect anything untoward. They haven't done so yet."

Michael exhaled roughly and straightened, keeping his gaze ahead rather than on her. "To me, Charlotte. If I am always tied to you, it will make things deuced awkward, if not impossible, to find a wife for myself. How can I attach myself to someone else if everyone assumes that the only woman in my life is you? You are not the only one seeking a change of situation."

Nothing could have prepared her for those words from him, and she could barely comprehend the meaning behind them. Was he saying he wanted to get married? When had that been decided?

Before or after she had decided to do so?

"You're pursuing matrimony?" Charlotte whispered. "When was this decided? You never said."

"I don't tell you everything."

They ate in silence, and the space between them might as well have held its very own blizzard for all the warmth there.

It wasn't right, her arguing with him about this sort of thing. She was pursuing matrimony, so why shouldn't Michael? Just because they had never spoken of it did not mean he should not, or could not. He was free to do as he liked without reference to Charlotte. It was entirely possible that her decision to marry had given him cause to consider the topic and, especially given his mother's wishes, give in and pursue the same.

Why should they fall out over it?

"No, of course," she murmured, unsure if he would hear her, or if he'd care to. "Nor should you have to." Forcing herself to brighten, she made a show of enjoying her meal. "Have you entered into a courtship with anyone? I shall have to give my consent to your choice, you know."

Michael grunted once, the tone flat. "No, I have not, and yes, I presumed as much. And I am not... That is... Marriage is not my primary concern, I am only allowing myself to consider the possibility."

Charlotte considered that with a playful tilt of her head. "Oh, by all means, consider away. Anyone in particular we are considering as yet?"

Now Michael looked at her in full, smiling in what had to be the first genuine manner all evening. "No, Charlotte."

"No what?" she pressed, the playacting growing easier. "No, you aren't considering anyone?"

"No, there is no 'we' in this scenario," he said simply. "No, I am not discussing any of this with you. No, you do not get to pick someone out for me. No, we will not be exchanging details of any future courtships either of us are engaged in as some sort of commiseration of its troubles. No, no, and no, Charlotte."

She giggled in spite of herself but sensed that Michael wasn't injecting as much humor into his words as she was. "But I can help, Michael. You know I can."

He shook his head firmly. "I have all the help I need. Besides, I've read every issue of the Spinster Chronicles. I know all of the advice on courtship and the like, and I'd rather not be so closely examined."

The message was unmistakable; Charlotte was to have nothing to do with Michael's impending yet currently hypothetical courtship. She was, in effect, to be excluded. Did that mean he wished to be excluded from her attempts, as well?

Charlotte absently fiddled with the base of her nearest fork, her throat working as she tried to find words. "And... if I would like some advice on my own courtship? When it happens? Might I ask your opinion on occasion? Having never been in a courtship, and knowing so little of men in truth..."

Michael stilled beside her, not even his breathing audible, if he was breathing at all. It didn't seem as though he was, and she was suddenly very carefully attuned to everything about him.

How did his not breathing prevent her from breathing as well?

"I would... prefer," he began slowly, "if you kept those instances to a minimum. If at all."

Charlotte's throat dried in an instant. "Michael..."

"You're my best friend, Charlotte," he said at once, his voice rough. "That won't change today or tomorrow or any day after. But

I cannot hold your hand while you court London Society in pursuit of marriage. I will not."

It was all she could do to blink, feeling cold without shivering, feeling warm without flushing. Why did her friendship suddenly seem so very different than it had only minutes ago? Why did it feel at an end, despite his vow that it would not?

She managed a swallow and glanced down the table as though looking for someone, more an act than anything else. "Well, so long as you don't sing…"

"I told you," he replied quickly, his tone warming, "I only sing for you, dear."

There was that, at least.

Charlotte's eyes fell on Mr. Riley and found his eyes already on her. For a moment, she only stared, her lips already curved in the benign, polite smile she always wore in public. He stared back, and then dipped his chin in a nod, now smiling at her.

That lightning sensation in her leg returned, this time making its way down into her smallest toe. Her heavy heart began to lighten, incrementally, and her polite smile turned into one less forced, less pained, less habitual.

It didn't solve her feelings of loss, nor her wistful longing of her friendship from days gone by, but it did give her a reason to smile and mean it.

At the moment, that was enough.

Chapter Eleven

One never knows what may be discovered over a simple game of cards.

-*The Spinster Chronicles, 19 December 1815*

"Sandford, you remember Mrs. Greensley? Formerly Miss Wilton, you know, but she married last year."

Michael smiled at the plain but friendly face of Mrs. Greensley, belatedly recollecting that, when she had been Jane Wilton, she had been Charlotte's favorite of the Wilton sisters. The most sensible, the most genuine, and the warmest by far. He could do far worse than reconnecting with her in this new chapter of his life, marriageable prospect or not.

Connections of any sort were his goal, and there was no telling who might know other people that could significantly improve his lot, his life, or his luck.

"Of course," he said as he gave a half bow in Mrs. Greensley's direction. "It is very good to see you again. How are you?"

She smiled and inclined her head, continuing to shuffle the cards in her hand. "Very well, Mr. Sandford. Will you and Mr. Sterling join us for a round or two of whist?"

He nodded once, pulling the chair out. "Certainly." He smiled at the woman across from Mrs. Greensley, a fair-haired lady with a warm smile currently directed at him.

Curious.

"Mr. Sandford, may I introduce my cousin, Miss Diana Palmer?" Mrs. Greensley said with a hint of a laugh in her voice. "She has come to stay with us from Derbyshire for the remainder of the Season."

Michael bowed before her, smiling without any effort at all. "A pleasure, Miss Palmer. Is this your first time to London?"

Rich, whiskey-colored eyes seemed to sparkle as Miss Palmer's smile deepened. "No, sir, though it is my first time in London for the Season. Even if it is at the end of it."

"Ah," Michael replied, taking his seat. "Well, the end of the Season is usually the best part, Miss Palmer."

"Is it?" She flicked a smile to her cousin, then returned her attention to Michael. "In what way?"

Michael folded his hands on the surface of the table, then shrugged. "The fuss and fervor that surround the opening of the Season has faded. Those wildly inclined to make a match have likely done so, or have at least selected their choice, leaving everyone else to enjoy themselves without any additional pressures."

Miss Palmer's eyes narrowed a touch, and he had the sense she was sizing him up, though he could not have said what for. "Is that what the Season should be about? Enjoying one's self?"

"I've always thought so." Michael continued to smile at her, charmed by her lack of silliness and intrigued by her lack of airs. She was beautiful, effortlessly so, but there also seemed to be a clever wit lurking beneath that fine façade, and therein lay much of his curiosity and interest, if he were totally honest.

"I suppose it would depend on what one does for enjoyment," Hugh added as Mrs. Greensley dealt the cards. "If the events and opportunities the Season can offer are of interest, one might find great enjoyment in it. If the country life is more suited, then alas..."

Mrs. Greensley chuckled softly. "Indeed, Mr. Sterling. I adore the ease of country life myself, but London does hold some pleasures for me in spite of this. Enough to bring me into town for a few weeks, at the very least."

Hugh chuckled as he pulled his cards towards him. "If you might convey that information to my wife, Mrs. Greensley, it would be much appreciated. She has no desire to remove to the country at any time, whereas I have lost my taste for London altogether."

That earned Hugh a sympathetic look from the woman as she finished her dealing of the cards. "I can understand that, sir, though it does sadden me on your behalf."

Hugh's smile was fleeting. "You are too kind." He glanced at the card she flipped over. "Trumps are clubs."

"What is my cousin talking about?" Miss Palmer asked Michael in an undertone. "Or is it too dear a topic?"

Michael flicked his gaze between the other two at their table, and, seeing their occupation with their cards, pretended the same. "Mr. Sterling spent a time of his adult life engaging in unsavory behaviors with unsavory people, though nothing particularly scandalous in his own case. One of his closest friends, a man cut from the same cloth, attempted to compromise Mr. Sterling's sister."

Miss Palmer could barely restrain her gasp, one shaking hand making a show of fiddling her cards. "Oh, heavens. Was she ruined?"

"Nearly, but not altogether. She is quite well and rather a popular girl now, but Mr. Sterling was shaken to his core."

"As any proper sibling would be." She looked at the man in question, biting her lip. "Poor man."

Michael nodded, clearing his throat and leaning closer. "He is most repentant now, and quite changed. So that, I believe, is why London no longer holds its former charms."

Miss Palmer shook her head, sighing. "I do hope his wife understands that. He should not have to remain if the memories are so painful."

"He is newly married," Michael informed her, finding himself smiling, "and rather inclined to dote on his bride, I think. The affection is quite mutual. I don't think either of them mind being anywhere, if they are together."

Something in his words made Miss Palmer smile, her dark eyes darting to him before turning to her cards. "What a lovely thought. Would that all matches had the same understanding."

"I quite agree, Miss Palmer," Michael murmured, smiling at her with increased interest. "Most heartily."

"Diana, my dear," Mrs. Greensley broke in, still holding a laugh in her voice. "Do you intend to follow my lead? Mr. Sterling has played."

Color raced into Miss Palmer's cheeks, and she looked at the pair of discarded cards quickly. "Oh, goodness, forgive me. I don't know where my head is."

"Don't you?" her cousin mused very softly, her words far too low for Miss Palmer to hear, though Michael caught them quite clearly.

His own cheeks began to flush, and he focused on his cards, lest he should get a similar hint from his partner.

The rounds continued in moderate silence for a handful of minutes, during which Michael became acutely aware of the woman next to him, and the eyes of their partners. He couldn't be sure, but he would have bet a good deal that the pair of them were watching Michael and Miss Palmer closely.

Were people always thrown into speculation upon the first meeting? It was an unnerving amount of pressure, despite the fact that he had just spoken of the lack of pressure during this time of the Season. The irony there was not lost on him, though he supposed he had earned his share of speculation and irony at this relatively late point of his life. He'd never been suspected of harboring romantic feelings for any lady, not even Charlotte.

Which was even stranger, as he had harbored the strongest feelings about her.

Had.

He paused as he laid a moderately scored card in the diamond suit, something stilling in the pit of his stomach. Had he lost his feelings for Charlotte? He couldn't have, they had been his constant companion for years, though not always in the forefront of his mind.

He'd told her not to bring her suitors to his attention, not to discuss anything of the sort with him, and she had seemed to agree. He could not deny that the dinner they'd shared at the Bonds' party had been awkward and painful, but it had been a conversation long overdue. And it was not as though he were cutting her off, as it were. More just giving them room to grow.

That was it. Room to grow and explore what other people might have to offer them.

No, his feelings for Charlotte were not gone, he decided. He only had to look a bit harder for them.

What an intriguing idea.

"Sandford, I am beginning to wonder about your strategy."

Michael blinked and looked across the table at Hugh. "Pardon?"

Hugh lowered his eyes meaningfully to the table before them, and Michael followed his gaze.

The cards there, while all diamonds, showed that Hugh had won the trick with a jack, but Michael, instead of keeping his cards low so that he did not sacrifice a potentially winning card later, had played the ten of diamonds. Their partnership had still taken the trick, but it was a waste of a card that could have won a trick later.

Moderately scored, indeed.

Michael stared at the cards, his mind spinning on various quips that might dissuade any discussion on his reasons for inattention. He forced himself to smile, then looked up at Hugh. "I am a terrible whist player. Didn't I say that?"

Hugh rolled his eyes and chuckled. "No, I don't believe so." He looked at Miss Palmer. "Won't you give up your cousin and partner me? You've clearly got an eye for the game, unlike someone else."

Miss Palmer smiled swiftly and began to carefully reorganize the cards in her hand. "I'm afraid not, Mr. Sterling. I am quite satisfied with my partner, and the current course of the game."

"That's because you're winning," Michael pointed out.

Miss Palmer's smile turned crooked, and she raised a brow. "Winning is a satisfying thing, and I'll not deny it. But I hardly think you can justify saying my cousin and I are winning when we have not even finished a round yet."

"No, indeed," Mrs. Greensley insisted with a light laugh. "It could all change in the next round, and I believe we'll still be enjoying ourselves."

"I certainly intend to," Miss Palmer agreed as she laid her card down. "Imagine if we only enjoyed the things we won at. Everyone would be miserable all the time!"

Hugh grunted once but smiled. "Spoken like a fair-minded woman. Men, on the other hand, are rivalrous to a fault, and are desolated when they lose." He held out a hand towards Michael. "Is it not so?"

Michael heaved a sigh, shaking his head. "It is so. Many a man has been called out for cheating when all he has done was win. We simply cannot accept anything less than victory."

Miss Palmer seemed to consider that, her expression still playful. "Perhaps this is why women live longer than men." She swept the cards to her, having won the trick, and shrugged her shoulders. "Contentment and proper enjoyment."

"Very likely," Michael allowed, "and a distinct lack of stupidity."

"That would depend on the individual," Mrs. Greensley chimed in, a devious glint in her eye. "There are plenty of females who lack intelligence in even the most basic of subjects."

"I could never say such a thing, nor will I be found agreeing to it." Michael shook his head very firmly, pointedly laying his card.

Miss Palmer giggled softly, the sound warm and natural rather than the forced trill of high-pitched tones he'd heard from so many other ladies. "But you won't argue against it?"

Smiling, Michael again shook his head. "I make it a point to never argue with ladies."

Hugh snorted softly, laying the final card and taking the trick. "Is that meant to be gallant or self-preserving?"

"Both, ideally." He offered the table a cheeky grin. "The only exception would be my sisters, and the older they get, the less likely I am to argue about anything at all."

"For gallantry or self-preservation?" Miss Palmer asked as Hugh shuffled the cards and prepared to deal.

Her wit earned her a smile from Michael, as well as an additional mark of respect, though such a thing was less easily displayed.

"Neither, in their case," Michael admitted fondly. "It's the utter futility of the thing."

That made her laugh again, this time more fully, and the sound was more captivating than anything he'd felt towards her yet. "Oh, Mr. Sandford, that is too perfect."

"As a brother to a sister myself," Hugh broke in, his tone serious, "I concur. There is no winning."

"It comes with sisters, I'm afraid," Mrs. Greensley admitted. She sighed and took a sip of the Madeira beside her. "The moment they learn the value of opinion, there is no stopping it."

Miss Palmer made the gentlest scoffing sound known to man and gave her cousin a look. "Come, come, you cannot think all sisters everywhere are like Lucy."

Mrs. Greensley grimaced, then looked around at them all. "Let it be known that I was not the one to mention a particular sister by name. I'll not take the blame, should rumors abound."

"So noted," Hugh and Michael said together, almost solemnly.

"But that would mean she would come against me," Miss Palmer pointed out, mock effrontery on display.

Mrs. Greensley gave her a pitying smile. "Alas, my poor cousin. I shall weep prodigiously at your funeral."

Michael chuckled to himself and looked between the ladies. "You never had the same trouble with another sister, Mrs. Greensley?"

She met his eyes, smiling congenially. "Not in the same way, no. Each sister has her own particular blend of mischief and mayhem, but I have found that each has some of both."

"Not Mary, surely," Miss Palmer protested.

Mrs. Greensley's look was answer enough, though she added, "Even Mary, my dear. We are so close in age that going to the dressmaker would cost our parents less because they would get half the number of dresses and expect us to share." She huffed, as if the memory of several fights on the subject still caused irritation. "It was a blessing when she married Captain Gracie, in a number of ways."

"I did not know she had married him," Michael said in surprise, smiling warmly. "My felicitations. When was that?"

"This winter," came the reply, "which is likely why you did not hear of it. They married and almost immediately set sail for the West Indies for his next posting."

"It was a beautiful service," Miss Palmer told the group. "Short, but lovely. And really, what is there to say besides the pronouncement of man and wife?"

Michael played the four of spades, looking at Miss Palmer with a rueful smile. "I do believe there are some vows…"

"One or two," Hugh added with a nod. "I barely recall mine. I was too distracted by my bride."

"You called?"

Michael groaned as Elinor approached, not that it should be an evil, but for the simple effect her presence would have on Hugh. As expected, his smile was doting, his wife's indulgent.

"Good evening, angel," Hugh said, taking his wife's hand and kissing it once.

Elinor winked, then turned to the table. "Jane! How well you look; I can see that marriage to Greensley suits you."

"It does, I'll not deny it." Mrs. Greensley returned her smile and gestured lightly. "And I would say that being Mrs. Sterling must agree with you. You're quite radiant."

Elinor blushed, glancing at her husband. "I am entirely under his influence, you might say. There is much to be said for a happy marriage."

"Amen," Hugh agreed softly, his eyes still on his bride.

"Is it a command that married ladies must compliment each other on being so?" Miss Palmer asked Michael in a low tone. "Or are we just fortunate enough to be witnesses to this particular exchange?"

Michael restrained a laugh, biting the inside of his cheek. "I really cannot say. I don't know that I would call Mrs. Sterling radiant so much as frequent to flush since her marriage."

"And my cousin has only found a softening to her features since her marriage, not an entire alteration to complexion," Miss Palmer added, flicking at something on her cream muslin. "I rather think that is due to a far better cook and less strife at home, not particularly owed to being wife to Greensley."

"Perhaps crediting marriage for the changes is a tradition," Michael suggested, watching the particular turn of Miss Palmer's lip while their companions chatted about all things matrimonial.

Miss Palmer hummed, her head tilting as she apparently considered that. "It's an odd tradition, I must say. And surely it only lasts the first year or two of a marriage. I cannot admit to hearing my parents say such things, though, admittedly, their marriage was not for love."

"Nor mine," Michael conceded, now eyeing Elinor and Hugh, wondering if such a match might have made a difference in his life. "Companionable enough, perhaps loving in the end, but not at the start."

"Mine was much the same, though my father was a good deal older than my mother." Her smile deepened almost wistfully. "It was his second marriage, though we were never made to feel like it. His other children were frequent visitors, more akin to aunts and uncles than half-siblings."

It was not an uncommon thing to find such a match and family in England, though Michael had never discussed such a thing so openly with anyone involved in one.

"Did you have siblings of your own age, as well?" he queried, setting his cards face down on the table and folding his hands in his lap. "I hope you had playmates, at least."

She turned more fully to him, nodding. "I have a brother just a year older than me, and a sister two years younger. And my half-niece is nearly the equal distance in age between us both, so the three of us were always together."

He smiled at the fond note her voice had taken on. "Was that never strange? A niece older than your sister?"

Miss Palmer shook her head. "No, never. We never knew that all families were not thus until we started making friends outside of our home and family. Millie is almost as much a sister to me as Mariah, and sometimes closer than."

Michael glanced over at Mrs. Greensley, who had now been joined by her husband, and the couple were still actively engaged in conversation with the Sterlings. They were not likely to continue their game for some time, and it seemed a shame to sit at the table and wait for them to return their attention to the game. Why not give all a chance to converse freely?

He looked back at Miss Palmer, who had done the same. "Will you favor me with a turn about the room, Miss Palmer? I do not think we will commence our game for a time."

"Please." Miss Palmer rose and brushed at her gown. "If their topic is to continue on the advantages of the newly married, I would much prefer to sample the punch."

"Happy to oblige you there." Michael gestured toward the table at the other side of the room where the punchbowl sat.

She inclined her head and began that way, though moved toward the edge of the room in what would take them both in a longer, more roundabout way than he'd planned.

He was not about to complain, though. He rather thought it was a brilliant diversion for them both.

"Do you object to matrimony?" Michael asked, stunned by his own boldness, though he did inject as much teasing into the words as possible.

Miss Palmer was not put off. "Is any woman truly opposed to matrimony? I have no doubt I will welcome the thing when it comes, but the idea that it should be my whole focus has never sat well. And I should so much prefer a match of true affection than one of ease and comfort."

"Cannot ease and comfort come with true affection?" he mused aloud, clasping his hands behind his back. "I agree with you, it is only a thought."

"I suppose it can," Miss Palmer allowed, "though I would not think it particularly common. And, I confess, it has always troubled me that the marriage vows in the church are the same for all marriages. How can an arranged marriage uphold a vow to love, honor, comfort, and obey? Does the definition of love change in that regard? And what of honor? Surely not all spouses honor each other."

Michael could honestly say he had never given the marriage vows a second thought, let alone with such depth, but now it seemed she had an excellent point.

"What would you have the vows say, then?" He allowed himself to smile, glancing about the room. "A marriage of convenience would vow not to kill each other and to ally themselves for the good of their families? A marriage of comfort that they would learn to love and behave with respect?"

She laughed quietly beside him, a measured step bringing them closer together. "I don't know, and I will not pretend to be overly cognizant of what vows to God should entail. But if I were marrying for love, I should like to vow that my love for him would grow day by day, hour by hour. That I should draw closer to God as I serve and give myself to my husband, and he to me. That we vow to walk through life hand in hand, come what may."

For the space of four heartbeats, Michael had no thoughts, let alone words. Her words circled about his head, seeping within it, and echoed within the cavern of his chest. There would never be vows like those said in a marriage ceremony performed in the classic sense, though one might find some leeway granted in Scotland, and more particularly in Gretna Green. The formality of the vows would ever remain, expecting the same of couples marrying for love as marrying for entirely material considerations. But what those vows meant to those uttering them might be entirely different based on the feelings and situations of those involved.

Miss Palmer, for example. And whoever was fortunate enough to win her love and her hand.

"You must think me a very silly creature for saying such things," Miss Palmer murmured, blushing prettily and lowering her eyes as they walked. "I'm far more practical than romantic, to be sure, but in this, I find sentiment outweighs sense."

Michael laughed softly. "I don't find you silly at all, Miss Palmer. In fact, I think you may be the least silly person I have ever met, male or female. More than that, I find you quite charming."

His cheeks instantly flamed as his words played back to him. "Your words," he was quick to correct. "I find your words quite charming. Marvelous idea, specific vows for specific circumstances."

Her warm giggle again met his ears. "I don't know how marvelous it is. I imagine a family engaged in a hastily arranged marriage would not like to have vows recited that reflect such a thing. The whole congregation would know, if they vowed to repent of their sins once bound together in matrimony."

Michael choked on a cough, a fist going to his mouth to stifle it. "Or," he managed when able, "to divide the dowry and inheritance of an heiress into specific avenues for a fortune hunter's marriage."

Miss Palmer snickered, biting down on her lip. "Vowing to stand against opposing relations in Gretna Green."

"Vowing to return to sea at least once a year if married aboard a ship."

She clamped a gloved hand over her mouth, her eyes squeezing shut in mirth. "Oh, Mr. Sandford, we will surely scandalize all. Our first meeting and we have talked of money, of marriage, and of scandal. What are we going to do?"

"Continue to meet, I hope," he ventured as they reached the punchbowl. "As I said… I find you quite charming."

She looked up at him, smiling in a way that expanded his chest rather grandly. "I find you rather charming as well, Mr. Sandford. I am happy to meet you again, if at all possible."

"It's possible," he assured her. "It is entirely possible, of that I am certain."

Chapter Twelve

A morning stroll is a marvelous gift to those intrepid individuals sane enough to seek it out. Provided one does not dawdle along it. There is no excuse for dawdling on morning walks.

-The Spinster Chronicles, 7 October 1819

There was something about a long walk. Charlotte wasn't entirely certain what it was, but her mother had always told her that the solution to any problem was a good cup of tea and a long walk.

Not that Charlotte presently had a problem, other than the obvious lack of husband, but people walked in Hyde Park frequently enough that it seemed the thing to do. She had no callers, so it was clear that she must do the venturing.

It was a maddening exercise, walking about and smiling at absolutely everyone on the off chance they may wish to speak with her. And to smile even more prettily at any men she happened upon, especially if they were remotely attractive.

That wasn't a desperate action, was it?

It felt desperate.

Having her mother as escort on this walk felt even more desperate.

"My face hurts," Charlotte grumbled through the pain of yet another brilliant smile at a young man on a horse.

"You're only out of practice," her mother told her without concern. "Why do you think I always wanted you to smile more?"

Forget desperate, this was maddening.

"What I wouldn't give for a mask."

"Yes, I think that quite often myself when in the company of you and your brother together."

Charlotte snorted loudly, covering her mouth.

"That was attractive, dear," her mother went on. "If that will not call all eligible bachelors to you, nothing will."

"You are not helping," Charlotte protested, giggling madly.

"Neither did that jig you danced with Lady Patton's godson last evening," came the quipped response. "Clearly, I have failed you."

Charlotte felt tears of mirth welling dangerously, her breath harder to come by as she continued to laugh. "I managed as best I could! I am dreadful at jigs, and he was an even worse partner!"

Her mother tsked. "Never blame the partner, dear. It is most unbecoming."

"Better to blame him than admit I am a poor dancer," Charlotte insisted, grinning and looping her arm through her mother's. "Oh, Mama, you do make me laugh."

"So I should hope." Her mother covered her hand, rubbing soothingly. "I know this is a bit of a trying time for you. Such confidence in all other respects, but in this, I think you might be just as insecure as any other girl in London."

Charlotte sighed and nodded once. "I'll only admit so to you, as you can already see it. Maddening business, finding love. I wonder that anyone succeeds in it."

"Most do not, I'm afraid."

That was unfortunately true. Charlotte barely avoided sighing again, looking out at other parts of Hyde Park as they strolled almost aimlessly. She had picked her ensemble this morning with great care, a lavender sprigged muslin and a plum walking coat, her bonnet a fine complement to both, and having to put so much thought into her appearance was wearing on her. What did any of it matter, in truth? She had been seen for years, and though being dressed elaborately and pinched into rosiness might have given her more attention, it could not change what they already saw.

She might never marry; would that be so dreadful? She'd never thought so before, but she hadn't particularly imagined being alone in her unmarried state.

Lady Hetty Redgrave would understand. It would likely be worth the visit to her to try and understand what she must prepare herself for, if the next few weeks did not provide her an adequate response. A tour of the Continent would likely be called for shortly, if she were disappointed. She'd never seen Switzerland, after all, and she rather thought one ought to be able to claim such things.

"Have you heard from sweet Prudence lately?" her mother asked beside her. "Surely she must be near her time."

Charlotte smiled at the mention of her friend. "Yes, only yesterday I received a note. She delivered a little girl on Friday. Cam says she has the sweetest disposition and rather dark hair. Small like her mother, but strong and hale. All is well, apparently."

"Oh, bless her! I'm so pleased. We must send gifts. Shall we see to Bond Street after this?" She dabbed at her eye discreetly with a gloved finger, sniffing softly. "I shall spoil the little lamb, mark my words. We cannot expect Marjorie Westfall to do any such thing, and Miranda Sterling will outdo me if I do not act first."

"Mama!" Charlotte laughed, nudging her gently. "You are a wonder. Yes, let's to Bond Street once we've walked more. I shall feel much more myself if I am needlessly buying something."

Her mother gave her a scolding look. "It's not needless in the service of others. Now, what is the child's name? Did Camden say?"

"He did," Charlotte confirmed. "They have called her Laura. Laura Mary Prudence Vale. Mary for his beloved cousin Molly, I believe."

"Lovely." Her mother nodded once. "Little miss Laura Vale shall have the best of everything, I do vow."

Charlotte narrowed her eyes as she looked at her mother. "Will you be so indulgent if Charles or I have children?"

Her mother patted her hand a few times. "I intend for you to become very cross with me some years hence for never upholding the punishments you see fit to inflict upon your offspring."

"I shall pencil in some spats for us, then." Charlotte hugged her mother's arm quickly, a surge of warmth and love filling her. While her mother often fit perfectly within the confines of proper distance from her children, as all mothers in Society seemed to do, at other times, she was inordinately affectionate and caring with them, and it was in those moments that Charlotte felt most herself.

Surely there was some significance to be found in that.

"I say, the pair of you do make a charming picture."

Charlotte looked up, smile in place, and surprise jolted through her as the sight of Mr. Riley approaching them struck her. He was just as handsome as he had been at the Bonds' party, and his smile more than ready. He walked rather than rode, which was convenient indeed for their purposes.

Her smile did not feel half so forced now. "Mr. Riley, good morning!" she greeted, curtseying when he neared.

He tipped his hat, bowing. "Miss Wright. The morning air does your constitution credit, if I may be so bold."

"It's not that bold, I concede that it does." She turned to her mother. "Mama, may I present Mr. Riley? We met at the Prestons' ball, and then again last week at the Bonds' dinner party."

"Delighted, Mr. Riley," her mother said with a bob of her head.

He bowed again. "As am I, ma'am." He looked at Charlotte, his smile almost sheepish. "I am sorry we did not have a chance to speak much at the party. My cousins do tend to monopolize me when I am in London."

"The Bonds are your cousins?" Charlotte exclaimed with a smile. "But of course, I can see the resemblance now. Do I take it that Mr. Bond is your relation?"

Mr. Riley nodded, grinning unabashedly. "He is, Miss Wright. My mother's brother. I have my own lodgings in London, but I find myself pressed upon to attend several meals with them a week. I cannot think why, I possess little of the refinements of Society."

Charlotte did not agree in the least, but she was not about to say so. "We ladies see enough of refinement everywhere else, Mr. Riley. What we are in desperate need of is good company."

"And refinement and good company are mutually exclusive?" he asked, his smile turning crooked, which was nearly impossibly handsome.

Struggling for wit amidst the flurry of butterflies within her, Charlotte shook her head. "Not always, but they are to be valued for themselves alone, regardless."

"And you seem to be quite good company, Mr. Riley,"

Charlotte's mother broke in. "Will you join us on our walk? Unless you have a pressing engagement, in which case, we would not dream of delaying you."

Charlotte could have hugged her mother to death for her suggestion and held her breath as she anticipated Mr. Riley's answer.

Blessedly, he nodded. "I would very much enjoy joining you. My business is not at all pressing, and a walk would be quite beneficial."

"It usually is," her mother agreed, stepping to one side to allow more room on the path and releasing Charlotte's arm.

Charlotte gestured to the spot on her left, smiling. "We are sometimes brisk in our strides, Mr. Riley. Leisurely strolls are not quite our pace."

"Charlotte, we can surely slow our steps if Mr. Riley wishes," her mother scolded from her right. "It is not as though we make haste for any purpose."

"As it happens," Mr. Riley informed them, "I have been known to take long strides at a certain pace myself. It irks my mother to no end. She always claims it is unnecessary to hurry along as I do, and I try to explain that it is not hurrying for hurrying's sake, it is only how I walk."

"Exactly!" Charlotte cried, laughing at being so neatly understood in such a simple thing. "I can never walk with my friends for that exact reason. They do tend to lag so."

Mr. Riley chuckled, the sound low and rumbling in the most delicious manner Charlotte had ever heard. "Would that be your friends from the Spinster Chronicles?"

Charlotte sobered just a little, nerves flaring at the question. "Yes," she replied with some hesitation. "Yes, it would."

Her mother reached for her hand and squeezed tightly before releasing.

"I have tried to my utmost," he went on, his dark eyes staring down at the path before them, "to identify which lady has written which article in the column, and upon my life, I have never managed it yet. Of course, I cannot be quite sure of the identity of the so-called Spinsters at any given time, so that surely does not help."

Relief surged through Charlotte's veins, nearly taking the strength from her legs. He did not disapprove, then. He did not judge nor harbor resentment, and he spoke of them as naturally as though they were any other set of women in the world.

What a find indeed was Mr. Jonathan Riley!

"You do not know who we are?" Charlotte inquired with a quick grin. "Mr. Riley, everybody knows who we are, you need only ask."

"And where would be the fun in that, Miss Wright?" he returned easily. He glanced down at her from his nearly towering height, smiling in a way that showed his nearly perfect teeth.

One must always appreciate nearly perfect teeth.

Charlotte hummed a laugh. "You take delight in trying to identify us? How did you know I was part, then?"

"Simple," he stated. "When I inquired about you, I was told. Imagine my surprise and delight that I could come to know one of the gifted writers of the column I'd been so fascinated with."

He could have proposed on the spot, and Charlotte might have accepted him. Such lovely words and opinions were so uncommon after the early strife they had faced from their column. While everyone in London, and several other parts of England, certainly read the issues as they came out, the writers of those issues had almost always faced criticism. That she was not doing so here was extraordinary.

Of course, he could have been giving her a false impression. It had been done before, and she had no doubt it would happen again. She only prayed it would not be here.

"And why would you wish to come to know me, hmm?" she asked him, keeping her voice innocent and light.

"Charlotte," her mother hissed, "what a direct question!"

Charlotte rolled her eyes. "Mama, if you intend to insert yourself into every moment of this conversation between Mr. Riley and myself, I'll thank you to take four steps behind us like a trotting chaperone instead of my dear mother."

Mr. Riley laughed heartily beside them, yet another uncommon trait in a gentleman of Society. "But it is precisely because of the direct questions, and your unflappable candor, that rendered me all the more curious about you, Miss Wright. And I take no offense, Mrs. Wright. I can assure you that I have had far worse in my own family, and I am quite comfortable holding my own."

"You must allow me to be a little embarrassed about my daughter's unconventional ways," her mother protested weakly, smiling at them both. "Not out of shame, but only because I am much less so."

"I will not think less of you for your motherly feelings," Mr. Riley assured her. "I only wish to reassure you that you need not fear my opinions or your daughter's reputation where I am concerned."

Charlotte's mother stared at him, then looked at Charlotte directly. "Well, then. Give him a hint on the Chronicles, Charlotte, and see if he is as loyal a follower as he claims."

Mr. Riley coughed a laugh as Charlotte giggled at the suggestion. "And you say you are not as unconventional as your daughter, ma'am? Upon my word, your very vocal support of her outspoken column betrays you there."

"I am quite proud of the Chronicles, sir," Charlotte's mother informed him. "And of my daughter and her friends for putting them out. I hope one day to write an article for them, if Charlotte will permit me."

"Mama," Charlotte groaned playfully, shaking her head. "She has been begging for years to do so, Mr. Riley, and will not give it up."

He only shrugged. "Then I say let her. What a lark would that be, eh?"

Perhaps, Charlotte thought to herself. Perhaps.

"Which article in the last issue was your favorite?" Charlotte asked him, moving on to the test her mother had suggested, and that Charlotte had considered administering herself.

"The trials of country dancing," he said at once.

"And what did you like best about it?"

He grunted. "It was spot on. I agreed with every word, and it had me laughing as well. I tend to prefer anything that makes me laugh where laughter is appropriate. The other articles were entertaining and good, to be sure, but that one was my personal favorite."

Charlotte hid a smile, flicking her eyes at her mother, who returned it. "And the issue prior?"

Without hesitation, he answered. "Quotes and Quirks. I haven't laughed so earnestly in ages, and I would swear I could pick exactly which member of Society had said what." He shook his head, smiling at the recollection, then looked at Charlotte in speculation. "Did you write either of those?"

"I did not," Charlotte was pleased to admit. She gave her mother a triumphant look. "I think we might have a true and loyal follower here, Mama. I did not write either article he praised, so this cannot be flattery."

"I concur, my dear," she replied with a sage nod. "You may proceed with getting to know him now."

"Was that in question before?" Mr. Riley protested.

Charlotte shrugged easily. "I cannot be too careful, Mr. Riley. Never fear, you have triumphed. In Society but not of Society, if I may."

"Nicely put," her mother praised. She looked around Charlotte at Mr. Riley, the pink ribbons of her bonnet almost matching her rosy complexion. "A rare find, Mr. Riley, given the draw of Society."

"Thank you, I think." He gave them both a quick smile, then sobered just a touch as they continued their walk. "I believe I may understand how I came to be so, if you care to know."

"By all means," Charlotte allowed, lacing her fingers before her. "How?"

"I was not raised in Society," he said plainly. "I'm from Rossendale in Lancashire, near the town of Haslingden."

Charlotte's jaw dropped. "You're from Lancashire? You don't sound like it."

Mr. Riley laughed and looked at her fondly. "I learned long ago that men of business do not take a man seriously when he speaks like a mill worker. When I am home, near my family, I can assure you, no one would doubt my heritage."

"Is it more natural to speak that way?" she asked out of outright curiosity. "You may do so now, if you like."

"Oh, I'm quite used to the finer accent now," he told her without concern. "When I'm perfectly at my ease, the accent slips in some ways, but it's still there. I hardly notice it now."

They walked in silence for a moment or two, while Charlotte tried to imagine the curious accent of the counties of the north in Mr. Riley's tone.

It was a rather warm, inviting, and particularly charming voice, in her imagination.

"I'm sorry," she said quickly, realizing she had interrupted his speaking. "You're from Haslingden."

"Yes." He nodded and tipped his hat at a passing phaeton. "My father was a rather driven, hardworking man, but distinctly middle class in Rossendale. He was a foreman in a cotton mill. Tough, but fair, and all the workers respected him greatly. You'll find that not all foremen are so, and mill masters sometimes less so."

Charlotte could not comprehend any such thing, being so far removed from any of the industrial camps and cities in the north.

"When the master of the mill decided to sell, my father went to him with an offer," Mr. Riley went on. "It was a daring move, some would even say rash, as he did not have even half of the funds requested for the sale. But my father is a canny thinker, and he had a plan."

"What was it?" Charlotte asked eagerly, caught up in the tale of this tough but kind man, seeing what his son had come to.

"A partnership," he said. "My father would put everything he had towards the sale, and the former master would continue to fund the mill until the agreed upon percentage of profits could pay him off outright, allowing my father to then claim sole ownership."

Charlotte gasped, shaking her head. "Unfathomable. Why would the master accept it, if he wished to retire from the task?"

Mr. Riley laughed and gestured down another path as they came to a fork. "Because he did not wish to retire in truth. His health did not permit him to continue on as he had done, so he thought selling was his only option. My father gave him the means to continue maintaining an interest and a share while his health would continue to decline, and by the time it was all paid, he might be ready in truth to retire in full. So, given how he respected and valued my father, he accepted."

"How marvelous!" Charlotte clapped and barely restrained herself from grabbing Mr. Riley's arm. "And? How long did it take?"

"Five years only," he replied with a proud smile. "He implemented some new ideas, found the latest machinery, increased production at an ambitious rate, and the mill flourished. A few years after that, he was one of the wealthiest mill owners in the county and can also boast the lowest rate of death and illness from his workers. He worked a mill as a child, you see, so he is mindful of the conditions of his own workers."

Charlotte's mother made a soft sound of approval. "Charity and ambition. Quite a rare combination, you must be proud."

"I am, Mrs. Wright." He nodded repeatedly, looking as though he might burst from it. "And while we, his children, never worked in the mill, he did insist that we try our hand at all the positions to learn how exactly things worked. We were frequently visitors to the mill, but never put in harm's way. He does not employ children, you know. Thinks it unnecessary and unscrupulous."

"Huzzah for that, I say," Charlotte praised. "And you? Are you taking over the mill?"

He smiled at the question. "I have inherited my father's visionary taste and drive to succeed. I am his partner now, and I've just finished finalizing a contract with a shipping company in Preston to expand our business and increase our holdings. In a few years, I shall be in a position to buy them out entirely, leaving my father with the mill while I oversee shipping. My brother has caught the drive we share, and time will only tell how he takes part."

Charlotte watched Mr. Riley in abject fascination, finding him far more interesting now than she had only this morning, and he had been marvelously intriguing then. "I find I'm rather impressed, Mr. Riley. To come from the working class and rise up the ranks in fortune and status to now be fairly wealthy, influential, and successful is an astonishing feat. And yet you intend to rise further still? Quite remarkable, I must say."

He looked at her with a quizzical smile, something akin to hesitation in his eyes. "You don't see me as somehow a lesser creature because my fortune comes from trade?"

"Why should that lower you?" she shot back. "I procure all sorts of things from trade, and it has never been logical to me that somehow the profit from my purchases and those of others should be of a lowering status to those who created them. No, I am rather fascinated with trade, and with those who know how to use it to their advantage."

"I have no breeding," he pointed out. "My grandfather worked in the mill all his life."

She raised a brow at him. "And my grandfather shined his own silver when his butler could no longer do so rather than sack him and find a new butler. Resourcefulness is not a crime, and is highly lacking in the upper classes, I find."

Mr. Riley grinned at her, outdoing the sun with its splendor. "You call me rare, Miss Wright. But I think you might be somehow even rarer."

"Oh, I doubt that very much," she scoffed, averting her eyes to glance around the park. "I'm the same sort of bird that flits around every ballroom in London."

"If you say so, but I've never seen a bird quite like you. Not ever."

Charlotte felt her cheeks warm and glanced up at him again, smiling with more warmth than she thought she could muster at this hour of the morning, or on this particular walk. "Would you like to accompany Mama and I to Bond Street, Mr. Riley? I should very much like the continued pleasure of your company."

"It would be my pleasure entirely, Miss Wright. I am quite at your disposal."

Chapter Thirteen

―――――――――― ⸙⸙⸙ ――――――――――

Balls are the perfect opportunity to meet new people, get better acquainted with those you know, and to experience new things. Mind you behave, however. There is nothing like a ball to start rumors.

-The Spinster Chronicles, 24 January 1820

Two weeks in Miss Palmer's regular company, and Michael thought he might just be the happiest he had been in four or five years.

What an unusual feeling.

Not that he'd seen her every day, or officially claimed courtship, but he had called on her three days last week and two this week, and were they not attending the same ball this evening, he would have called tomorrow, as well. He'd have to make his suit official soon, or speculation would do the thing for him.

If he did take on a courtship, and he was quite sure he would, he could have been at the Greensley home at this moment waiting to escort them all here. Instead, he was standing by and watching the entrance to the room, waiting for them.

At least Lord Eden provided well, and the supper would prove exquisite when it was time.

Tyrone had begged Michael to come early, though as yet, Michael had not seen his friend to inquire as to why the request had been made. It was most unfair. The musicians were still tuning their instruments, so there was not even dancing as yet to distract him from what seemed to be endless waiting.

He caught sight of Lieutenant Henshaw striding by and smiled. "Henshaw."

The man turned at his name, then returned his smile with a quick one of his own. "Sandford, good evening. You haven't seen the Mortons yet, have you?"

"I have not, but we are among the early arrivals, you and I."

"True, true, I suppose," Henshaw muttered distractedly, tugging at his pristine cravat. "Waiting is torment."

Michael nodded in agreement. "I was just thinking the same thing."

Henshaw looked at him with some interest. "Who are you waiting on?"

"Miss Palmer," he said without shame, not seeing a need to keep the truth from a friend like Henshaw. "She's a cousin of Mrs. Greensley."

"Are you courting her?" Henshaw asked, smile returning.

"Not yet, but…" Michael trailed off with a shrug.

Henshaw now grinned. "Very good, Sandford. About ruddy time you courted somebody proper."

Michael lifted a brow. "I could say the same for you, Hensh."

"I know," Henshaw grumbled as he averted his eyes. "Believe me, I'm doing what I can about that."

"Are you?" Michael nodded in approval. "Is it who I think it is?"

Henshaw's thick brows snapped down. "How should I know who you think it is, Sandford?"

Michael pressed his lips together, understanding all too well the irritability that came with being too directly questioned about romantic intentions that were not yet to fruition. "If your intentions are not clear or obvious, Henshaw, you're going to have to adjust things. Trust me, lack of understanding can hamper everything, and leave you with nothing."

Henshaw blinked at him, his expression clearing. "Why do I suddenly believe every word you say?"

"Because I know of what I speak." Michael smiled bitterly, a twisting sensation in his stomach returning after weeks without it.

Silently, Henshaw continued to watch him, then slowly nodded. "Right. I'll take that into consideration." He looked around, frowning again. "Why in heaven's name did Demaris ask us here early? I hope he hasn't promised Eden we would lead the dancing. I don't mind dancing, but I do prefer to choose when and where I do so."

"And with whom," Michael concurred, eyeing the ladies present. None of them were truly objectionable, but neither were they ladies he would have thought to seek out. "If we can convince him to keep the first dance short, perhaps…"

"You both came. Good."

They turned as one to see Tyrone approaching, his brother, Lord Eden, just behind him.

"This isn't good," Michael muttered to Henshaw.

"No, it is not."

Tyrone and his brother bowed quickly. "In an attempt to promote dancing this evening," Eden started, "I would ask the two of you, as well as my brother, to dance the first three dances. After that, I don't care if you take yourselves off to the card room. My wife is worried there will be no dancing tonight, and I ask you to help me assuage those fears."

Michael stared at Lord Eden, who looked exactly like Tyrone, only taller and but for the brighter shade of his waistcoat was dressed identically.

He'd have told off Tyrone for doing this, and would have told off Eden, too, however…

"You had to bring Lady Eden into it, didn't you?" Henshaw said in the blandest tone known to man.

Eden smiled without humor. "I know I hold little sway anywhere, but if I mention my wife…"

Michael shook his head, sighing heavily. "For Lady Eden's comfort, I will dance the first three dances."

"As will I," Henshaw added. Then there appeared a devious quirk to his mouth. "Provided you and Lady Eden dance the first with us."

Eden grimaced in response. "That was already determined, thank you. In exchange for your sacrifice, you all get a half a crown lead on any gambling you do in the card room."

Michael snorted softly. "Can I just get half a crown? I'll lose it in the first hand if I gamble."

They all chuckled and Eden thanked them again, before moving to the musicians.

"You were supposed to refuse!" Tyrone hissed when out of his brother's earshot.

Henshaw gave him an incredulous look. "When he asked us to help make Lady Eden more at ease? Just how heartless are you, Demaris?"

Tyrone scowled and shook his head. "Just enough for my own self-preservation. Now, if you'll excuse me, I'm going to procure my partners for these ridiculous dances to ensure I survive them." He bowed dismissively and strode away.

Michael and Henshaw watched him go, then looked at each other. "Is Annabelle Wintermere here?" he asked Henshaw.

"No," Henshaw replied with a confused frown. "Why?"

"No reason." Michael glanced at the door to the ballroom, seeing Sebastian and Izzy Morton entering, followed by Sebastian's sister, Kitty. He smiled to himself and indicated them with his head. "The Mortons are here now, Hensh. If you're still in search of them."

Henshaw left him at once, moving directly for them, leaving Michael laughing to himself.

Unfortunately, Diana had not arrived yet, so he would not have the same pleasure as Henshaw in the dancing of the first three dances.

"Right," Michael muttered, looking around at available options. "Better see to it."

An hour later, his duty done, Michael exhaled and desperately wished for a chair to rest himself for a while. But supper wasn't for a time yet, and gentlemen did not generally sit at a ball. He'd have to increase his endurance where dancing was concerned if he would be expected to continue in this vein.

Three dances in a row was not his usual routine.

"You look quite done for."

Michael laughed to himself and glanced at Hugh Sterling, now nearing him. "I feel quite done for. But my duty is discharged, so I can be satisfied with that."

Hugh nodded and handed him a drink. "Well, you did garner some attention for yourself, you know, doing those dances at the beginning of the evening. Several young ladies are asking questions about you."

"Are they?" Michael toasted to that with his friend, then surveyed the dancing, now that his help was no longer needed to ensure it went on. "Have you seen Miss Palmer this evening?"

"As it happens, yes," Hugh said with a knowing chuckle. "She's chatting with my wife. Piqued your interest, has she?"

Michael only smiled. "I've called on her a time or two. I may venture to court her in truth."

"Really?" Hugh queried, sounding impressed. "Well, well. What do you know of her family?"

"Not all that much," Michael admitted with a wince. "Outside of Mrs. Greensley's family, none at all. Our conversations have been more on interests than on personal details."

Hugh sipped his drink, cocking his head. "How very modern of you. Most men wouldn't dream of calling on a woman without knowing exactly how her dowry is settled."

"Did you ask Elinor's dowry before you ventured?" Michael countered without missing a beat.

"My situation was different," Hugh insisted. "I was stranded at her family estate at Christmas."

Michael's expression turned dubious. "You could have kept to your rooms or kept a polite distance, but you still romanced her."

"This is not about me!" Hugh laughed, grinning at him. "But I take your point well enough." He sobered suddenly, eyes widening. "Would you let Elinor look into Miss Palmer? She's been rooting out information on bachelors for years for the Chronicles, it would be no trouble to find details on her."

The offer was a kind one, but Michael could not help but feel uncomfortable with such an intrusion into Diana's life. He knew it would not be that invasive, all things considered, but what difference would it make? He already liked Diana, thought of her by her Christian name rather than the more formal address Society would prefer, and was ready to offer her courtship.

What would change if he knew her dowry or how her family was set up? He had no need to marry a fortune, so money was of little matter. His family was already respected enough, so he did not need to marry into an established bloodline. All he needed was to marry a woman he would enjoy spending the rest of his life with. Diana could fit that quite nicely.

Two weeks of association was not long enough to be sure of such things, of course, but he knew enough to desire to know more. To know if she could fit. To know if he wanted her to.

"If she likes," Michael settled on, a simple smile remaining on his lips. "It won't sway me one way or the other, but if she would feel more comfortable knowing the information, I'll not stop her."

Hugh gave him a careful look. "She only wants you to be happy, you know, and to see you well situated in that happiness."

Michael's smile spread with fondness as he glanced over in Elinor's direction, though he couldn't see her clearly for the dancing. "I know. She is kind for caring so, but, as I said, it will change nothing for me."

"And that, I think, will make her even happier to do it." Hugh thumped him on the back in encouragement. "Shall we go to them?"

"Lead on."

The pair of them moved about the onlookers in Lord Eden's ballroom, nodding at several people and pausing for brief words of politeness with some. And Michael could not fail to notice that several young ladies watched him move, eyeing him in a far different manner than Roslyn Lawson had some weeks before.

"What in heaven's name is so fascinating about me now?" Michael hissed when he and Hugh had escaped yet another pause for short words. "I feel as though I am on display and about to be bid upon."

"You might as well be," Hugh replied with a light laugh. "And for all our whining about it, Miranda's efforts have not been in vain with your apparel. Quite smartly dressed, you are. A marked improvement."

Had they not been in public, Michael would have thrown his hands up in exasperation. "Nearly all the men in here are dressed the same, Sterling."

Hugh held up a finger. "There are many differences, Sandford, if you would really take a look. And it is your failure to notice such things that led to her interference anyway. But all is mended, and you are undoubtedly the best dressed gentleman in the room."

"I feel so comforted by that," Michael told him dryly.

They reached the ladies then, and Michael bowed to Elinor and Diana as one. "Ladies, I hope your evening has been enjoyable thus far."

Elinor smiled up at him. "It has, Mr. Sandford, thank you. Though, shockingly, Miss Palmer has not danced a single dance yet this evening."

Michael looked at Diana for confirmation and found the lady blushing just enough to be even more maddeningly attractive than she already was. "Is this true, Miss Palmer?" he demanded.

"I've not been here long," Diana insisted in her soft manner, "so it cannot be so very shocking."

"It is shocking," Michael insisted playfully, forcing himself not to smile. "I must see this remedied at once. Will you dance the next with me?"

Diana smiled prettily and dipped her chin, her golden hair plaited into a sort of crown around the top of her head, small white flowers interspersed throughout. "I thank you, yes, Mr. Sandford."

He smiled in return. "And, if it is not too bold, the supper set as well?"

Her fine lips parted in surprise, then formed a beaming smile that stole his breath. "I would be pleased to, Mr. Sandford."

Pleasure spread from the center of his chest to the tips of each finger and toe as he nodded. "Good."

Michael and Diana clapped with the rest of the dancers as the supper set finished, grinning at each other with the breathless amusement that comes from exuberant dancing.

He'd never enjoyed a dance more; he was convinced of it.

He'd speak to Greensley about courting her tomorrow. Perhaps the day after, if the ball went far into the early morning hours. But he was determined now that he would do it, and the anticipation of it was exhilarating.

"Ladies and gentlemen, if you will please proceed into the dining room, we will have supper momentarily," Lord Eden announced from somewhere in the room.

"Good," Diana gushed, moving a golden ringlet from her brow to behind her ear. "I am famished. Is that improper to confess?"

Michael shook his head, grinning. "Not to me." He offered her his arm, and she took it, the feel of her hand on his arm so natural it ought to have been a sign.

A sign of what, he couldn't say. That she was perfect for him? That he was right to pursue courtship? That all of this had been worth it to have her in his life? It could have been any of these things, or all of these things. Only time would tell.

The dining room was full of splendor, the plates and bowls rimmed with gold and the cold meats already set out for their consumption. Crystal goblets waited pouring for the guests, and a dozen or more footmen stood at the ready along the walls.

Michael gestured to a chair for Diana, pulling it out and helping her to sit before sitting beside her and looking at the meal before them. "White soup. That's quite a treat indeed!"

"Perfection," Diana murmured as she discreetly inhaled the scent. She glanced up and down the table shaking her head. "Ham, goose, salmon, cheeses, glazed vegetables, fruit... How will anyone be able to dance after this?"

"And we are destined to have desserts, too," Michael pointed out. "What can I get you to drink, Miss Palmer?"

She pursed her lips, considering the options. "I think ratafia, if I may."

Michael chuckled and gave her a look. "I think you may." He reached for the decanter of ratafia to find another hand there first. "Oh, pardon me."

The gentleman across smiled and gestured. "Please, you first."

He nodded and filled Diana's glass before handing the decanter across the table, freezing as he caught sight of the woman directly across from him.

Charlotte.

She was already staring at him, eyes wide and round, the white ribbon with a cameo at her throat bobbing with a swallow.

He would have given anything not to have seen her.

But dash it all, she was stunning. A little pale at the present, but her dark hair had been dressed in the most attractive manner known to man, and the gown she wore blended white and blue together across her bodice and sleeves in a perfect impression of the sky itself. The heavens literally wrapping themselves around her.

He couldn't look away.

"Miss Wright," he said in a too-rough voice, dipping his chin in a nod.

Again, the cameo at her throat moved tremulously. "Mr. Sandford." She cleared her throat, then smiled, although it looked a bit forced. "Do you know Mr. Riley?" She gestured to the man beside her, who had offered Michael the ratafia decanter first.

The man was certainly good-looking and had none of the airs the dandies of the day usually possessed. More than that, he was giving Michael a welcoming smile of introduction.

That called for politeness.

"I do not," Michael admitted, returning the smile. "A pleasure."

Mr. Riley nodded. "Thank you, sir."

"This is Miss Palmer," Michael said quickly, indicating her. "Miss Palmer, this is Mr. Riley, and Miss Wright."

Diana nodded at each, then froze, her eyes fixed on Charlotte. "Miss Charlotte Wright?"

Charlotte's brows rose, and she flicked her eyes to Michael before returning to Diana. "Yes…"

The gasp that escaped Diana startled Michael to such an extent that he jumped, but somehow, Charlotte and Mr. Riley maintained composure.

"I never thought I would get to meet you, Miss Wright!" Diana said in a voice higher than her natural one. "I've read every issue of the Spinster Chronicles from the very first edition. We get the London papers at our home in Derbyshire, and I adore every word. I find them extraordinary, and I cannot begin to tell you what an honor it is to sit across from you."

If Michael could have left the table, he would have done so now. Stormed out of the room and never returned. Diana had heard of Charlotte, and was apparently an ardent admirer of her? What did Michael do to deserve this?

"You are too kind, Miss Palmer," Charlotte murmured, a slight smile on her face.

Michael knew that smile. Charlotte was amused and uncomfortable at the same time, and her good nature would not let her make Diana feel that she had erred or misstepped in any way.

"What made you wish to write the Chronicles?" Diana demanded without shame. She turned to Michael, brow furrowing. "How do you know Miss Wright? Oh, you must move in the same circles in London, of course you do."

"Actually," Charlotte broke in, her voice gentle but firm, "Michael here is one of my oldest friends."

Oh, gads, did they really have to do this?

Again came a gasp from Diana. "You are? Oh my goodness, how did you meet? Were you children?"

"We were, yes," Michael said quickly, hoping they could end this painful interlude sooner rather than later. "I was seven or eight, wandering the edges of my family estate, and Charlotte was swinging on the branches of a large weeping willow on her family's pond."

"Were you really?" Mr. Riley asked Charlotte, laughing as he looked at her. "Why does that not surprise me?"

So Mr. Riley already knew Charlotte well enough to know how unconventional and daring she could be when she wished.

Marvelous.

"I was," Charlotte conceded as she looked at Michael quickly before dipping her spoon into the white soup. "It seemed a rather good natural rope to swing on to me."

Diana and Mr. Riley laughed, while Michael only smiled, though the smile pained him. "I believe I asked what she was doing," he told them, "and she said something of the sort, then insisted I try."

"And how did you fare?" Mr. Riley inquired, still grinning.

"At first, well enough." Michael poured himself a glass of Madeira, focusing there rather than on any of the people near him. "She took another turn, and then I did, and then..." He paused, looking up at Charlotte.

She picked up the story at once. "And then I dared him to go further, which Michael did, only to lose his grip and fall directly into the pond."

Mr. Riley laughed while Diana gasped and giggled. Charlotte

smiled, though she glanced at Michael repeatedly.

He forced his mouth to relax into a set smile that took minimal effort to maintain. "The pond was not deep, and I could swim well. I believe our adventure ended there, and we both went home, planning to meet again another day."

And Michael had started falling in love with Charlotte from then on.

But that part would remain unsaid.

"And meet again we did," Charlotte went on. "We got into all kinds of scrapes, sometimes bringing my brother along. One of Michael's sisters may never forgive me for some of our tricks."

"It's true," Michael added before he could stop himself. "She reminds Charlotte of it every time they meet."

They shared a smile, then both looked down at their meals.

"What a charming pair of scamps you must have been!" Mr. Riley exclaimed, drawing Michael's attention back up.

The man was looking at Charlotte with warmth and familiarity, and she was looking back at him with the same.

"I don't know how charming our parents thought we were," Charlotte laughed, "but they certainly learned we were inseparable. For a while, at least."

"Yes," Michael murmured, feeling himself grow colder the more Charlotte and Mr. Riley gazed at each other. "For a while."

He swallowed and turned to Diana, smiling through his coldness. "The soup is marvelous, is it not?"

Supper lasted an interminable length of time, and it was even longer before Michael could escape to the card room. Not to play or to gamble, but to drink. He needed an excessive amount of drink, indeed.

Unfortunately, all Eden had to offer was port and various wines. So Michael sat at a lone card table, no cards in sight, and drank.

"What in the name of bloody blazes are you doing?"

The question came from Hugh, but Lord Sterling and Tyrone Demaris likely thought the same as they stood on either side of him.

Michael squinted as he poured more wine into his glass. "I am trying to get wildly intoxicated using what Eden left at our disposal."

"Why are you trying to get drunk?" Lord Sterling inquired in a surprisingly mild tone.

"Because I want to."

Hugh hummed in a doubtful tone. "I really don't think you do."

Michael slammed the bottle of wine down, jostling his glass and spilling some of the liquid onto his sleeve. "Yes, I bloody well do! I have never been well and truly soused, it was always reckless and irresponsible, and right now reckless and irresponsible is exactly what I want to be!"

The three men looked at him, then at each other. "He can't stay here and get soused," Tyrone murmured. "It would take ages, and there are witnesses. We can take him to the club."

"Surely you're not going to indulge this," Lord Sterling protested.

Hugh frowned. "Better we indulge him under our care than leave him be and let him fend for himself. I'll make certain he doesn't get too far gone."

Michael shook his head, swallowing a bitter taste in his mouth. "You can shove me in a hack and send me on my way when I am too drunk to walk on my own, and not a moment before!"

"Right," Hugh muttered, wiping his hands together. "Tyrone, we need a discreet way out. Francis, can you explain to my wife? It's going to be a long night."

Chapter Fourteen

A conversation with a friend may straighten everything out. Of course, it could also ravel things more so, make things more complicated, and bring in too much drama, but that is where selection of friends comes into play. Take great care that the friend you converse with will improve matters rather than magnify them.

-*The Spinster Chronicles, 11 October 1815*

"I don't know what I did, but Michael is not answering any of my notes."

"Why do you suppose it is something you did? Most men do not answer notes in a timely manner."

Charlotte shook her head, sitting in the drawing room of Georgie's home, watching her infant son crawl about the floor. "Not Michael. He always responds, and sometimes just appears, if he is in town. I know he asked not to know about my suitors and courtships, but…"

Georgie sat up straighter on the divan she was on, staring at Charlotte with round eyes. "Wait, he did what?"

"I told you," Charlotte insisted, clasping her hands before her, her yellow muslin creasing as she sat forward. "Surely I told you."

"I would remember hearing about something like that," Georgie retorted. She tucked a strand of her fair hair behind her ear and fidgeted with her fichu. "Michael said that?"

Charlotte nodded, her cheeks coloring, choosing to look at the cherub-cheeked Thomas Sterling as he crawled towards his mother's legs. "At the Bond dinner. We were sat beside each other, and he told me he did not wish to know about my potential courtships. He would prefer to know nothing about any of it. It was a most uncomfortable conversation."

Georgie shook her head slowly. "I can easily believe that. Interesting." Her brow furrowed and she lowered her eyes.

"What?" Charlotte demanded, having looked at her friend during her response. "What are you thinking?"

She bit her lip. "Has he been distant only since that conversation?"

Charlotte frowned as she considered the question carefully. "I think so… No, that's incorrect." She shook her head firmly, sighing and slumping in her chair. "No, I became so wrapped up in preparing myself for earnestly looking for love and marriage that I never wrote him, sent for him, or saw him. I thought that had all been on my end, but now I see that he had made no effort, either."

"I wondered if that might have been the case." Georgie gave her a sympathetic smile. "Surely you cannot blame him. He'll lose your friendship the moment you take your marriage vows."

"He would not!" Charlotte folded her arms, grumpily wrenching her gaze to the fire. "I would stay his friend until the day I die. I do not understand why everyone believes a man and a woman who are married to other people cannot be friends."

Georgie laughed once. "Do you not? How would it look for Michael to visit you in your husband's house? Or for you to visit the home he shares with his wife?"

"Michael isn't getting married," Charlotte told her without looking. "He may entertain young ladies for his own amusement, but I know him. He'd never want a wife."

"I think you had better revise your opinion," Georgie suggested. "Elinor says he is growing very fond of Diana Palmer."

Charlotte made a face. "She is a dear girl, but not right for Michael. At any rate, everyone knows the nature of things between Michael and me. No one should think anything of us visiting each other."

The heaving sigh Georgie released ought to have warned Charlotte off, but she wasn't about to budge. Why should her friendship with Michael change? Yes, a natural distance would fall between them, and she had felt that at the supper the other evening, but she refused to let it be an end. She was stubborn enough to fight it every step of the way, and when she was on her mettle, nothing stood in her way.

"You are not a naïve woman, Charlotte," Georgie said firmly. "You know Society in a way that few can claim. Despite what people know and claim, do you really think that you would be safe from the gossip that such an action would stir up? Why wouldn't you and Michael start an improper relationship, given the history you share? It is not too great a leap in logic, and you should know that."

Well, when put that way...

Charlotte imagined the scene Georgie had painted for her, that of Michael coming to visit her in the home of her husband, perhaps with a child or two about. He wouldn't care about visiting her husband, unless the pair of them became friends, he would simply maintain the same warm companionship they always had.

But what would her servants think? They would see their mistress keeping company with a man who was not her husband, and without an additional set of eyes in the room, as a married woman did not require a chaperone. Any passersby would see Michael entering the house at regular intervals, and it would not take much for such a thing to be mistaken for an assignation.

Such was the nature of Society that Michael's reputation would not suffer much, as men could carry on in all sorts of improper ways without even blinking. But Charlotte would be ruined. Charlotte's husband would be mortified. Charlotte's children would suffer.

And what of Michael's wife? If indeed he married.

Michael married...

What if he did marry?

"I don't want things to change," Charlotte whispered as she belatedly came round to Georgie's way of things. "Why must I give up Michael in order to gain a husband?"

Georgie offered her a small smile. "I don't think it is an exchange in the way you're describing."

"It feels that way."

"No..." Georgie trailed off, pursing her lips in thought. "No, I think it is different. I believe that the sort of match you are looking for, one of love and mutual respect, would ideally have your husband becoming your best friend. Replacing Michael, in a way, but only due to the depth of your feelings and the companionship you develop. It is only natural that Michael should then have a different standing in your life. I cannot think that he would give up your friendship entirely, but he will have to make room for the man you choose to spend your life with. I think he knows that."

Charlotte felt tears welling in her eyes, the pressure of them tightening her chest. "I hate seeing the distance between us. Thinking of him making room for someone else in my life. Changing the way things are between us, the way things have always been."

"Then perhaps you ought to marry for convenience, dear." Georgie lifted a shoulder, then bent to pluck her son from the rug and set him on her lap. "That way, Michael would always be your best friend, though he still would not be able to call."

It was true, Charlotte knew it well, but the idea of marrying for convenience to keep Michael to herself did not sit well either.

Could not.

"I cannot do that," Charlotte murmured. "I won't marry for the sake of being married. I don't have to do that. I simply don't want to be alone, if I can help it. I see what all of you have found, and I wonder why I have been so unfortunate as to not find it yet. Why I stand alone in this now."

Georgie bounced Thomas on her knee, giving Charlotte a look. "One of us was always going to be last, Charlotte, no matter what happened."

Charlotte rolled her eyes briefly. "If we married, yes. But we never thought we would, so I don't know that we ever really thought about it. And…"

"And you were never supposed to be last," Georgie finished.

"Does that sound so very horrid?" Charlotte asked with a wince. "So snobbish and cold?"

Georgie shook her head, smiling still. "Not to me. You're right, you and Grace were the mysteries of our bunch. Were we betting on our fates, I would have bet the pair of you to marry and have children before I ever managed a true courtship."

Charlotte snickered, shaking her head as she thought back. "That certainly would have made the most sense, given our situations. But I wouldn't trade it. While I hate being last, I wouldn't trade the loves you all have found purely to satisfy my needs. You've all made splendid matches, and that is not something I would ever find regret in."

"Thank you, Charlotte," Georgie responded, her voice growing rough, blinking rapidly.

"No, don't!" Charlotte protested, holding up a hand as though to shield herself from Georgie's emotion.

Georgie laughed and focused her attention on her son. "Fine, fine, I'll rid myself of these tears shortly."

"See that you do!"

Moments later, they shared a smile before Georgie looked back at her son. "How is it going, Charlotte? Are you having any success?"

Charlotte allowed herself to smile ruefully, though not for Georgie's eyes. "Well, I'm not anticipating a proposal, if that's what you mean."

"Is that what I mean?" Georgie replied without any sharpness, though there was a distinct tone of understanding in her voice.

It wasn't fair when she did that. Georgie had the same ability as Charlotte's mother; that of being able to perceive the truth of someone's thoughts in the most important times. She'd never blatantly announce such things, but she would certainly allow herself to guide her friends to the proper realization.

If they would be guided.

"I'm not in love," Charlotte told her, hoping it would be enough to keep her from prying further, "and I am quite sane and sensible. If my witnessing the romantic journeyings of you all has taught me anything, it is that nothing is too serious if I still have my wits about me."

"I did not realize that love had rendered us witless!" Georgie laughed, which made her son turn and reach for her face. She took his hand and kissed it, then directed the next words to him. "Auntie Charlotte thinks the frantic, mad rush of love makes us all fools, my lamb."

Charlotte frowned at her words, though they were clearly meant in jest. No, that wasn't what she thought, and that wasn't what she wanted, either. She wanted more than that. Saw possibilities beyond that.

Craved higher than that.

"I don't want the frantic, mad rush of love," she managed in a low voice.

Georgie paused, looking at her with some concern. "What? I thought…"

Slowly, Charlotte shook her head. "I want that love that exists between a man and a woman who have been together for years, the couple that knows each other intimately and completely, good and bad, inside and out. The love that tells of trials and triumphs, victories and failures, and spectacular fights with tender apologies. I want the tangible love of those who have entwined their lives so completely with another that no individuals exist. Just the pair of them together. Two hearts, one life." She fought hard for a swallow. "That is what I want, and my heart breaks at the thought of missing it."

There was no sound in the room but of Thomas softly babbling and the faint crackle of the fire.

Charlotte couldn't look at Georgie now, felt her own emotions growing harder to manage. How could admitting what she wanted aloud have such an effect on her? Conveying the deepest feelings of her heart to someone other than herself, allowing that vulnerable wish to become known. It was terrifying and freeing, yet it made the whole thing far more real. Far more of a risk.

"I thought you wanted a love to bring you to your knees," Georgie murmured, seeming confused.

Typically, Charlotte would have had a witty reply to such a statement, but she simply could not manage her usual antics at the moment.

"If it brings either of us to our knees, so be it," Charlotte told her, keeping her voice low. "But more than that, I want a love that makes me feel whole."

"Charlotte, that sort of love takes time."

She swallowed, nodding once. "I know, and I can't seem to find the man I want to spend the time to find that love with."

"What about Mr. Riley?" Georgie pressed gently. "I thought the pair of you were getting on rather well."

"We seem to be," Charlotte allowed with a faint smile. "He's terribly good with Mama, and never makes her feel as though she is conspicuous as our chaperone. I am finding myself more comfortable in his presence, which is lovely." She wrinkled up her nose and shrugged. "I don't know, Georgie. What am I supposed to feel?"

Georgie smiled at the question. "At the beginning? Awkward."

Charlotte scoffed and allowed herself a droll look at her friend. "Fair enough, I think we can say I have felt awkward."

"One usually does." Georgie's smile turned wistful, her eyes taking on a far-off look. "Then you find yourself comfortable, but with an excited edge that doesn't quite make sense."

"That would describe what I feel right now," Charlotte told her with a nod. "I could talk with him for ages, and yet I seem to fidget constantly."

Georgie snickered, bouncing her son again. "It's the anticipation, isn't it? Wondering if something will happen, wanting it to and yet not wanting it to…"

Charlotte nodded over and over, then huffed to herself. "Maddening stuff. Tell me it gets better."

"I am so sorry, it doesn't." Georgie made a face, shaking her head. "Things only get more complicated."

"Lovely. I see I have much to look forward to." She plastered a false smile on her face that made Georgie laugh. Charlotte groaned and put a hand to her brow. "Why did I want this again?"

"Because we have been led to believe that love is the most enviable of all things," Georgie answered simply, "and it is. It is also rare and unusual, and there is something to be said for those people who claim a marriage of convenience is a far easier matter."

"Is there?"

Georgie nodded. "Yes. It's true. That would be easier."

Charlotte narrowed her eyes. "But…?"

"But a love match is so very satisfying," Georgie admitted with an almost dreamy smile. "So lovely. So enjoyable. And complicated though it is, I cannot think my happiness could be any more than this if I had married for other reasons."

"I want that ease and happiness," Charlotte confessed. "I want it so much."

"I know, dear." Georgie smiled as she hugged her son to her. "You do like Mr. Riley, don't you? I'd hate to think that you were trying to force your emotions to fit into a mold of love rather than let it grow naturally."

Charlotte nodded quickly. "Of course I like Mr. Riley. I do not see how anyone could not like Mr. Riley. He is handsome, charming, and excellent company. I've never had a better dance partner, and he seems to only get more interesting the more I get to know him."

Georgie grinned at her, setting Thomas back on the ground when he fussed. "Charlotte! That is wonderful to hear! And certainly a very promising start."

"Do you think so?" Charlotte rubbed her hands together in more of an anxious habit than a speculative one. "I want to smile whenever I see him, Georgie. I don't always do so, but I want to. My lips simply want to smile when he is near. But he's not said anything about courtship or affection to me. Do you think that is a sign?"

"No, I think it is perfectly right," Georgie assured her. "Mr. Riley does not need to be proposing from the first moment he meets you and continuously until you accept."

Charlotte snickered at the idea of Mr. Riley doing something so ridiculous, like one of the dandies of London. "I cannot see him doing any such thing. Going to his knees and dramatically asking for my hand or begging me to be his wife. He's got far too much taste and sense for any such thing."

Her friend dipped her chin in a knowing nod. "You see? You have grown so accustomed to receiving proposals from any man who has spent three minutes in your company that you cannot recognize the genuine attentions of a gentleman worth considering. Once you are both more sure of your feelings, you may be surprised by the speed at which things happen, but there is no set timeline, Charlotte. You must do away with the idea that there is some sort of deadline to love or courtship. It will not be any less sweet if Mr. Riley should propose next spring if it means that he is convinced you are the perfect choice for him."

Charlotte's cheeks heated at the idea of Mr. Riley feeling so much for her. They had seen each other almost every day, but she couldn't say it had been for an excessive amount of time. He was always very cognizant and aware of the time he spent at her home during calling hours, and whenever they met in the park on a walk, which seemed to happen more regularly, he took great care that a respectable amount of time be spent together, and did not overextend it.

It all sounded very polite when she thought of it in such terms, but she would not have called Mr. Riley a particularly polite man. He was never rude, of course, and would never come close to earning such an insult, but he did have a bit of a wicked sense of humor that rendered him just amusing enough to keep around, for the surprise, if nothing else. When he and Charlotte had spent too much time together, they were quite the amusing pair. No one else would be able to attest to any such thing, as they hadn't been out in public much, but they soon would be. What might they become with even more exposure to each other?

Charlotte sighed as she thought of him, smiling to herself.

"What is that smile for?" Georgie demanded.

"I'm simply smiling!" Charlotte insisted, tucking her thoughts of Mr. Riley into the deepest recesses of her heart.

"And the sigh?"

Charlotte quirked a brow. "An exhale with audible aspects. Nothing more."

Georgie's eyes narrowed. "I don't believe you. You are hiding something, and I insist that you tell me what it is."

"All right, Miranda," Charlotte replied pointedly.

Georgie gasped dramatically, then burst out laughing. "Oh, very well, I'll leave off teasing you and prying. I'm only hopeful and encouraged where Mr. Riley is concerned. Is that too much?"

"Not at all," Charlotte assured her. "You are a true friend, and I am anxious for him to meet you, to meet all of the Spinsters, so that you might all like him as well."

"I already like him," Georgie laughed. "The moment you find it acceptable, I'll invite him here for supper. I think he and Tony might find a friend in each other, and it would do well for Tony to have other friends than Morton or Hensh."

Charlotte grinned mischievously. "Why does he need to spend less time with Hensh?"

"He doesn't. Only Hensh seems determined to spend all of his time with the Mortons, and Tony feels quite left out."

"Hensh has a plan, and he is determined to see it through." Charlotte smirked to herself. "Good man. I'll have to do more to enhance my chances of winning. New tactics, and greater effort."

Georgie frowned. "Winning what? What tactics? What have you and Hensh done?"

Charlotte only smiled all the more cheekily. "Never you mind. What are your thoughts on chaperoning me to the theater this week?"

Chapter Fifteen

Behavior at the theater ought to be studied with more focus and interest. This author could tell all sorts of tales from observation alone, but why risk the ruination of so many?

-*The Spinster Chronicles, 16 July 1817*

"Are you certain we may use the box? It is no trouble to me to sit in the general seats, you know. I am quite used to such things."

Michael smiled down at Diana for at least the fifth time that evening. "I am quite certain, Miss Palmer. I have had many assurances that it will not be occupied tonight, and that all will be available for our use. What else can I do to put you at ease?"

Diana blushed in her pretty way, her smile only heightening her beauty. "I am perfectly at ease, I assure you. I am only excitable and so delighted to be at the theater." More color rushed into her cheeks and she lowered her eyes. "With you."

The sweetness of her words filled his lungs, could have given him wings, would have spurred him to run extreme distances for the promise of her smile. It was a strange sensation, and certainly the first time he had experienced it from her hand, but there was also a thrilling sense of victory in it.

He had done it. He had found a woman who made him happy, who made him feel things, who saw him for the man he was and enjoyed being in his company. He could come to love Diana Palmer, and it would not take too much effort at all.

What an astonishing thought... and a sobering one.

He'd need to start thinking matrimony and details before too long. That would require several meetings, but it should be fairly straightforward, all things considered.

But first, there would need to be courtship.

He smiled at Diana, though her eyes were still cast down. "I'm rather pleased to be here with you, as well," he told her in all sincerity.

Her nearly amber eyes rose to his, an innocent light glowing there.

Michael nodded in encouragement, then smiled. "I feel rather fortunate, actually, to have such a vision of loveliness on my arm."

The flattery made her laugh, and she averted her eyes again, though no one would have denied Michael's words.

Diana had dressed herself in pale green silks, which gave her eyes a more magical hue, and the cut, fit, and styling of the gown, none of which Michael understood, seemed to heighten her figure magnificently. Her golden hair had been curled and plaited, ribbons and flowers darting here and there in the fair tresses. She was a complete vision, and he defied any man in this theater to find her anything less than stunning.

"You are lovely, Diana," Mrs. Greensley insisted behind them. "Come, come, you must accept your due praise."

"Please, cousin," Diana pleaded with a smile. "Mr. Greensley, will you not give a word of sense?"

Greensley, accompanying his wife to the theater on chaperoning duties, shook his head. "Afraid not, Diana. You outshine all ladies here save one."

"I'll accept that!" Diana said with a quick laugh. "Who supersedes me?"

"My wife, naturally," Greensley replied without hesitation as he smiled at the woman beside him.

Mrs. Greensley gave him a playful look, then shook her head. "Chivalry, but no sense. Alas for Mr. Greensley."

Michael chuckled and continued on their promenade in the theater, the pressure of Diana's hand on his arm a strength and a comfort, though he hadn't realized he needed either.

Being with Diana was certainly a revelation in more ways than one.

Their small group walked on, all smiling and nodding at other guests milling about with them. Michael was pleased to note how many of those nodding at him he could actually name. He had grown so used to only keeping track of names as they affected Charlotte, keeping stock of each of her would-be suitors, no matter how unlikely, that any individuals that might have impacted *him* in some way had been completely ignored. Now, however, he was only meeting people for his own interests, and the sheer volume of names had taken some getting used to.

What a relief to know he was equally capable of managing his own social connections.

"I believe we should come to our box shortly," Michael assured the others. "I trust you will be quite pleased with the view of the stage. I do not think there is a single seat in the box that will be a poor one, and we are assured of enjoying the performances."

"I will confess to not knowing much of opera," Mr. Greensley said to no one in particular, "but the reviews of this one are most encouraging. Very entertaining, this."

Mrs. Greensley laughed at her husband's words. "Well, it is an *opéra comique*, my dear, so one would hope it would entertain."

"I always marvel at the talents of opera singers," Diana commented before the thread could continue. "All ladies are expected to have some ability to sing, and some are better than others, but what would it be like to have a voice of this brilliance!"

"Rather busy, I would think," Michael replied with a quirk of a smile. "You'd likely be asked to sing at every gathering you attended, even if there was no other music planned. Mothers of daughters would ply you with questions about your training in the hopes that their daughters might somehow follow the same course. Ears of music lovers would strain for your voice, knees weakening as they neared your presence, and all would fall before your feet."

Diana stared at him, eyes wide, then her lips moved into a soft smile. "You're right. That does sound busy. I think I'll keep to my middling voice after all."

Michael laughed at the quip, as he tended to do whenever Diana's wit was on display. She kept that skill rather private, which allowed one to appreciate it all the more when it did appear, but what a brilliant wit it was! Perhaps that was due to her quieter nature, perhaps it was that beauty and wit were such a rare combination, or perhaps it was that he did not expect any woman outside of Charlotte's circle to possess much by way of wit.

Whatever it was, the pleasure of once more having female wit in his company was a true delight.

"Ah, here we are."

Michael stopped cold as the voice he knew well said the exact words he had been preparing, and his eyes blinked twice before he could believe the sight before him.

Charlotte stood there, her hand in Mr. Riley's arm, Tony and Georgie Sterling behind them.

At the same box they were preparing to enter.

Which, all told, was not surprising, as it was the Wright family's usual box.

But Michael had received permission from Mr. Wright to make use of the box tonight. Had the man forgotten his own daughter was going to use it? Yes, they had fit a number of people into the large box before, but this…

"What are you doing here?" Charlotte asked without any politeness, apparently not noticing any of the others.

"Your father gave me use of the box," he told her without any defensive airs, which was a feat in and of itself. "He assured me it would not be in use."

Charlotte's expression did not change, but he caught a flash of a wrinkle in her brow that belied her calm. "Clearly, my father needs to speak with my mother at more regular intervals. She granted me use of the box this evening."

Michael grit his teeth, praying he could keep his composure intact in the presence of Diana and the Greensleys. "Well, we certainly don't wish to impose…"

"Not at all," Charlotte said quickly, looking at the group finally and smiling at them all. "There is plenty of room, and I've had larger parties than this in our box without the slightest bit of discomfort." She gestured towards the box, her expression all benevolence and generosity now. Her eyes fixed on Diana, and her smile widened. "Miss Palmer, I am so pleased to see you again."

As Michael feared, Diana beamed in return. "You as well, Miss Wright. I had no idea we'd be using your family's box. Is this where you sat when you imagined the article about secret behaviors at the opera? It is one of my favorite pieces."

Charlotte cocked her head with a bemused smile. "How did you know I wrote that one, my dear? I know Michael couldn't have told you, I never give him advanced insight into my articles."

Diana blushed and bit her lip. "I have made a study of the articles. I can usually tell which of the Spinsters has written which thing."

"Can you, indeed?" Mr. Riley said with a laugh. "Miss Palmer, you will have to enlighten me. I've never been able to properly identify the authors, though I confess to not knowing the identities as it is."

"Miss Palmer," Charlotte broke in quickly, "may I present Mr. and Mrs. Sterling? Mrs. Sterling is also one of the writers."

Diana all but squealed. "Oh, Mrs. Sterling, what a delight! I'm honored to meet you."

Georgie smiled with her usual kindness, though there was also amusement in her features. "Miss Palmer, I've heard much about you, but none of it measures up to the reality. What a pleasure. Shall we take our seats?"

Michael could have kissed Georgie in gratitude for suggesting it. Chatting about the Spinsters in Charlotte's presence while standing outside of the box at the theater was not something he was enjoying, and the sooner they could return to his previous designs of wooing Diana the better.

Having Charlotte about only heightened his resolve to begin his courtship in truth. He'd speak to Greensley tonight and call on him in the morning. The only reason he had not done so following Lord Eden's ball was due to a foolhardy night spent in a club consuming more alcohol than a man was designed to hold, then spending the following days in bed sicker than a dog. Were it not for Hugh Sterling, Michael might have had a spot of trouble there, but he had been well tended.

Stupid, but at least cared for.

He wouldn't wait any longer. Tomorrow, he would take the first step.

The four couples entered the box and began rearranging their seats accordingly, faint shuffling as they tried to find the best arrangements, the murmur of the other theater guests adding a layer of sound above that of the orchestra near the stage as they played the overture of the opera.

Michael tried his best to smile, to be congenial, to pretend as though his entire evening hadn't been completely upended with one simple misunderstanding. But the truth of the matter was that he was perfectly and acutely aware of every move Charlotte made. Her exact distance from him, every breath she took, the smiles that crossed her face as she settled herself.

He couldn't bloody recall what Diana was wearing unless he looked at her, because in his mind, he could only see Charlotte.

Dressed in white, she was fully angelic, porcelain in almost every respect. The bodice of her dress was wreathed in pink cords and lace, a pattern of leaves on the fabric itself. Folds and ripples there streamed into the length of the gown, reappearing with the cords and lace again at the hem, more folded pink material waving in a pattern he could have studied for hours in sheer fascination. Flounces, he thought, though he didn't dare look back to confirm. The sleeves were small, which matched the low bodice, though he couldn't deny the perfection both captured in Charlotte.

Curls had cupped either side of her face, while the rest of her hair seemed to be almost haphazardly curled and fastened up with combs he had never seen her wear, long ringlets streaming from the crown of her head, yet never quite made it to her neck. She wore a head-dress and flowers, too, though all he could think of were those long curls draping behind.

He knew what Charlotte looked like at any given time and in any given place. For pity's sake, he had studied her face, figure, and form nearly every day of their friendship until nothing about her looks was a mystery. Yet he had never seen her look thus. Hadn't felt this pain in so long.

Had time away from her only made his longing worse?

It couldn't be. He shouldn't be longing for her at all. He needed a clean break, needed even more distance, needed to drown himself in Diana Palmer or any other woman until it was Charlotte who faded, not them.

Yet he could not act with haste. He had seen all too often what happened when feelings of passion or desperation were indulged. He could not, would not, subject the woman he married to such a future, and to such inelegance of feeling on his part.

No more, he thought. After tonight, no more Charlotte in any form.

It wasn't for his sake he would do this. It was for Diana. If not her, the woman he courted after her. Whoever she was, wherever she was, the woman who would replace Charlotte in his affections deserved no competition.

He smiled at Diana as he took his seat beside her, turning his form just enough that he could see nothing of Charlotte at all, and she would only see his back, should she have looked. The position brought him closer to Diana as well, which was undoubtedly safer, and better for all concerned.

He exhaled slowly as the overture ended, and the opera began.

Charlotte was dying.

Slowly and without any ado, she was going to die.

Michael was done with her. That was abundantly clear, and she had no time or space to mourn the loss of him. She had just come round to the idea that they would not be as close as they had been previously, but she hadn't thought they would cease to be friends entirely.

She hadn't reveled in the thought of sharing the family box with him tonight, particularly when he was clearly courting Miss Palmer, and it would be far more difficult to encourage Jonathan when Michael was around.

It was amusing; she had only just begun to think of Mr. Riley as Jonathan, not that he had given her permission to use his Christian name, and in considering him in such a way, she felt the ties between them tighten. Felt closer to him than they undoubtedly were. Gave her an interesting scene to imagine in her unoccupied hours.

Finding that scene was nearly impossible at the present, though the man who played in it sat beside her, laughing in all the correct parts of the opera.

She forced herself to laugh, though anyone paying attention would notice she was a notch or two delayed in doing so.

She was too focused on whether Michael was laughing. If Miss Palmer was laughing. If they were paying any attention to the opera or if they were more enthralled with each other than in any of the performances.

How many evenings had she and Michael spent in this box, surrounded by other people, but always gravitating towards each other? Enjoying good performances and commenting on them, mocking poor performances and criticizing them, laughing in muffled tones that her mother was constantly scolding them for. Michael had always been there, and she'd never had reason to think that would change.

The memories in this box enveloped her, robbed her lungs of air, and her eyes began to sting with tears.

They hadn't reached the interval yet, but Charlotte suddenly felt choked by the sensations here.

Michael leaned closer to Miss Palmer to whisper something that made Miss Palmer smile in what had to be the most beautiful smile to ever grace a face.

Whether Michael loved, or would love, Miss Palmer was irrelevant. What was entirely relevant, and entirely evident, was that she was now more to him than Charlotte was.

She could not watch this, could not see him like this with her, could not stand to be confined in this space with him.

She got to her feet and stepped around Jonathan quickly.

"Are you all right?" he whispered quietly, his features wreathed in concern.

Charlotte nodded, forcing a smile. "I only need a bit of air. I won't be a moment."

"Shall I come with you?" Georgie asked, beginning to rise.

Charlotte waved her down. "It's only the fit of my gown. I'll return presently."

Fearing Tony would follow, as he had threatened once before,

Charlotte rushed out of the box and hurried down the corridor. Her slippers made no sound at all on the carpet, though her skirts rustled enough to direct anyone to her position, should they be searching.

Blessedly, the family box was situated near one of the square rooms in the theater. It was generally reserved for use by members of the peerage or members of Parliament, but Charlotte did not care enough to avoid it. She needed a space to breathe and recover, and she refused to hunt for an alcove. Every story of poor behavior at a theater occurred in an alcove, which struck her as odd, as alcoves were not nearly so plentiful for such things, nor did they allow for necessary privacy in most cases.

A square room, however...

Charlotte entered and moved directly to a chair, sinking into it and slumping forward, stripping her gloves off and pressing her hands against her face. Her breath came slowly and unsteadily, each inhale painful and each exhale draining. She had never been particularly skilled at playing a part, and here she was, acting a role while burying her natural inclination and disposition at the same time.

She was incapable of doing so.

Until she found some control over her emotions, she would not be able to maintain the necessary façade for the evening.

Once this evening was over, she'd be able to create a strategy to avoid seeing Michael more often than society would dictate, and especially in a more direct setting such as this. She had enough connections and allies to inform her of guest lists, so planning would be easy and essential. All she had to do was survive the evening, uncomfortable and unplanned though it was, and then she need never experience this again.

She slid her hands to her mouth, swallowing hard, shuddering another exhale as she sought control.

"What is it?"

Charlotte closed her eyes, fighting the wild inhale that would completely undo her and forcing her breathing to find a steadier pace, limited though it would be.

She opened her eyes and lowered her hands to her chin, allowing herself to smile at Michael as he stood in the doorway of the room, his hands at his side. "You needn't have followed me, you know.

You're here with guests, you should go back to them."

Michael did not react but for the fingers of his right hand rubbing together. "What is it?"

She ought to have known he would see through her politeness. Still, she was not about to confess her pain to satisfy his curiosity. "My dress," she lied easily, just as she had to Georgie. "The bodice is particularly fitted, and I feel rather trapped in it. Nothing drastic, just my lack of fashionable training to give me the proper stamina."

His brow wrinkled, and he took four steps into the room. "Why do I not believe you?"

Charlotte managed to quirk a brow and dropped her hands to her lap, elbow at her knees, still slumped over inelegantly. "Because you've never worn a gown that requires a tighter setting of your stays than is reasonable."

He blinked once. "I generally don't wear stays at all, so I can agree with you there."

She grinned without meaning to, his usual dry quip doing more to set her to rights than anything else could have, even if his voice lacked an encouraging tone. Quickly, she sobered and straightened in her seat.

"I like Miss Palmer, Michael," she told him, the words nearly choking her, true though they were.

Michael almost smiled but didn't quite manage it. "That's because she's nearly obsessed with you and the Spinsters."

"Well, that does help her win more favor," Charlotte admitted with another smile, this one more controlled. "It shows her excellent taste."

"It certainly shows something, I grant you." He moved further into the room, watching Charlotte.

That searching look, the eyes that could see more than she wanted, was more than she could bear. She rose and turned her back to him, rubbing her palms together. "She seems rather lovely," she told him, her voice perhaps a touch too loud. "Sensible, intelligent, and good-natured. Have you known her long?"

"Charlotte, we're not going to talk about Diana in here."

His use of her Christian name slashed through Charlotte painfully, seizing her chest with a chill that took a number of heartbeats to recover from. "I'm trying, Michael," she whispered harshly, glancing over her shoulder without actually looking at him. "As your friend, I'm trying."

"Don't," he said, the word almost a bark. "Don't try to enjoy this. Don't try to make it better that I'm doing this, that you're here with Riley, that we can't avoid each other here."

Charlotte closed her eyes again, her throat moving on a lump she simply could not swallow. "I didn't know we were avoiding each other. I didn't know you were shutting me out. I didn't know we were ending our friendship as we pursued love for ourselves."

Michael didn't respond, which prompted Charlotte to turn to face him.

His expression was hooded, his fingers now fists at his sides, his eyes on her.

Anger roared within Charlotte, and she took two steps forward. "I didn't know," she snapped, "that my best friend was replacing me with a pretty girl ten years his junior. I didn't know that, in spite of cutting me off, you still feel entitled to ask my family for favors."

Michael's mouth opened as though he would retort something, but Charlotte wasn't finished.

"I didn't know," she went on, "that you wouldn't be laughing with me anymore. That we couldn't even look at each other anymore. That I would begin to lose years and years of memories with you because you could not stand to be near me during one of the most terrifying times of my life."

"What else am I supposed to do, Charlotte," Michael cried, his hands splaying out before him in an almost desperate gesture, "when I am still madly in love with you?"

Whatever Charlotte had been about to say vanished, and her heart plummeted into the pit of her stomach, making her toes tingle ominously. "What?"

Michael shook his head, exhaling what seemed to be a laugh, though torment lay in his features rather than humor. "You *still* don't see. After all this time, you still don't..." He shook his head and strode forward, jaw set.

Charlotte stuttered back a step or two, her breath hitching in the face of his determined approach.

Then his mouth was on hers, his hands on either side of her face, his body flush against hers. She couldn't move, couldn't think, could not comprehend that Michael... *Michael*...

Instinctively, Charlotte relaxed against him, began to move her lips against his, sighed against the exquisite pleasure such an action gave her. Michael held her closer, kissed her deeper, and Charlotte felt her pulse begin to pound in her ears and her lips, taking over everything else she could feel. She snaked her hands up to his neck, tugging him closer without thinking.

Michael groaned and began to kiss her as though life itself was at an end, wild and intense, overwhelming her with passion and need, sending her thoughts and emotions swirling in a thousand different directions. She would never breathe again, would burst into flame on the spot, would forever crave this madness... Would never feel herself whole without it...

With a gasp that sprang from one or both of them, Michael shoved away from her, causing them both to stumble.

Charlotte panted in a haze of desire and confusion, staring at him, waiting for the fog to lift, wondering if they might continue the foray...

Oh, blessed saints above...

A hand went to her mouth as realization dawned, cold and terrifying. Michael's eyes were wide and staring back at her, his chest heaving, horror rampant in his expression.

He shook his head quickly, swallowing. Blinked. Shook his head again, much more firmly.

Charlotte mouthed his name, not sure what she meant by it. Apology? Pleading? Assuring?

All of them at once?

She'd never been kissed in her life before this, and instinct had taken over. That it happened to be Michael was both the best and the worst possible option. He would never tell, would never think less of her, would never see her ruined for it.

But nothing could be as it had been after this.

Not ever.

Michael slowly backed away from her, his fingers again fists, then turned and strode from the square room at a clip that she could not hope to match while her legs continued to tremble.

Inhaling deeply, exhaling the same, Charlotte glanced down at the floor, willing her pulse to slow and steady, waited for her face to cool, and tried for logic. She had been kissed by Michael, and she had kissed him back. Attacked him, really. Rather unfair to lay that upon her with her inexperience.

Still, now she knew what a kiss was like, and knew that she was weak to it. Rather susceptible, if she could kiss Michael in such a way, of all people. She'd have to behave with more care in the future.

Another insight in her journey to love.

That was all.

It had to be.

Chapter Sixteen

It is often said that how one reacts to adversity is rather telling. In this author's opinion, it is not the reaction itself that is telling, but the intention. Intention is the root of all things.

-The Spinster Chronicles, 30 August 1816

Michael hadn't been to church this much since his sisters fancied the young clergyman in their youth, and he'd been forced to escort them to any service they attended.

His heart was in a far better place now than it had been then, but a desperate need for repentance would do that for a man.

He had kissed Charlotte.

Well, that was putting it a bit mildly, considering he had practically attacked her, but the distinction really wasn't all that necessary.

Years and years of wondering what it would be like, and in one reckless moment of desperation, he'd given in and kissed her. Kissed her soundly while the woman he was planning on courting sat watching the opera, no doubt wondering where he had gone.

He couldn't even remember what excuse he'd made for following Charlotte, likely some simple line about checking on her, which was true.

What was also true was that he could not help himself.

He had spent nearly the entire first half of the opera completely ignoring Charlotte. He'd kept his back to her and focused entirely on the opera and on Diana. He'd begun to feel rather proud of himself, thinking his efforts had been a success, when a rustling behind him had drawn his attention there, seeing Charlotte disappear out of the box. No rush of emotions, no evidence of distress, she'd simply left the box before the interval had begun.

Michael had shared a look with Riley, who had shrugged, and with Georgie, who looked after Charlotte almost at once.

It was enough to force Michael to leave, as well.

A habit borne from years of following Charlotte. Observing Charlotte. Caring for Charlotte.

Loving Charlotte.

But how could he have known that she would express such feelings about his behavior? That he had been disappointing her, hurting her, and she still did not comprehend his motivation. She could do exactly the same to him, had been doing so for years, and he had accepted it as his lot. As his fate, knowing she would never love him.

When he began to live independent from her, she erupted in a tower of indignation. And in response, he had confessed something he had kept from her for years. It should have settled everything, but instead, she had been shocked by it.

What had he been doing with his life? How could he have spent all this time with her, around her, and thinking about her, and yet never make it clear that he had been doing it for love of her?

The moment had taken over his sense and his control, there was no other explanation for it. Heady, passionate, and stunning though it had been, it had been a mistake of the grossest manner. A betrayal of his pride and honor, his plans, and his self-respect. He'd been half tempted to abandon the entire party at the opera and take himself off to his country estate, but, thankfully, he'd regained enough sense to calmly return to the box and resume his seat beside Diana.

He hadn't talked to another soul the whole evening but her.

Charlotte returned to the box at some point, but he'd forced himself not to notice, not to care, and even now could not recollect at what point she'd returned.

That had been several nights ago, and he still hadn't officially established a courtship with Diana. He thought it only right that he should be free of his feelings for Charlotte before he did so, and that he should feel he had done penance enough to expunge the mistake from his soul.

And that brought him to this chapel a stone's throw from his London home, sitting quietly in the pew.

Praying.

"I'm beginning to think you ought to have become a clergyman."

Michael smirked to himself and raised his head, glancing to the aisle where Miranda Sterling stood. "I'd have been dreadful at it, I can assure you."

"That doesn't stop a great many clergymen, which proves you would have been decent enough." She smiled and flicked her fingers, indicating he move further down the bench.

He did so, gesturing for her to sit beside him. "What makes you think I come here often?"

Miranda's lips curved into a knowing smile. "I've seen you, Michael. You've taken to coming around the same time every day, and it happens to be when I come."

He cocked a brow at her. "You attend church daily?"

"I'm a devoted Christian, my dear, but even I am not so pious." She scoffed and turned her turbaned head towards the front of the chapel. "No, I meet with Mr. Jenkins on the regular. It is astonishing how abandoned the poor of each parish are in London. One would never dream of such in the country, but we forget all manners in London. So I come for a daily assignment to assist where I can."

Michael frowned at her, though the generosity in her words touched him greatly. "I didn't realize this was your parish in London."

Her mouth quirked to one side. "It isn't. Mr. Jenkins is a cousin's son, so I pay him a special attention. Don't tell the Lord, I daresay we aren't permitted favorites among his shepherds."

"I'll keep your secret, if secrets from the Lord do not damn us."

She chuckled and nodded in approval. "Brava, Michael. Now, will you tell a friend what brings you to the hallowed halls of the church so often? Not family cares, I hope."

Michael sighed, knowing that Miranda was as wise as she was eccentric, but also knowing her devotion to the Spinsters, and therefore to Charlotte. It would be a risk above anything to confide all, and he dared not do it. Only Miranda could pry so personally and not offend.

"No," he told her simply, "my family is well. This is…" He twisted his lips, searching for words. "Seeking guidance, I suppose. Forgiveness. Inspiration. Motivation."

"That seems a great deal for the Lord to do at one time," Miranda tsked. "Is He accustomed to so fervent a list from you?"

Michael had to laugh at that. "No, actually. I was just considering that. I attend services as often as any good Christian, but my devotion is certainly lacking."

Miranda harrumphed softly. "Then I hardly think this would be the place to find the answers."

"Are you telling me to cease my diligent prayer?" Michael inquired dryly, feeling more relaxed by the second as they sat here, which was astonishing in and of itself.

"I would never," she vowed solemnly, crossing herself in dutiful fashion. "But I've always thought the Lord expected us to act as well as pray, and you seem to only be doing the one. Rather difficult for the path to be made clear if you are not walking."

There was an idea, and a rather sound one. He had felt quite trapped by his indecision, and by his guilt, so he had chosen to do nothing for fear of making another false step. Yet what good would that do him? Nothing would change if he did not move, and change was what he sought.

Michael turned to the woman beside him with a warm smile. "You are a wealth of wisdom, Miranda."

She dimpled with an almost matronly pride. "Yes, I do try to tell people so, but alas…" She winked and rose, gracefully stepping out of the pew and moving towards the front of the chapel. "Go do something, dear. It will do you good."

He smiled after her, watching as she moved to the rooms off of the chapel to meet with Jenkins. The moment she disappeared, he slid out of the pew himself and walked out of the church, wearing a true smile for what had to be the first time since attending the theater.

He could have gone home and changed, and probably should have, but he had a sense that if he returned home before his errand was complete, it would not, in fact, get completed. Besides, he was dressed finely enough. It was part of his habit now, which would have delighted Tyrone's valet to no end. He was fully presentable to meet with Greensley for the appropriate conversation, and it was not as though Greensley would judge him for what he wore even if he had not had his entire wardrobe exchanged for finer things.

"This is excellent timing. I was just coming to your house to call on you."

Michael glanced at the approaching Hugh Sterling with wry amusement. "I'm beginning to think I am being followed by the Sterlings."

Hugh's high brow furrowed. "Why?"

"Nothing," Michael muttered, shaking his head. "And it is rather good timing, as I would not have been home when you called."

"Are you not going home now?" Hugh asked, gesturing the way. "It is the right direction."

Michael laughed once. "I'm aware of that. But we are turning, you see. Here." With great emphasis, he turned the corner and continued down the street, Hugh walking along beside him.

"Where are you off to, then?" his friend inquired with mild interest.

"Greensleys," he stated. He grinned at Hugh quickly. "I'm going to request permission to court Miss Palmer."

Hugh's mouth dropped in surprise before spreading into a smile. "Are you, indeed? My felicitations, old fellow. She's a beautiful lady, to be sure, and I hear only praises of her."

Michael nodded in agreement. "She is lovely in every respect. I cannot say yet if it will lead to marriage, but…"

"You have hopes?" Hugh prodded, his smile turning teasing, if not suggestive.

"I do, I'll not deny it." He shrugged a shoulder, a sense of pride welling within him. "I think she likes me, Sterling."

Hugh guffawed without shame. "I should ruddy hope so! I'd heard the pair of you had been seen together, but nobody could make heads or tails of it. A courtship would certainly do the trick."

Michael frowned at the phrase and glanced at him. "For what?"

"Well, for my wife, for one."

"Elinor? What does she need convincing of?"

Hugh rolled his eyes but continued to smile. "Nothing. She's just

171

battling Charlotte and her foul mood."

Michael's stomach squeezed into a tight fist within him. "What's Charlotte upset about?"

Fleeting prayers ran rampant as he considered that Elinor could know exactly what transpired at the theater, that all the Spinsters could know.

Oh, gads, how would they work a reference to his behavior into the next issue, if that were the case? They would put it in, he had no doubt. They were just the vindictively creative sort to allude to the event in such a way that only he would understand, but it would be all too clear for him.

"Hang me if I know," Hugh admitted with a sigh, shaking his head. "Elinor comes home three days a week speaking of nothing but Charlotte's sour mood, and how she offers a dozen explanations, but nothing seems to make sense to any of them."

There was some relief in that, but Michael still wasn't satisfied.

"Why would my courtship with Diana have any bearing on Charlotte's mood?" he asked sourly, the prickles of discomfort intensifying in his chest and extending into his arms.

Hugh gave him an odd look. "Jealousy, I should think. She's terribly determined, you know. Don't you think it would irk her to no end that she had decided to marry and then you entered into a courtship before she managed to? Blimey, she'd bring down thunder from the heavens, I'd expect."

Relief was so sweet it was almost sickening, and it was all he could do to place one foot in front of the other. If that was all Hugh thought that would give Charlotte fits about the situation facing them all, Michael was safer than he could have imagined.

It appeared that Charlotte truly was not sharing the details of what had happened, and he wasn't sure he'd ever appreciated discretion more. He'd do the same, of course, and would have had she been the only one with a potential courtship to hand, but he'd have thought Charlotte would tell the Spinsters, at least. Charlotte was all well and good where secrets were concerned with other people, but the Spinsters...

Well, it would not surprise him if they knew everything about their relationship from the very beginning, including Charlotte's very clear and concise thoughts on the matter.

"It would, you're quite right," Michael managed around the odd taste in his mouth. "She was livid when Elinor married before her, so why should it not be the same with me?"

"I thought we weren't extending to marriage yet," Hugh teased.

Michael's face flamed, making his friend laugh and wave him on as he approached Greensley's home. His cheeks seemed to cool with each step towards the door, even as his heart pounded further.

If he wasn't sure of his course before, he was now.

The door was opened at once, and he was let in with all due politeness as he extended his card to the butler. It wasn't but another moment or two that Greensley appeared from his study and walked with him to a drawing room.

"What can I do for you, Sandford?" he asked with a friendly smile. "You find me all alone this morning."

"That is just as I would hope, Greensley." Michael inhaled, hesitating only a moment, then ventured, "I would like your permission to court Miss Palmer."

"What lovely flowers, Charlotte!"

"All six bouquets of them."

"I thought we weren't entertaining all the men anymore."

Charlotte smiled rather smugly as she raised her tea to her lips. "We aren't. Those are all from Jonathan."

"Jonathan?" Grace repeated with wide eyes. "Since when do we call the man by his Christian name?"

Charlotte sipped slowly, then placed the cup on its saucer rather demurely, if she did say so herself. "Since I have agreed to his courtship."

There was a long pause as her words sunk in, and she watched the expressions of each of her friends as they began to have an impact.

"What?" Georgie cried first, her hands slapping in her lap.

"Courtship?" Izzy followed with a squeal of delight.

"You agreed?" Grace repeated in abject disbelief.

"Finally!" Elinor crowed as she raised both hands in the air.

Charlotte laughed at that one. "Finally?" she said with a look at her friend. "Have you been waiting for me to do so?"

"As a matter of fact, yes," Elinor replied without hesitation, grinning at her. "He's simply marvelous. Handsome without being distracting, wealthy enough to not be a fortune hunter, and charming without being insincere. And I think he's rather amusing, which would follow if he's got an interest in courting you."

Charlotte made a playful face, but allowed that, as it was undoubtedly true. A man would not get far with her if he did not possess humor and wit, and he would have to have a decent quantity of both in order to take her on. She would not deny that Jonathan possessed a sort of natural perfection, which, rather than distance himself from mortals, brought him to a more believable level. He was as genuine a person as she had ever met in her life, and what flaws he could possibly possess were beyond her imagination. Of course, he was not perfect in truth, but neither did he have any faults of such a magnitude as to make him an improper suitor.

It was rare that Charlotte could not find a particular mark against a man, particularly when considering them in a more romantic sense. She was harsh in her judgments, and rarely changed her mind when one was made. With Jonathan, she hadn't been able to do so.

He was patient, but he was no saint. He was polite, but he was no paragon. He was clever, but he was no scholar. He was a gentleman, but he was anything but stuffy.

He might not have been perfect by Society's standards, yet he was perfect according to Charlotte.

What was more, she liked him.

It was astonishing how free she felt in having accepted his courtship. Liberated, really. In a simple answer, she was able to relate to him that she had enough romantic interest to wish to know him on a deeper level. She was able to express her wishes, which Society usually discouraged, not that Charlotte obeyed. She was able to claim the man as hers, for the time being, and the more possessive side of her thrilled with that victory. For however long it lasted, Jonathan Riley was hers.

Was it so very selfish to have that delight her?

"Did he meet with your father?" Izzy asked as Georgie began pouring tea for them all and handing cups around. "How did it happen?"

Charlotte smiled at her, bringing herself back to the moment. "He came for supper and asked to court me between courses."

"While you and Charles were sitting there?" Grace laughed. "Rather unconventional, but I like him more for it."

"So do I," Charlotte admitted, wrinkling her nose in a faint giggle. "I had an inkling he would, he'd hinted around it on our last walk of Hyde Park, so it wasn't a terrible surprise."

Elinor shook her head, taking her teacup and saucer from Georgie, leaning forward, and plucking a biscuit from the tray. "How did your father respond to that?"

The memory made Charlotte grin once more. "It's my father, Elinor. He looked at Jonathan, looked at me, drummed his fingers on the table, then asked if I wanted him to say yes."

Snickers and giggles resounded in the drawing room, and Charlotte sipped her tea as they did so, feeling quite satisfied with herself. There was something quite gratifying about knowing that a man she was intrigued by, that she was growing to like and admire very much, felt the same way about her. She hadn't had the pleasure of mutual affection in her life, not in the romantic sense, so this first adventure was full of surprises and secret pleasures.

Whether she and Jonathan would wind up making matrimonial vows with each other remained to be seen, and she refused to anticipate any such thing for fear of ruining things. She was determined to enjoy each moment of this courtship as it happened, not wish for more or for different. She may only get the one courtship, and would it be so terrible to be ignorant as to what it could have been?

Sudden flashes of memory and sensation lit her mind, and her lips tingled as images of Michael's kiss replayed. She could recall the taste of him on her tongue, the feel of his hands against her cheeks, the heat of his body pressed to hers. Her lungs began to burn as they had then, her head swam and her fingers itched to cling further, to pull him in, to drag them both into the spirals of anticipation coiling in her.

Charlotte cleared her throat, forcing herself to sip her tea again, if only to wash the taste of him out.

Would kissing Jonathan be a more delicious experience than that?

Surely it would be, given how different her emotions were with him. Perhaps he would be a gentler sort, his kisses more ticklish, or his attentions more focused. Perhaps he would prefer to let her have her way, generously accepting whatever she saw fit. Perhaps he would prove a masterful tutor, and the pair of them would have the sort of romance to rival and overshadow all loves of tales, myths, or poems. She could have a child every year or so just to prove to the world that their affections were rather histrionic, and wouldn't that shock Society?

The more she thought on the topic, the more amusing it became, yet the anticipation of it seemed rather pale compared to the entertainment of it.

That could not be the way it was supposed to be.

But then, their courtship was new. The more passionate aspects would develop as their mutual admiration did.

How could any woman not be passionate where Jonathan Riley was concerned upon growing closer to him?

"What does Michael say to all of this?" Izzy asked, laughter still adorning her features.

Charlotte's eyes snapped to her, cheeks flaming, heart thudding into the pit of her stomach. "Michael?"

Georgie shushed her cousin quickly, throwing a meaningful look her way. Izzy's eyes dropped to her tea and she sipped without another word. Elinor focused on her biscuit, her expression composed.

Only Grace stared at Charlotte without shame, clearly still expecting her to answer the question.

This was why she should never keep secrets from them, and why she should never tell one of them something she had not told the rest.

What would Michael say?

How was she to know what Michael would say? Michael was apparently in love with her, if he was to be believed. Michael clearly hated that he loved her, though he was intent enough in his kisses that she should feel it. Michael had no intention of being friends with Charlotte anymore, even if he was madly in love with her.

If Michael was so in love with her, why was he not attempting to court her? Why was he determined to have Diana in his life? Why hadn't he said something before now?

He had, her mind suggested.

Images of a spring morning appeared, younger versions of herself and Michael in one of the sitting rooms in Brancombe. Michael sat beside Charlotte on the sofa and took her hands. "Charlotte, will you marry me?"

She recollected the panic that had seized her chest as she'd searched his fair eyes, seen the earnestness in his face, and hated that she felt nothing but anxiety in the moment.

"Oh, Michael," she'd said, rubbing her thumbs over his hands. "I couldn't think of you as a husband. And you couldn't marry me, not if you wished to continue thinking well of me. You'd hate being wed to me. Say no more about it and take it back."

And take it back he had.

But what had his expression been when he'd done so? All she remembered was her relief and delight, but he…

Well, what did it matter now?

Charlotte cleared her throat and spoke directly to Grace now, as everyone else was pretending to be occupied. "Michael knows nothing about it, and cares nothing for it. And I would very much like to keep it that way."

Grace only blinked before taking a sip of her tea, and the others had nothing further to say on the subject.

Small mercies.

"But why six arrangements of flowers, Charlotte?" Elinor asked as she looked around the room at the flowers. "Mr. Riley doesn't strike me as a man of excesses, but this really is too much."

"Is it?" Charlotte replied, trying and failing for a comfortable, nonchalant air. "I rather like it myself."

Chapter Seventeen

———— ❧ ❧ ————

Surprises are not entirely logical, nor entirely desirable.

-The Spinster Chronicles, 1 August 1818

"I had no idea the park was so vast!"

"Did you not?" Michael laughed, looking down at the lovely woman beside him. "I thought you told me you and your cousin walked through it every day."

Diana peered up at him with a bemused expression. "Through the park. Through. Not in. We've never walked the whole of it, or simply done so for pleasure."

"Ah," he mused, returning his attention to their path and the beauty of the morning around them. "Well, in the interest of fairness, we are not walking the whole of it this morning, either. We are simply walking."

"But walking with you is far more enjoyable than walking with my cousin," Diana insisted with a sweet frankness.

"I heard that," Mrs. Greensley called from behind them.

Michael and Diana both chuckled at that, then Diana turned to call back, "You must allow me to prefer his company to yours, Jane. They are hardly comparable."

"But I think my pace is better," Mrs. Greensley suggested with a light laugh.

"Haste is frowned upon in a courtship," Michael informed them both, bringing more laughter from both. "I've taken the guidance quite literally."

Diana put her free hand atop his arm, though she already had the other looped through it. "I find this pace rather perfect. And what a lovely day to be walking here! I've only seen the Serpentine from a distance, so I had no idea it was the size it is!"

"It's hardly as impressive as some of the bodies of water in the countryside," he assured her, "but for London, it is a lovely sight."

"What is your country estate like?" Diana asked, her voice taking on a note of longing.

Michael smiled at the question. "Do you prefer the country to London, Miss Palmer?"

Her cheeks colored as she smiled. "I find I do, though London certainly has diversions enough. The sedate pace of the country, the simpler manners, and the generosity of time and energies by people of all stations are too fine a temptation to completely resist."

The simplicity of the statement struck a chord within him, and he found a poignant truth in it.

"Yes," he murmured, nodding to himself. "I never feel so accomplished or satisfied with my day as when I have exerted efforts on my estate. London is for entertainment, but the country is for contentment."

"Is your family on the estate? Or are they somewhere else?" Diana pressed.

He smiled fondly. "No, they are all there. My father passed a few years ago, but my mother, my sisters, and my brother, when he is not at school, are all at Crestor Grove."

Diana hummed in thought. "Are your sisters out? Surely one of them must be."

"Eliza has been to London for two Seasons," he told her. "I offered to bring her with me this year, but she declined. I think she may come next Season, though."

"Unless she is sweet on a young man at home," Diana pointed out in a light, teasing tone.

Michael scoffed, shaking his head. "Oh, I doubt that very much."

"Why?" she demanded. "Would she tell you if she were? Are there no young men she could grow fond of?"

He paused in the act of rebuttal, thinking quickly.

No, actually. No, she wouldn't tell him, and there did happen to be young men around Crestor Grove that certainly could have attracted her attention.

He wasn't prepared to think about that.

"Oxfordshire is a beautiful county," he said quickly, desperate to change the subject and not caring how obvious it would be.

Diana laughed merrily beside him, and he had to smile at the comfort in the sound. "Is it? I know nothing of it."

"Yes," Michael confirmed, lifting his chin proudly. "In fact…"

He broke off as a phaeton approached ahead of them, and he gently guided Diana aside to allow them to pass, Mrs. Greensley following close behind.

He reached for the brim of his hat, preparing to greet the passersby with all politeness, but froze in the process.

The startled, dark eyes of Charlotte Wright clashed with his.

The phaeton pulled to a stop, and it was all Michael could do to refrain from howling for it to continue to move on.

"This is a pleasant surprise!" Mr. Riley exclaimed, grinning madly down at them all and inclining his head. "What a fine company of walkers you all make."

Diana, possessing none of the bias and more of the kindness than Michael had, returned the smile. "And what a lovely team of horses, Mr. Riley! I am quite envious."

"Are you a horsewoman, Miss Palmer?" He chuckled and gestured to them. "If you are, please, feel free to touch them. The one nearest you is Annie, she'll purr like a kitten. The other is Bonnie, and she's more judgmental."

To Michael's surprise, Diana moved to the horses and began to rub their noses, speaking softly. Then she smiled up at the phaeton passengers. "Good morning, Miss Wright. I do hope you don't mind the delay in your ride."

"Not at all," Charlotte assured her with a genuine smile that shocked Michael further. "I have little enough appreciation of horses myself, but it is clear you have a way with them. You should be a country woman, Miss Palmer."

"I intend to," Diana quipped, her eyes darting to Michael almost hesitantly before returning to the horses. "Mr. Sandford and I were just talking about the country, as it happens."

Mr. Riley gave Michael an interested look then. "Really, Sandford? Are you a man of the countryside?"

"I believe so," Michael replied, forcing his tone to remain even for the man who had no idea how or why Michael disliked him. "I grow fonder of my estate day by day, and it may surprise people how deeply I love it. I've spent so long in London, they'd never know. I think I may stop pretending that I don't love being there and start keeping myself in the place I am happiest."

"What?" Charlotte's voice broke through his fervent avowal and drew his attention back to her. "I didn't know that. Why didn't you tell me?"

Michael met her eyes squarely, his throat tightening with the memories of the heat and sweetness her lips had held. "It never seemed the time. But it is so."

Her expression shuttered, and her lips formed a tight line. No one seeing her would think anything amiss, but Michael saw the discomfiture before she could clear it.

Then her face became shockingly blank, and he knew nothing about what lay beneath. "Jonathan doesn't have much experience in the country," Charlotte announced with a playfully sad note to her voice, snaking her hand around his arm and smiling at Mr. Riley. "He comes from the mill towns of the north."

Mr. Riley shrugged, smiling as he released a heavy sigh. "Alas, I will never know the thrill of the hunt, and all else that a gentleman does when in the country, the details of which completely escape me." He winked at Charlotte, then looked at Michael. "I am quite envious, Sandford. It sounds idyllic, I will confess."

"It is," Michael responded shortly, his smile strained. "But I imagine you find great satisfaction in your work where you are. Perhaps our paths are ours for a purpose."

"Amen to that, sir." Mr. Riley nodded in approval, genuine enjoyment appearing on his features. "I fear I would not last more than a few days in the country before I would yearn for the sounds of the mills."

The discrepancy in tastes made Michael's smile more easy, full of irony though it was. "And I would be fascinated by the mills, but within days, long for the pastures and farms."

"Yet the world spins for us both," Riley added, picking up his reins. "And, no doubt, is better for our different spheres."

"One can hope," Michael murmured.

Riley prepared to snap the reins, then paused, looking down at them again. "Do you all plan to attend the dinner party at Ingrams' tomorrow?"

"Yes," Diana replied before Michael could offer his own reply. "I'm so delighted to have been invited!"

"She's looking forward to meeting you, Miss Palmer," Charlotte told her, still smiling.

It would appear Michael would be going as well, though he hadn't intended on it purely to avoid Charlotte.

"Then it appears we will be seeing each other there." Riley tapped the brim of his hat to the group, smile growing as he did so. "Excellent. I'm a terrible bore at parties, so allies are much appreciated." With a flick of the reins, his horses moved on, pulling the tidy phaeton behind them.

Michael watched them go, wondering if he might be sick shortly.

"What a striking couple!" Diana said with an almost disbelieving shake of her head, her bonnet ribbons swaying against her as she did so.

"Yes," Michael muttered, thinking striking was an excellent choice of word.

He rather did feel struck when he saw them together.

He did not care for that at all.

"Shall we continue, Miss Palmer?" he offered, gesturing back to the path. "I think you'll enjoy the paths coming up."

"Hensh, I may be ill."

"What? Why?"

Charlotte swallowed, shaking her head.

"Erm... please don't?"

She forced herself to exhale slowly, her hands laying almost feebly against her stomach as she and Hensh surveyed the room. "I may not have much control over such things," she admitted weakly.

"I find that hard to believe," he protested in a boastful tone. "You control all things. Command your body to be well, and to cease such abuse."

Charlotte managed a weak laugh. "If only I could."

Hensh turned to her, his expression furrowed. "What's the trouble, Charlotte?"

"I cannot say," she whispered, heat flooding her cheeks. "I'm afraid…"

"Of what?" Hensh pressed. "The Ingrams are hosting creditably, your beau will arrive shortly, and you are not expected to do or say anything. What are you afraid of?"

Charlotte looked at him, eyes wide. "Michael will be coming. With Diana Palmer."

Hensh raised a brow. "And what about that frightens you?"

"I don't know how I feel about it," Charlotte admitted, one of her hands pressed further against her stomach, the pressure oddly comforting. "Diana is a lovely girl, and she adores the Spinsters."

"A sure sign of intelligence and taste, I must say." Hensh smiled rather indulgently, nudging her side with familiarity.

Charlotte returned his smile weakly, the thing wavering as much as her knees presently were. "But Michael seems to focus on her especially when I am near. I do not know how their courtship proceeds in privacy, but at our last two meetings, he does his best to ignore me and devote all of his attention to her."

Hensh blinked at her words, his brow creasing. "Have you inquired about this? Why he might appear to do this?"

There was no easy way to reply to the questions, given what had happened when she had made an accusation on the subject, but she could trust Hensh with private concerns, and sensitive manners.

"He said…" She bit her lip, the words nearly choking her before she could even speak them.

She couldn't do this.

Couldn't admit this.

Couldn't say it.

"He doesn't wish to discuss our courtships," she told Hensh instead, finding small comfort in the fact that she was not lying about the situation. "At all. He told me we would still be friends, but I rather feel as though he's changed his mind there."

Hensh made a face, but he said nothing immediately.

Something about his hesitation made Charlotte curious, and she stared at him with more patience than she usually possessed.

That could have been the impending feeling of sickness, however.

"Well?" she finally prodded without any sharpness.

Hensh's eyes flicked to hers before averting again. "I have a number of thoughts, Charlotte, but only one of them is supportable at the present."

"And that is?"

He sniffed, staring ahead. "I don't think Sandford knows how he feels, either. He's courting Miss Palmer, and therefore cannot be seen with a preference for any other women. That likely includes you, as rumors and jealousy can create all sorts of controversy."

Charlotte frowned, taking a sip of the lemonade she belatedly recalled still sat in her hand. "Miss Palmer doesn't seem to be the envious sort..."

"Can you account for rumors?" Hensh shook his head, exhaling roughly. "And that may not even be the case. It may only be that he wishes to prove his loyalty to Miss Palmer. Sandford is an honorable man; do you think he means to behave maliciously, or is he simply foolhardy?"

Unless she wished to confess more than she was comfortable, there was only one answer she could give that was honest.

"Both," she grunted, forcing herself to smile, though she did not feel the thing. "Michael's a terrible boor when he's not getting his way, particularly with me. I wonder if he isn't trying to find his own match before I do. A competition, if you will."

Hensh met her eyes now, merriment dancing in his eyes. "Now who would be idiotic enough to wager on a thing like matrimony?"

Charlotte's smile became less forced in an instant. "I haven't the faintest idea. How go your efforts?"

His mouth curved into a small smile, something rather sweet that Charlotte had never seen on him before. "Well enough."

"Ah," Charlotte mused, nudging him now. "Has she learned to pay you attention instead of the stage?"

"Who told you about that?" he demanded without irritation. He waved a hand quickly. "Never mind, it does not matter. The point is that she seems to be aware of my particular interest now."

Charlotte beamed and gripped his arm, barely restraining a squeal. "Hensh! How is she taking it?"

His smile turned teasing then. "Do you know, Charlotte, I don't think I want to discuss my courtship with you, either." He winked and strode away, and it was only then that Charlotte noticed the Mortons entering, Miss Morton following behind in a pale pink muslin that rendered her luminous.

And she looked around the room in a very searching manner.

Apparently, Miss Morton was taking it very well, indeed.

Strangely enough, the attention shifting to Hensh and his situation had erased Charlotte's ill feelings, and she now only wished for Jonathan to arrive so she might have someone besides the Spinsters to converse with. Hensh would be lost to her for the rest of the night, as he well should have been, and Grace was hostess. That left Izzy, though she would likely need to be chaperone for Kitty, Georgie, who was chatting with Miranda near a window, and Elinor, who had yet to arrive.

Miranda Sterling caught her eye and flicked her fingers in a beckoning gesture.

That settled that, then.

Charlotte moved across the room, grinning unreservedly at her friend and her stepmother-in-law, both of whom had chosen to wear shades of green this evening. Miranda's was, of course, more elaborate and fine, yet Georgie's was perfectly suited to her looks and timeless in its loveliness. Both of the Sterling women were visions of beauty, there was no question about that.

Luckily, Charlotte had no pangs of jealousy there, and could still feel that her dusky, red-striped satin bore enough elegance to render her sufficient attention.

"Lovely picture you present, my dear," Miranda praised, holding out a hand. "Are those silk bands at the hem? Simply marvelous, and what a full skirt! Goodness, I shall request an identical one in gold tomorrow morning."

Charlotte laughed and took the proffered seat beside Miranda.

"You will undoubtedly wear it better than I, though I do recommend avoiding netting in the headdress." She scratched at her own quickly, wrinkling her nose.

"Oh, don't upset it!" Georgie pleaded. "It's simply stunning. I rather like the netting of it."

"Then you wear it, and may you have joy of it." Charlotte sighed and snapped open her fan. "Has anybody seen Jonathan?"

"I wish I had, my dear," Miranda said without shame. "Marvelously handsome, that man. Will you marry him?"

"Miranda!" Georgie cried, a gloved hand going to her cheek in embarrassment. "You don't have to answer her, Charlotte."

But Charlotte adored Miranda and her frankness, finding the whole approach to life and conversation rather refreshing. "Well, he hasn't asked, Miranda, so I really cannot say. The point is irrelevant if the offer is not made."

Miranda smiled knowingly, her eyes narrowing. "Charlotte, my dear, you could ensure that the offer is made by Wednesday, if you set your mind to it."

"I take that as a compliment," Charlotte quipped. "Though I have little desire to rush Jonathan. I'm rather enjoying courtship. Only last evening he came to family dinner, and we all of us were awake far into the early morning telling tales and laughing for ages. Then this morning, I come down to breakfast, and there were two more bouquets of flowers."

"What a lovely gesture!" Miranda simpered. "Two bouquets for you? How charming!"

Charlotte grinned and shook her head. "No, Miranda. One bouquet for me, and one for my mother."

Miranda and Georgie clapped in delight, making Charlotte laugh. "All the better! You must marry him, Charlotte. I wish it."

"If he asks, I may," Charlotte replied, still laughing.

"Ladies and gentlemen," Aubrey, Lord Ingram, intoned from somewhere in the room. "I'm delighted to provide you some entertainment before dinner, and more particularly for the surprise it will be to us all. At the request of Miss Palmer, Mr. Sandford will oblige the company with a song. My wife will accompany him. Please."

Charlotte blinked as the other guests began filing over to a corner of the room, but she could not move. Her limbs had no strength, her frame no warmth.

Michael was here? And he was going to sing?

I only sing for you, dear.

The pianoforte struck up, Grace's nimble fingers no doubt dancing along the keys, and, a moment later, Michael's voice filled the area.

Memory after memory assaulted Charlotte's mind the moment he began; vocal duets the two of them had attempted, playful ditties Michael had sung to break her out of sour moods or to make her laugh, relaxed days of hearing his voice across the room while she pretended to read...

Each one darkened and dimmed as his voice floated among the guests. Only she had ever truly known the power, sweetness, and delight of his voice before this, and he had claimed to have kept that gift for her alone. Now that was gone, the secret revealed, and nothing remained between them that was only theirs.

The last link between them was gone. Broken by his own acquiescence. She did not believe Diana had coerced him into singing, even if she had known about his vocal abilities. Michael would only have done this if he had wished to.

He wished to sing for them, not only for Charlotte anymore.

"Charlotte?" Georgie murmured from beside her, somehow having gotten Miranda to leave. "Charlotte..."

Charlotte sniffled and shook her head, rising to her feet. She had to face him. She *would* face him while he did this. Because he did this.

The song soared as she approached, which would usually have brought her unending delights. It brought her nothing now.

Finding a small break in the gathered guests, Charlotte fit herself into the space, pressing forward as much as she would without being in any way forceful. She would show no desperation, display no overt emotion, leave no sign to anyone that her heart was full to the brim with this betrayal. She would carry on this evening as she would have done otherwise. She would smile and laugh with Jonathan, finding and taking comfort in his presence. She would praise Grace and Aubrey for their excellent dinner service and delightful friends. She would even encourage some light dancing later, if she thought others might join in.

But in this moment, one person needed to know, needed to acknowledge, what he was bringing about.

She saw Michael through the break then, lifted her chin as he grandly sang for them all. He was dressed in better finery than she had seen him in, which seemed to suit, and saw more people smiling for him now than ever had in his life. And then there was Diana, just a few feet away from him, beaming with pride and delight.

Something sharp and cold lanced Charlotte's heart, but she would not crumble and fall. She was too well-practiced in all things Society to do anything so publicly.

She could withstand this.

Michael's eyes cast about the guests as he sang, then, at last, met Charlotte's. Aside from a stilling in his form, he left no obvious sign of distress. His voice did not waver, his complexion did not wane. But a faint crease appeared in his brow, and his head lowered perhaps a half an inch. He knew. He knew what he was doing, and he knew what it would do.

And still he sang.

Charlotte dipped her chin in a nod, then backed gracefully out of the group.

"Charlotte," Georgie whispered, her voice hitching in concern.

Charlotte ignored her again and moved to a footman she recognized from previous visits. "Thomas, would you be a dear and fetch me a glass of Madeira? I've a fearful headache, and I don't wish to disturb his lordship before supper."

"Certainly, Miss Wright." He bowed and departed at once.

Exhaling, Charlotte turned back around, preparing to endure the rest of Michael's singing thus until her drink arrived.

Would to God it was something stronger.

Chapter Eighteen

When we dance, we find the conversations we cannot have, the feelings we cannot share, and the confessions we cannot make. Often, we also find trouble.

-The Spinster Chronicles, 5 April 1819

"She didn't say anything? Are you sure?"

"No, Sandford, I'm not. But I refuse to interrogate my wife, and you forbade me to have her ask the specific question."

Michael growled as he strode from the card room back into the ballroom at Lord Attley's home, wanting to tug at his cravat, but knowing he needed to make a good impression. "Because if she does not know that I'm concerned, I don't want her to know. I feel I am to blame, and I will make amends. But if she does not know, then I do not need to do a thing. You see?"

"Not in the least. You've talked me in a circle, and I'm wondering when you'll get to the point." Hugh Sterling sputtered to himself, no doubt irritated by Michael's pestering on this topic. "And I dislike keeping secrets from my wife, so kindly don't insist on any more."

"I can agree to that," Michael promised easily, nodding at a few other guests. "You don't even understand this one."

Hugh grunted once. "Not even a little. So you sang for company. Why should that offend? Are you that horrid?"

Scowling, Michael glanced over his shoulder. "No. But only Charlotte had heard me sing before... What is the point in explaining it?" He shook his head and returned his attention forward. "Nobody else will understand."

"Ah, so *that's* the issue. It's something special between you."

If hearts could shrink, Michael's did then for a moment or two. "Yes," he muttered. "It is. Or was."

"And Miss Palmer?"

His heart expanded, warming just a little. "Diana is the sweetest girl I've ever met. She'd never heard me sing, and I thought... I thought..." He exhaled slowly. "It doesn't matter what I thought. I shouldn't hurt one while pleasing the other, should I?"

"You cannot balance the feelings of both in your hands your whole life, either."

That, at least, was unfortunately true.

"Is that what I'm doing?" Michael murmured to himself, not expecting an answer from Hugh or anyone else.

Probably, his saner side replied. After all, mere hours after deciding he could let Charlotte go forever by singing for company, he was desperate to repent of the deed and to make amends.

But should he?

"I should have gone back to the church," he hissed to himself.

"Pardon?" Hugh queried from behind him.

"Yes, I need one." Michael shook his head and sighed, pausing as he looked out at the dance. "Do you see Diana?"

Hugh came up beside him and began scanning the guests. "No, but you've already had one dance with her tonight, so unless you want more rumors..."

"I can dance with her once more, and after that, I will need to propose, I am well aware." He pursed his lips, eyeing the rather full ballroom. "I'm not necessarily looking to dance, Sterling. I only need her location."

"Simple enough. She's dancing with Demaris."

Michael looked at the dancers, and, sure enough, the fair-haired woman he was pursuing was there, a lovely paradox of her present partner, dark and brooding as he was. They attracted the admiration and attention of several onlookers, and, quite frankly, it was right they should have. They danced marvelously well together, and no other couple in the dance could compare.

Even Michael was momentarily captivated watching them.

"You aren't jealous, are you?"

Michael smiled to himself and shook his head. "No, not at all. Should I be?"

"Honestly, yes."

The answer made Michael frown, and he looked at Hugh in confusion. "Why's that?"

Hugh seemed more bemused by the question than anything else. "The woman you are courting is dancing, delighted, and distracting at the present, in the company of a man who is not you."

That did not make anything clearer.

"And...?" Michael prodded, drawing the word out. "I have no fear of her affections straying to Demaris, and it is only a courtship, not an engagement. If she should find she prefers another, why should that upset me?"

Hugh blinked at Michael's statement, his smile wavering. "Sandford, you are supposed to be possessive and uncomfortable if any person of the male sex should come within three feet of her, whether you know him or not."

"I don't see why." Michael looked out at Diana again, smiling as he saw her laugh during the jig. "Her happiness prompts my own. I feel proud when I see her, not possessive. I know that I am courting her, and that she has agreed to my suit. We are becoming better acquainted, and I'd say it is going well. But I have no claim on her. By all rights, she is free."

There was no immediate response, and, when it lingered, Michael thought it best to check that his friend still stood beside him.

Hugh stared out at the guests in the ballroom, but he seemed not to see any of them, his head shaking back and forth without any haste or energy.

"What?" Michael groaned, feeling he had failed to come up to snuff somehow.

His friend's jaw tightened for a moment. "How would you describe your feelings for Miss Palmer, Michael?"

He did the lady the justice of collecting his thoughts before replying. "Admiration. Great esteem. Respect. Affection. What description are you looking for?"

Hugh raised a brow. "Something that does not also apply to your mother."

Michael scowled at him. "I don't mean affection in that sense."

"Yet it was the word you chose. Not attraction, not passion, infatuation, or devotion. Certainly not love." Hugh shrugged and smirked as he continued to watch the dancing.

"You cannot judge all relationships by the same standard," Michael insisted. "I've never been in a courtship before, so perhaps this is how I feel as it proceeds."

His words had Hugh nodding slowly. "But you have been in love before, Sandford. You cannot claim ignorance to the emotions and sensations involved there."

Michael ground his teeth so tightly his jaw ached.

Not this again.

"That is behind me, Sterling," Michael insisted. "And before you can suggest it, my desire to find Charlotte now is purely to ensure that my actions have not given her undue pain. It has nothing to do with how I may or may not have felt."

"Fair enough." Hugh turned to stare rather frankly at him. "But if you think the polite feelings you described for Miss Palmer will ever amount to the same as you felt for Charlotte, you do all three of you a disservice. Charlotte is by the terrace door, by the by." He dipped his chin in a nod, then strode by Michael in search of some better company.

It was worth a moment's pause to consider Hugh's words, even if Michael did not necessarily agree with them.

After all, what had his feelings for Charlotte ever done for him?

He was far more inclined to trust the more sedate feelings he was growing for Diana, and the deep, abiding course they could run, than any passionate outburst for Charlotte he could not control.

A nagging inkling began to prick at his mind, and Michael was quick to shove that aside before it could formulate. He did not need doubts, rationalizations, or fond memories to shake his present state of mind.

He had a wrong to right, and then this could all end neatly. He could resume his proper courtship of Diana without obstacle, wiser for his mistakes, and searching what other feelings Diana could rouse in him, if only he'd open himself to them. And if nothing resembling the heat of fire arose, so be it. A comfortable, steady, loyal marriage was not something to be laughed at, especially if one's partner was well chosen. He could do far worse, and there were several examples of that in this room, as well as in London as a whole.

But he was still far from offering marriage, for himself more than for Diana. He needed to be sure. Committed and sure.

And for that, he needed a clear conscience.

The dance presently came to an end, and rather than go to the woman he was courting, he waited in place for her present partner to deliver her to her friends.

If he kept his distance, no one would know he was courting her at all, and he saw no issue with that. He was a fairly reserved man, preferring his privacy to popularity, which Diana did not seem to mind. Or, at least, she had not complained as yet.

He'd been seen calling upon her. He'd walked with her several times in Hyde Park, and been seen doing so. He'd escorted her to the theater, to card parties, and to various other entertainments in Society, and been seen.

He did not have to be at her heels all night for Society to know his interest lay there. He would go there shortly, of course, but surely his entire evening did not have to center on one woman when he had other concerns to attend to.

Gads, he was making himself ill with his justifications, and no one had asked for them.

Why, then, was he making them?

Michael shook his head and moved around the nearest crush of guests, some of whom seemed almost to dance where they stood, so in want of a partner were they. Others would have become one with the wall if the wall would only accept them into its fold. He'd never once been the former but had plenty of experience in the latter.

It occurred to him that he may never enjoy being so again, should his courtship come to fruition.

What an odd thought.

"Quite the lively dancer, your nearly intended," Tyrone praised with an almost wild smile, given their location and setting. "I rather enjoyed myself."

"So I see," Michael replied, wondering if he should frown or grumble, or perhaps threaten his friend.

His indecision was apparently fitting, for Tyrone's brow snapped down. "Trying to decide if you want to warn me off?"

Michael would have made a face were they anywhere but a ballroom. "I'm not…"

"Allow me to take advantage of your internal debate and make myself scarce on the off chance you decide on a violent defense." He bowed playfully, starting past him.

"Wait." Michael put a hand out to stop him, forcing aside his indecision in favor of firmness in another matter. "Can I beg a favor of you?"

Tyrone flicked his dark eyes to Michael. "I daresay you can, though the begging of others has never done me any good."

Michael ignored his snide remark. "Dance with Charlotte Wright next. I'll partner anybody you approve of, but you must dance with Charlotte."

"Why must I?" Tyrone replied in a bland, uninterested tone. "I'll barely be dancing with her at all, considering which style of dance it is."

"Exactly." Michael waited for his friend to understand his meaning, gesturing slightly.

Tyrone's expression turned into a scowl as realization set in. "This is not a favor. This is striking up a brawl in a ballroom."

Well, not ideally, but it was possible.

Michael blinked. "But will you do it?"

Tyrone shook his head but sighed. "I will accept copious amounts of very strong beverage in recompense for my part."

"Done." He all but grinned, clapping Tyrone on the shoulder. "Good man."

Tyrone only sputtered and turned to set his course in motion, grumbling incoherently.

Michael nodded to himself, satisfied almost into smugness, before going to find the fairest woman in his closest vicinity, if only to soften Tyrone's temper as he provided the exact opportunity needed to put all this to rest.

"Why is Tyrone Demaris coming over to me?" Charlotte asked of her friends, eyeing the approaching man with some speculation.

She had nothing against Tyrone, nor against the idea of dancing with him. He happened to be her favorite of Janet Sterling's cousins, but their association was more polite than preferable. And they had never danced together in all the years they had been in Society together.

It seemed an odd time to start now.

"Miss Wright." Tyrone bowed, smiling in a manner she refused to trust. "Would you dance the next with me?"

"If you've the energy," Charlotte told him, still wary of him, but not averse to a dance. "You've only just completed an exuberant jig with Miss Palmer, might you not prefer to rest a moment?"

He smirked at her point. "Perhaps, but I must insist on a dance with you at this time, if you will consent. Then I may rest contented."

Charlotte raised a brow at the flattery. "Or the more fatigued."

"Which makes the rest more contented, as the rest is more well-earned." He held a hand out to her, keeping his smirk in place.

She placed her hand in his, exhaling her reluctance. "What is your plan, Mr. Demaris? And do my intelligence the respect of knowing there is one."

Tyrone chuckled as he led her to the floor. "I'm certain there is, but as it is not my plan, I cannot tell you what it is. My plan is to dance with you and earn myself a significant amount of drink."

Now *that* sounded far more plausible.

But Tyrone Demaris was not the sort of man to admit something that would offend her, which meant this had not been conceived maliciously.

"Was a dance with me so monstrous a prospect?" she inquired as they took their places.

"Not at all," he said without airs, which spoke of honesty if nothing else did. "Only the instigator and the motives. I'll dance with you again next week to prove it is not personal."

Charlotte had to smile at that, enjoying the frankness in his manner that so few gentlemen employed in Society, let alone around her. "If it's a waltz, I'll agree."

Now he scowled as he looked at her. "Of course, you would be particular. I ought to have been more specific."

"Indeed, Mr. Demaris, the fault is clearly your own." The first motions began, and they took hands to follow the pattern of the dance.

"A statement I hear rather frequently in my life," he told her without much concern. "I'm growing accustomed to the idea."

Charlotte laughed as she returned to her position. "There are greater sinners than you, Mr. Demaris. Never fear."

She turned her attention to the corner of the square the dance formed between them and the couple neighboring, and she nearly sagged in misery at the gentleman who was now approaching for the motion.

Michael.

"Speak of the devil, and he shall appear," she muttered, catching Tyrone's stifled amusement out of the corner of her eye.

He bowed in the dance and held out his hands.

She waited half a beat longer than she ought, a thrill of satisfaction lighting her chest at his wide-eyed reaction to it.

"Please don't make a scene," he asked as they turned.

"Why would I make a scene?" Charlotte replied, releasing his hands to do-si-do. "I have a reputation to consider." She threw a glower at Tyrone as she faced him, earning a sheepish attempt at a grin in return.

"I need to speak with you," Michael insisted.

Charlotte harrumphed, shaking her head. "He says as if he were not speaking. This is an extraordinary way to bring it about."

Michael's expression turned almost scolding as they turned once more. "I didn't think you would agree if I approached in any other way."

"Oh, so he has got some intelligence." She forced a bright smile she did not feel. "How refreshing."

The dance sent them back to their corners, and Charlotte looked down at the floor while Tyrone and the woman beside her took their turn in the center.

Why in the world did Michael need to speak with her? What could he possibly have to say after what had passed between them?

After what he had proven at Grace's party, there could be no mistaking the status of their relationship.

It had been neatly terminated, and there was nothing of friendship remaining.

So much for his vow that they would remain friends. The best of friends, if she recalled correctly.

How had they gotten to this point?

She returned to Tyrone's side as they promenaded down the line and around to the back. "You may owe me more than a copious amount of strong drink for this, Mr. Demaris."

He hissed under his breath. "I did promise a waltz."

"Somehow, I don't find that as satisfactory." Charlotte gnawed the inside of her cheek as she took up her new position, preparing to face Michael again.

He wasted no time when he came to her. "I apologize for singing."

That was it? Not for breaking their longest-reigning understanding? Not for breaking her heart? Not for scrubbing her out of his life? Just singing? As if singing alone was a crime?

Charlotte felt a cool composure ripple across her being, and she found a polite, formal smile crossing her lips. "I apologize for singing, as well. It's a beastly business, singing. Almost nobody does a fair job of it, and it is so mortifying. Such a vulnerable experience, which is why I never do it."

Michael frowned. "I'm not apologizing for the existence of singing. I'm apologizing that I sang for company."

She pretended to be surprised. "What's it to me if you wish to sing for company? You are free to do as you like."

"Charlotte, that was our secret."

"Surely not ours alone," she protested, maintaining wide-eyed innocence. "Your mother knows you sing, yes? Your sisters? Cousins?"

"Well, yes…"

She trilled a merry laugh. "Then it can hardly be our secret. You are a gifted vocalist, why should the world not know?"

She heard his short exhale of frustration. "I only want to say that I am sorry if I hurt you in doing so."

"You didn't."

"I can see that, but the apology stands," he insisted.

"Then your conscience is clear. That should be enough."

"Do you accept my apology?" he ground out, evidently growing weary of her game.

"Do I need to? After all, I have told you, I was not wounded."

Michael retreated to his place, but his attention remained on her with an intensity that was almost unsettling. This time, Charlotte stared back at him, daring him to find something weak, flawed, or wounded in her. What her heart felt was no longer his concern. What hurts she carried would no longer be known to him. What familiarity they shared could no longer be.

He had done this, and he would be the one to feel it.

Wordlessly, expressionless, she watched him, waiting to see him accept the strength she was showing, the detachment from any emotions he could rouse, and the beauty she had worked so tirelessly to array herself in this evening. Let him see Charlotte Wright as she was, not as the girl he'd thought her to be.

At that moment, Michael's eyes dropped from her own and, starting at what seemed to be the toes of her slippers, slowly examined every inch of her all the way up. An accompanying shiver raced through Charlotte on the exact same path at precisely the same time, as though his eyes had power over her limbs and frame. When his eyes reached hers again, something hot and blinding screeched from the core of her down into each of her toes, curling them in her slippers. Rays of it raced upwards through her, singeing each hair on her head and incinerating her ears.

She watched his eyes shift across her face, felt the fire of them in each place, and her lungs began to quiver in panicked anticipation.

Of what? What did they expect? What did they fear? What did they want?

What did she want?

Her fingers shifted anxiously against each other at her side, the sensitive skin of each feeling abraded by the smooth fabric of her gloves. Everything was heightened somehow, everything on edge, and staring at Michael made her better and worse in equal measure. Equal burning, searing, breath-stealing measure, and she could feel her composure unraveling with each beat of her rampant heart.

She blinked and recollected the dance, turning to promenade with Tyrone again, trembling in his hold.

"Steady," he murmured, no hint of sarcasm in his tone. "You all right?"

"In a manner of speaking," she whispered. "Would you care very much to douse me in a glass of port?"

"Douse you? In what way?"

"Over my bloody head," she managed to say, her voice hitching on the words.

Tyrone tsked softly. "Sorry, pet. Port does not do well on silk, and I've a valet that will summarily execute me for marring such exquisite fabric."

"More's the pity." She parted from him with a tight squeeze of hands and prayed she could finish the dance without embarrassment.

This time as Michael came to her, Charlotte wished she could have fled. She would have run from the ballroom, out onto the terrace, and into the gardens. She'd have run all the way home, into the house, up the stairs, and flung herself under the bedcovers in her room until she felt more herself.

At the present, she barely felt human.

Her hands reached out for Michael's the moment they were able, and her eyes locked with his. He said nothing this time, and neither did she. Neither *could* she. There were no words for such an experience, such a captivation with one person whose touch was the breath of life to her. There was only the feel of his hands in hers, the heat of his body as she passed it, brushed her back near it, passed it again to face him once more, a delicious friction with nothing touching at all.

It was a dizzying, drowsy feeling, weakening her knees and squeezing her lungs until each breath took more effort than it rightly should. Yet the pace of all was as it should have been, her heart a cadence for the dance, her lungs natural in their rhythm. A cacophony of sensations in and around her, with only her eyes to tell her which way was forward.

Forward was Michael.

Forward was right.

Michael was right?

She blinked unsteadily, the spell breaking as she resumed her position, her mind reeling. What had just happened? What had she felt, what had she realized? Something had been decided, she felt sure, but there was no insight into what that might have been. Only that it was Michael.

Michael…

Charlotte couldn't look at him, not the rest of this dance, not the rest of this evening. Could not be clouded when she needed clarity. Clarity and certainty.

And a glass of port.

Chapter Nineteen

Denial is not a powerful defense. When it is gone, a person is rather exposed. Better, then, to choose something else for one's fortress. You won't want to be in denial when it comes tumbling down around you.

-The Spinster Chronicles, 29 December 1818

"Michael, what are you doing?"

"Reading. Why?"

"There's a card party going on, and the people are out there."

"Which is why I prefer to be here."

Elinor Sterling plucked the book out of his hand and gave him a severe look.

Michael peered up at her. "What?"

She shook her head. "I had such hopes for you. The better clothing, the more social activity, the courtship. You were doing all the things a gentleman does, finally, instead of being lost in the melee of it, as you did before. Questions were being asked about you. Interest was aroused. Only last week, you stepped foot into the ballroom, and any young lady would have begged for a dance with you."

"I hardly think it was that extreme," Michael scoffed, waving a hand.

Elinor's expression showed she was not amused. "I heard them, Michael. You were watched the entire evening. Your jaunt into the card room after a few dances was noted. Your reentry was praised. Your return to dancing gave them hope."

At least the dance with Charlotte wasn't mentioned. Or the dance where Tyrone danced with Charlotte. Michael hadn't danced with her.

Officially.

He couldn't explain what had happened, but it rather felt like their experience in the square room of the theater. The same breathlessness, the rush of energy and feeling while being powerless to resist, the inability to think or comprehend anything but her. Yet they had been constrained by the dance, by the parts they had to play there, and by the company they were in, feeling so much while being unable to act as instinct demanded.

It had been somehow more powerful than kissing her. Then again, he'd only kissed her the one time. Several times, but the one occasion. One occasion, but one much repeated in his mind.

Resisting such thoughts was getting rather old.

"And you danced a second time with Diana Palmer," Elinor went on, completely ignorant of the content of his thoughts. "And had my husband dance with her so you could have additional moments in the dance with her."

Michael smiled as she brought that up, given he'd done the exact same thing so he could dance with Charlotte, yet it was not remarked upon.

"People are wondering about a proposal," Elinor pointed out, her arms folding before her. "Are you engaged?"

"No," Michael told her easily. "Not yet, at any rate."

Her eyes narrowed at him. "Is there an understanding?"

"That is between her and I, thank you." He batted his lashes, knowing it would irk her, as it would have his own sisters.

"Are you bound to her in any way at this present time?" Elinor demanded, not put off at all by his lack of answer.

He frowned at that. "No..."

"Then come with me and attend the card party," she insisted, gesturing to the door. "I did not invite you to keep my books company."

"I thought your husband invited me," he suggested ruefully.

He really should not test her further; she was beginning to look like Eliza did when she was about to hit him over the head. "Hugh made suggestions, but I approved all invitations. So come with me now and pretend that you are pleased to be here. Or have you given up on actually appearing in Society as an individual?"

Muttering to himself, Michael pushed up out of the chair he had been occupying pleasantly since his escape. Not that the card room had been so very dreadful, he'd only lost interest in participating in the conversations occurring there. Diana had pleaded a headache, so she had chosen to remain at home to rest. He'd grown used to only appearing to further their courtship, but he hadn't cried off himself purely for the sake of Hugh and Elinor and this first informal event they had hosted.

Much of the company was filled with people he admired well enough; he was simply not feeling the thing. Was that so wrong?

"Thank you," Elinor chirped, taking his arm.

"Does your brother feel so badgered by you at times?" Michael inquired with a tilt of his head as he led her down the corridor.

Elinor nodded once. "Of course. He has four sisters, after all. And just so you are aware, Eliza wrote to me and bade me to keep you out of mischief."

Michael coughed in mock effrontery. "I *never* make mischief! She had best mind what she says to people, given the favors I have agreed to do for her while in London. I've a mind to tell her she can come fetch her own fabrics."

"She doesn't care about fabrics," Elinor laughed as they reentered the card party. "It's all about the... Never you mind. Send me her demands for the modiste, and I'll see to that in exchange for your good behavior tonight."

"Done." He patted her hand, giving her a smile. "See? It wasn't for naught that I went to the library."

Elinor nudged him hard before stepping away to return to her guests.

Michael chuckled and began to amble about the room, forcing himself to look as pleasant as he could. Several people smiled, returning his nods of greeting, and some of the young ladies, he did note, lingered in their smiles.

Intriguing. Was this because Diana was not in attendance, and they knew no engagement had been set as yet? Perhaps Elinor hadn't been exaggerating after all.

He smiled further still when he caught sight of Mrs. Partlowe, Elinor's sister, sitting alone nearby. He moved in that direction, feeling some sage conversation with her would be preferable than forcing politeness elsewhere. Emma had always been a creature of sense, not carried away by fancy like her sister or some of her friends, yet she was also one of the originators of the Spinster Chronicles. She had left the fold to marry her husband, choosing not to continue with the column, which had injured some to a degree, though no one had taken it harder than Charlotte. He remembered well the rant Charlotte had made over the comfortable marriage and departure, but he had not felt the same.

On the contrary, it had made perfect sense to him that Emma had chosen such a course.

"Mrs. Partlowe," he greeted, bowing when he reached her. "May I take the seat beside you?"

She smiled up at him, and for the first time he noted faint lines in her features that had not been there only a few years ago. Yet they suited her, and her loveliness was not diminished by them. "Please, Michael. It would be a pleasure."

He sank down, sighing in relief and at once as comfortable with her as he had ever been. "You look tired, Emma. Can I say such a thing?"

She laughed softly. "Perhaps only to me. And I feel tired, thank you. The twins are anything but content these days, and I find myself in an interesting condition at an inconvenient time."

"Congratulations, and my condolences?" he suggested with a wince, chuckling to himself.

"Yes, quite." She sighed, shaking her head. "It is a blessing, of course, and many women have dealt with such a condition inconveniently, but I think I shall need another version of myself in addition to manage it all."

He smiled with some sympathy. "We'd only be so fortunate."

Emma's smile quirked crookedly. "Flatterer." She turned her attention across the room, and her smile deepened. "Now there is a pairing for us."

Michael followed her faint gesture and saw Lieutenant Henshaw and Kitty Morton sitting in a pair of chairs near each other, deep in conversation, both seeming on the edge of their seats.

"At last," he said on an exhale, crossing one knee over the other. "I wasn't sure they would ever get there."

Emma laughed to herself. "Should I warn Izzy that her sister-in-law is sitting too close to him? Or that they are holding each other's hand?"

"Absolutely not," Michael retorted. "Miss Morton looks delighted with her present situation, and Henshaw might burst. Leave them. That's as it should be."

"Is that how it is for you?" Emma's question was much softer, and while it carried the same inquisitive direction her sister had used earlier, he felt none of the impertinence or prying of it.

More than that, he needed to think about the question.

"I couldn't say," he eventually replied, considering his feelings for Diana and the relationship they were cultivating. "It's... different."

"I can understand that," Emma murmured, looking down at her fingers. "I never had the frantic part of love. The breathless, unable to sleep, romanticized and publicized version of it. I did not even marry for love, but I found it all the same."

Michael took her hand, squeezing gently. "I hoped you would."

She smiled up at him, her eyes and smile warm. "There is more than one way to love, and to feel love; even romantic love. Some feel it loudly and cannot contain it. Others find it quietly, deep into their souls. And all can be everlasting."

He released her hand and sat back, nodding. "I'm beginning to see that. But it makes me glad to hear that you found love in your own way."

"My sister thinks you'll propose within the week." Emma turned her body to face him more. "Will you?"

Now he laughed, finding the prying edge that he was accustomed to with the Asheley sisters. "Not this week."

Emma snickered beside him. "What, do you have a previous engagement?"

"As it happens, yes," he replied with a jaunty smile. "I've an errand to see to in Derbyshire this week. Very important, very secret."

"To whom and for whom?" Emma pressed with a grin. "Yourself, I hope."

Michael pretended to consider his answer. "In a way, I suppose it is. It has more impact on another person's happiness, however, but their happiness should promote my own."

"Very gallant." Emma nodded her approval, then leaned forward just a little. "You won't give me a further hint, will you?"

"I cannot," he said firmly, still amused by her interest. "Far too much work has been done with my solicitors and other important men to risk word getting out before all is settled."

Emma shook her head in apparent disappointment. "Very well. Shall we see if one of the card games is free? My husband, bless him, is still in conversation with Mr. Chadwick, and I am in need of a partner."

Michael rose and offered a hand to help her up. "Yes. Let's."

"Mama, have you seen my blue spencer?"

"Lottie, my lamb, you have at least three. Which one are you seeking?"

Charlotte rolled her eyes. "The one I've worn this year, Mama! Honestly, I am not hoarding endless amounts of clothing in the same shade."

"Sure about that, are you?" her brother quipped as he passed, flicking at her ear.

Charlotte lashed out a quick smack of her hand against his upper arm, the tips of her fingers whipping sharply there.

"Ouch!" he bellowed, the cry echoing through the house. "Mama!"

"I do not want to hear it!" she bellowed back. "One of you started it, and the other retaliated, and that is the end of it!"

Charles looked nearly affronted at the statement and turned to Charlotte in shock. "I think we broke her."

"Children!" their father hollered. "Don't make your mother yell!"

Charlotte scowled, shaking her head. "We broke her years ago.

That she no longer cares is the greater issue, I think."

"Agreed. Can't see what did her in, though. We're such angels."

"Probably my courtship. Too much of a change, she simply cannot adapt."

Charles moved to the wall and leaned against it, fiddling with the end of an unlit cheroot. "How is that courtship, Lottie? Accepted his proposal yet?"

Charlotte looked at her brother rudely. "He has not asked, I'll have you know."

"Can't say I blame him."

Plucking up a vase nearby, Charlotte held it in the air. "So help me, Brutus, I will chuck this at your head and pummel you thereafter."

He winked at her, grinning cheekily. "I know. Put it down. Truce."

Charlotte gave him a warning look as she slowly lowered her weapon to the console table beside her. "We have not discussed the subject of marriage, Jonathan and I. And I don't mind it. I am enjoying being courted, learning more about him and he about me. He is… he is a good man, Charles."

"I know," her brother said, surprising her. "I've tried finding all of the negativity in his reputation I can, and damned if I can find a single thing."

"He's not perfect," Charlotte assured him with a laugh. "He simply keeps his sins and errors small."

Charles shook his head, smiling. "He's a better man than I am."

"We knew that." Charlotte returned his smile and shrugged. "At any rate, I'm content."

"Good. And Michael?"

Charlotte's smile vanished. "Michael has sins."

Charles rolled his eyes, his head rolling dramatically in accompaniment. "Yes, I know, Lottie. I was present for many of them. What I mean is what will he think of it?"

"Who cares what he thinks of it?" Charlotte asked, her eyes narrowing at her brother. "My courtship is not for his pleasure, nor for his approval. If I want to marry Jonathan, I will. If he has an issue with it, he should perhaps have thought about not abandoning me from the very first day."

Her brother pursed his lips, then nodded once. "Right," he said slowly. "I'm going to leave now before you throttle me in his place."

She returned his nod and waved him off, turning on her heel to go sit in the drawing room. Jonathan was due in an hour or so to take her for a drive in his phaeton again, and she had nothing to fill the time. And now, thanks to her brother, she was in a sour mood again.

She'd had some reprieve from that in the last day or two, once she'd given up on trying to decipher what had happened in her dance with Michael that had really been a dance with Tyrone that Michael had commandeered for his own purposes. She didn't feel in any way settled by it, but the more she tried to settle it, the more unsettled she felt, which seemed to defeat the purpose.

Whatever it had been, she refused to let it happen again.

Perhaps it would be a lovely time to visit Jonathan's family and home. Her mother and father would love a trip to the north. And it would leave London behind, which was far more enticing.

She'd suggest it to Jonathan this afternoon.

"Mrs. Partlowe, Miss Wright."

Charlotte blinked at the announcement and sat up. "What?"

Emma entered the drawing room with a flash of a smile. "Good morning, Charlotte. I hope you don't mind, I was passing your house and realized how long it had been since we'd visited."

It had been long. It had been an age, and until seeing her now, Charlotte could not have said how much she missed it. "Yes, it has. Please, come sit." She rose and took Emma's hands as she came closer. "You look wonderful."

Emma groaned, her brows lifting. "I look tired, as I have been repeatedly told of late, but the interesting condition of my body would have it that way."

Charlotte beamed and sat, Emma coming beside her. "Another baby? Oh, you must be delighted. What does Partlowe say?"

"Not much," Emma admitted with a slight wrinkle of her nose that was quite charming. "He doesn't, usually. But I could see how pleased he was. It was very moving, actually. I think he truly loves being a father, which I had seen a little when I married him, what with his girls from his first marriage, but being part of it now... I think I may love him more for how he adores his children than anything else."

"You love him?" Charlotte made a soft noise of surprise. "I didn't know that. Did you think you might when you married?"

Emma tilted her head at that. "I don't know. Perhaps I saw that I could love him if all worked in my favor. I'm not sure I was aware of that at the time, but I certainly felt more than simple comfort in it." She smiled sadly at Charlotte. "I know you didn't approve…"

Charlotte shook her head. "You know better than to consider what I say for more than three seconds at a time. If you were happy, that meant more to me, even if I did not say so."

They shared a smile and Emma's eyes turned brighter. "I saw you and your Mr. Riley the other evening at the ball. You make a striking couple, I must say. Do you like him?"

"Very much," Charlotte admitted, "and it feels so strange to say such a thing. He's coming to take me for a ride in his phaeton shortly, if you'd like to meet him officially."

"I cannot. I'm due to meet Elinor in Bond Street. We're shopping for Eliza Sandford on her brother's behalf."

Charlotte snorted once, even as her stomach seemed to flip. "Well, that will see her far better arrayed, but why is Michael not doing it himself?"

Emma snickered. "He did Elinor a favor, and she traded this duty. Besides, he's away on business in Derbyshire."

That seemed odd, and Charlotte blinked at it. "Derbyshire? What business could he have there? His estate is in Oxfordshire, as our family's is."

"He wouldn't say," Emma told her, tone apologetic. "Only that it was very important and very secret. I asked, but he said it would upset a good deal of work with his solicitors if it was made known prematurely. Oh, and that it was not just for himself."

Charlotte frowned, looking down at the rug in the room as she thought. "He's not the sort to take up a risky venture, he's only interested in certainty. What could take him there?"

"I wonder if it might have to do with Miss Palmer," Emma mused. "I think that is her home county, but he doesn't seem…"

Her voice faded in Charlotte's ears as her mind spun the pieces of information together.

That was it. Michael was going to Derbyshire to meet with Diana Palmer's father. He was going to offer marriage, and he had been arranging things with his solicitors to accommodate her dowry. He was settling matters for the rest of his family, now that he would be taking up residence in Crestor Grove with his new bride.

He was going to marry Diana.

Michael was getting married.

But that couldn't be. Michael couldn't get married, Michael loved Charlotte. He'd said so. He still loved Charlotte while he was courting Diana. He couldn't marry one while loving the other. He couldn't make Charlotte feel the way he did from just a dance and marry someone else.

She couldn't let him.

Let him.

She had no power over him. She'd shut him out, after all. She had assured herself that he knew she had no feelings for him, that his actions did not affect her. Why shouldn't he marry the young, beautiful, sweet Miss Palmer?

Even Charlotte thought Miss Palmer was lovely, so why shouldn't Michael marry her?

Because Michael couldn't marry anybody. Michael had to stay a bachelor. It would ruin everything, absolutely and utterly everything. London would not be London if he retreated to the country for good with his country-loving wife. It would be the worst possible thing if he married her and left London.

No, he could not marry anybody at all… except Charlotte.

Her lips slowly parted, her eyes widening.

Marry… her?

A single pant of breath escaped her lips, her lungs seeming to collapse with the force of it.

Heavens. She loved Michael.

She had always loved Michael.

She had lost Michael.

The breathless smile that had started shifted into a gaping expression of horror.

No! No, he couldn't! She needed a chance to… She'd only just…

One hand flew to her mouth as she began to shake. She'd done everything in her power to put distance between them, to shut out the hurt he had caused her, and only now realized that the cuts had been so painfully deep because she *had loved him*.

Their friendship, the most treasured of her life, had turned to love at some point, some slight shift that she hadn't even known. There had been no mad rush of it, no breathless anticipation of his touch, only the steady, comforting, abiding assurance of his care to accompany her every day. Knowing he would be there, that she could confide in him, that he would do anything for her. More than that, knowing that she would do anything for him. Not that he would ask, but that she would.

They had felt just as strongly about each other, only he knew what it was. Her change had been so subtle, her attraction to him so gradual that until this moment, she had been entirely unaware of it.

Well, perhaps not entirely. There had been that electrifying kiss, after all, and she had been more than pleased to engage in that with him.

Because it was him.

The madness she had felt would not have been the same were the man anyone else. The unrelenting waves of passion crashing over her in his arms had been a dam of emotions she hadn't known she'd been holding inside her.

How many times had he tried to tell her he'd loved her, and she hadn't seen? Or hadn't wanted to see? How many opportunities had she wasted due to her ignorance?

Now it was too late. She'd given him the closure he needed in order to finalize his plans with Diana. He was finalizing it now. Might have already done. He could even now be on his way back to London with her father's permission. Bound to her already.

Michael would never jilt Diana.

It was over. She had lost. She hadn't even begun, and already she was done.

"Charlotte?"

Charlotte blinked and slowly looked at Emma, and only then realized a pair of tears were slowly making their way down her frozen cheeks. "I love him."

Emma's brows creased and she put a hand on Charlotte's arm, looking her over. "What?"

"I love Michael," Charlotte said clearly. Then she burst into tears and crumpled against her friend as her heart shattered.

Chapter Twenty

————⸎⸎————

The ability to converse well is a gift and blessed are they who know when and how to employ it.

-*The Spinster Chronicles, 25 August 1815*

He couldn't believe he was doing this. Could he really tempt fate further than he already had? Madness, this was, and there was no other word for it.

He couldn't help himself, couldn't resist, but it was mad.

Anyone would have said so.

Michael shook his head as his coach pulled up to the Wright house, just as it had so many times before but had neglected to for several weeks.

He couldn't stay away now. Habit, tradition, and good manners guided him, insisted that he call.

Charlotte was unwell.

Or so he had been told.

A supper party at the Morton home had revealed that to him. Charlotte had not attended when all the other Spinsters had, and questions were raised. The simple answer had been that Charlotte was unwell but would soon recover herself. She had not been seen at any event since.

She hadn't been seen in Mr. Riley's phaeton, in Hyde Park, or in Bond Street. More than that, she had apparently also been too unwell to attend any of the Spinster gatherings for over a week.

That concerned him more than anything. Her friends did not

seem overly concerned, but he couldn't take their word for it. Something was wrong with Charlotte, and until he saw her with his own eyes, spoke with her himself, he would not be satisfied.

Of course, that meant calling upon her. He'd begged off on an outing with Diana to do so, which could mean anything.

He'd risk that.

She might throw him out of the house without letting him say a word in true kindness.

He'd accept that.

He smiled as he was let into the house, nodding and offering his hat and gloves to the servants. "Is Miss Wright well enough for a friendly visitor?"

"I think so, sir," the butler said with an indulgent smile. "Mrs. Sterling is already with her in the Blue Room, and I daresay they have been laughing enough to be in quite high spirits now."

Michael chuckled to himself. He should have known Georgie would have come to visit her friend and manage to raise her spirits in the interim. At least he could not receive the excuse that she was not accepting visitors, given that she presently had one.

At least he was well enough known in the house that he did not warrant formal introduction. He was fully free to walk around the place as and where he may without raising any brow or questions. There would be no opportunity for Charlotte to escape facing him on this occasion, no matter how she might wish to.

He made his way to the Blue Room, his pulse starting to pound with nerves. What if she was still so upset with him that she sent him away? What if she had no interest in anything he had to say? Just how unwell was she?

He heard the laughter before he reached the room, and the sounds of it made one thing perfectly clear.

Georgie was not the Mrs. Sterling that had called upon Charlotte.

Now his smile was entirely helpless, and a little uncertain, as he entered. "This is a fine surprise. I come to call upon the invalid and find she is already aptly cared for."

The ladies within turned, faces still wreathed in smiles. "Michael, dear," Miranda greeted, rising to face him.

Charlotte's smile turned to a very small, very tired one, and he saw how pale and thin she looked, though still she was the most beautiful woman his eyes had ever seen.

Strange, that.

He hadn't thought of her in that sense for some time. He'd known it, of course, but it wasn't often he was struck with the impression. Even rarer that he thought it when she was completely unadorned and unwell. There must then be an odd truth to it.

Interesting.

He bowed to them both, then waved Miranda back down. "Please, sit, Miranda. I have no intention of monopolizing Charlotte's time and sending you out."

"Marvelous," Miranda replied, making no move to retake her seat. "I do so hate being sent out, and even more so by someone not of the house. I resist in every respect. Fortunately for you, I have quite finished in my ministrations to the sick and weary in this place." She turned and winked at Charlotte, who giggled at some private joke between them.

"Do not leave on my account," he pleaded.

He glanced at the floor below the sofa where Charlotte lay, smiling to himself at the sight of Rufus laying there. The dog seemed perfectly at ease and relaxed, breathing the deep and rumbling sounds of sleep with no clear indication that he would ever leave.

Miranda smiled indulgently. "I never would, Michael. You're a dear, but I do not think of you before acting in my own behalf. The truth of the matter is that I should have left a quarter of an hour ago, and simply could not break away from the conversation. Your arrival provides a natural break that suits me quite nicely."

There was no course but to grin at that, which was usually the way with Miranda, and Michael made a playful almost bow. "Then I am happy I could oblige you."

"Most kind." Miranda reached out a hand to Charlotte, who took it at once. "Get some rest, dear Charlotte."

"I will," she replied easily. "Rufus will see to it."

Miranda glanced down at her beloved pet with a smile. "He certainly will. And I trust the pair of you will keep quite perfect company together." She nodded, then turned and glided from the room, winking at Michael as she passed.

He watched her leave, then looked back and saw Rufus still sleeping on the floor where he had been. "Is she loaning out Rufus now?"

Charlotte's hand dropped to the dog's head, and she scratched lightly. "She thought having him here might comfort me. And she is venturing out to her estate tomorrow, but the visit will be of short duration, so she saw no need to trouble Rufus with the journey."

"Because troubling Rufus should always be the utmost priority where travel is concerned." Michael rolled his eyes but smiled all the same. "Do you think he will be of some comfort to you?"

She looked down at the bloodhound with a warm smile. "Yes, I do. I may have to get a Rufus of my own." Her eyes tracked back up to Michael's and the smile remained, which seemed a miracle. "Come, sit down."

Relief lit his chest, and he nodded, taking the chair that Miranda had vacated. "I wasn't sure if you would wish to see me. Or agree to it, as it were."

Charlotte tilted her head at him, her smile soft. "I'd always agree to see you. For curiosity, if nothing else." She laid her head back against the pillow, her eyes closing for a moment. "I'm sorry to not be better company."

"Are you very unwell?" he asked, keeping his voice low. "Should you be in bed? I'll carry you there, if need be."

She hummed a laugh, her eyes opening again. "No, it is quite a relief to be out of bed, thank you. And as for being unwell, it is more a matter of fatigue than anything else. Quite listless at times, and it does make my head ache so."

"I'll not stay long," he promised. He leaned forward, elbows resting on his knees. "I'm sorry, Charlotte. I've not behaved well towards you of late, and I acknowledge that."

Charlotte's smile curved crookedly. "Nor have I towards you. Hardly fitting behavior for best friends, is it?"

"Not ideally, no." He gave her a wry smile. "We never discussed either one of us getting married, did we?"

She swallowed before shaking her head. "No, we did not. It... Well, it never came up in a natural way, as far as I can recall. We were content as we were."

Michael nodded slowly, the palms of his hands rubbing together absently. "That we were. Until we weren't."

"I am sorry for that," Charlotte murmured, focusing her attention on scratching Rufus again. "I feel that what happened stemmed from my insistence that I marry, and blindly taking up the charge to make it so. It seemed so important to join my friends, to not be the only spinster left, but I had you, didn't I?"

He wasn't entirely certain how to answer her, given that, at the time she'd decided to marry, he had loved her. Considered her the only woman he could ever love, and she'd always had in him that regard. But she had never been interested in his love, so his friendship had been the lifeblood of their relationship.

She'd always had that, too.

"Yes, you did," he told her roughly, resisting the urge to reach out and touch her hand. To touch her cheek. Her arm. Her hair. Anything. Just to connect with her physically as he sensed the emotional connection rebuilding between them.

Charlotte shook her head, her eyes steady on his. "That should have been enough."

He gave her a sympathetic smile. "I couldn't fill every role in your life. You've always wanted the wild romance, something that brings you to your knees. There was nothing wrong in seeking that. Still isn't."

"But I shut you out to do so," she insisted, her voice breaking a little, dark eyes luminous with welling tears.

He did reach out now, setting his hand safely at her arm. "Charlotte, I closed myself to you first. I couldn't imagine losing you to another man, or for anything to change between us in any way. It was selfish and naïve, not to mention shortsighted."

Her lips curved in a smile again. "Might we be friends again? Not as we were before, as so much has changed, but friends all the same?"

A tear lingered at her cheek, and he gently brushed it away, ignoring how his finger burned from the contact. "Of course," he said as he sat back, breaking the connection between them. "We will always be friends."

"Good." She exhaled, the sound seeming a sigh of relief, and her smile turned more to the one he was used to from her. "I've missed you. Conversation is never quite as stimulating at events without your input."

Michael laughed in disbelief. "I barely contributed at all. Far too much of a lurker in Society, which, unfortunately, has been lost to me now."

"Lurker or no, you always had something to say that was worth hearing." Charlotte shrugged against the cushions propping her up. "It will be nice to have that again."

He shook his head ruefully, giving her a wry look. "You might be the only person on earth to find me interesting, Charlotte."

She was completely unruffled and dipped her chin in almost regal, classic Charlotte fashion. "That's because I am exceptionally perceptive and have marvelous taste."

"I know." He smiled, exhaling his own sigh of relief to find this easy way between them again.

There was something new in the way she looked at him, something softer and warmer, something that made him long to stay and desperate to leave at the same time. Had the loss of who they had been affected her that much? He'd felt it keenly, but what had it done to her?

"I'd better go," he heard himself say. "You need your rest, and I only wanted to see that you were not too ill."

Charlotte blinked, somehow appearing smaller and more fatigued now than a moment ago. "Not too unwell. Just unwell enough."

"That sounds about right." He smiled and rose, looking down at her with a torrent of emotion filling him. "Take care of yourself, Charlotte."

"I always do." She returned his smile, but it seemed to waver.

He couldn't think about that, couldn't dwell on it, had to forget it. Not wonder what it meant.

Bowing, he turned and left the room, the tips of his fingers tingling strangely as he did so.

"Ah, good. You're up."

Charlotte looked at her mother without emotion as she entered the drawing room. "Yes, I do get up on the regular."

Her mother ignored the comment and took up a chair next to her. "I count each morning you get out of bed as a victory. You had me dreadfully worried those days you did not."

"I did not mean to worry you," Charlotte told her, instantly contrite. "I could not think of anyone but myself at the time, and myself had no desire to leave the comfort of my bed."

"It is a wonder you did not take with fever." Her mother shook her head, smiling as she drummed her fingers on the arm of the chair she was in. "I daresay Society thinks you must have. We even sent for the doctor a time or two for appearances."

Charlotte laughed in surprise. "When was that? I don't remember."

Her mother winked. "We always sent for him while you slept. It made your symptoms far less suspicious."

That was the most beautifully devious thing her mother had ever said, and Charlotte grinned for the first time in weeks.

"Will you not now tell me what dropped you into such depths of despair?" her mother inquired, her face filling with concern that would have broken Charlotte's heart had it not been broken already.

Charlotte shook her head firmly, giving her an apologetic smile. "I will not. There is nothing to be done about it, so I must let myself break so that I may heal. I must learn to live with what has broken me."

"You are not broken," her mother protested, each word harsh with emphasis as her eyes skewered her. "You are strong, and you are impenetrable."

"Impervious, too, apparently," Charlotte murmured, more to herself as a faint memory shot through her mind, making her smile. "Alas, I am also human, Mama. And humans were made to hurt."

A wrinkle formed in her mother's brow. "But I'm your mother. It is my calling to soothe your hurts and set things right."

Charlotte sighed sadly. "This is not something that can be put right. It is not so simple. And besides," she paused to pat Rufus down on the floor before her, "Rufus soothes me. A cup of chocolate soothes me. Being home soothes me."

"Well, as long as that helps…" Her mother winked and bent to pet Rufus herself. "I must say, he is a marvelous creature. Far better than any of the hounds your father kept. I may get a dog for myself; one that your father cannot claim."

"That would suit you, Mama." Charlotte smiled at her, raising a brow. "But why now?"

She shrugged. "You'll be getting married eventually. I should like some soothing company to replace you."

Charlotte sobered and sank back against the sofa. "Not too soon, Mama. I've no plans at the present."

"It will happen, dear. One way or another, it will happen." She rose and moved to leave the room, then turned back. "Georgie Sterling inquired if she could call. I told her yes. She will be here presently."

"Ugh, Mama, I do not feel like entertaining," Charlotte groaned, slapping the sofa cushion beneath her. "My head aches, and if I have to force a smile I do not feel, it will only worsen."

Her mother nodded. "I'll have a tea tray sent up, and make sure Cook includes some honey biscuits. I know they are Georgie's favorite." She left the room without another word, leaving Charlotte to silently stew.

That was just like her mother, to interfere without being the least bit perturbed. If she had any inclination as to why Charlotte had been so unwell and depressed, she would understand that Charlotte only wanted to be alone.

There were exceptions, of course, but entertaining friends was so exhausting when she had to continually avoid discussing what had happened to her.

Only Emma knew the truth of things, and she had sworn not to tell anyone.

Charlotte could not bear the embarrassment and mortification of admitting to anyone that she was in love with Michael Sandford, after all they had been through, put each other through, and seen each other through. That he should have known he loved her for years, and she had only known it a matter of days. That he had proposed to her years ago, and she had refused him.

If only she had seen then. If only she had known.

She might now be his wife, have his children, and they might be happy together. But he was to be happy with Miss Palmer, it was all but certain, and she was only waiting for her friends to tell her it had been announced. She had avoided Society to spare herself, but also to keep from having to be in company with Jonathan. Or being seen to avoid Jonathan. Or to think about what she would do about Jonathan. Really, she had simply kept out of Society to avoid anything and everything surrounding Jonathan.

And Michael, too.

Oh, she had to avoid Michael. Her heart would burst if she saw him, her expression would give her away, she would do something desperate like beg him to marry her instead of Diana.

And then he had come to her home, and she had been so tired, so weak, so broken that the sight of him gave her joy rather than pain. For those few minutes, he had been returned to her as the dear friend she had known for years. They could be as they were, comfortable in each other's company and free with their words. She could stare without being forward, reveal more than she could in public with her eyes and expression. He could touch her...

The touch of his finger on her cheek as he wiped away her tear would sustain her for ages, and there were no words for how pathetic admitting that made her feel. He had given her wings that day, though he had also given her a cage.

They had never talked of marriage, he'd said. No, and she hadn't intended to talk of it then, but his bringing it up had confirmed her worst fears.

He was getting married.

There were no more tears to shed on the subject, but the ache of it would take far longer to fade.

Her mother was sure she would marry, but Charlotte could not see how. Even Jonathan, for all his goodness, looks, and prospects, was not Michael. But someday, when the ache did not seem so gaping, he could fill the space well enough.

Would he wait that long?

Who would she find after him, if he would not?

"Oh, you look better than I expected. That is quite the relief."

Charlotte looked up as Georgie entered the room, bobbing a polite curtsey of sorts, and moving over to her. "Was I supposed to be at death's door?"

"Something rather like," Georgie quipped, sitting just across from Charlotte. "Or wallowing in abject despair, hair streaming loose and rumpled, your nightgown stained with broth you would not take."

"Goodness," Charlotte replied. "You've put a great deal of imagination into my condition. I feel I must disappoint."

Georgie smiled in her customary mischievous way. "Reality usually does."

"Your tea, Miss Wright." Charlotte smiled as the tea tray was brought in, enjoying the way Georgie's eyes widened.

When they were alone again, Georgie gave Charlotte a look. "I feel as though I was anticipated."

"Mama insisted we have your favorite honey biscuits." Charlotte gestured to them, sighing. "Help yourself."

Georgie immediately set about making tea, but surprised Charlotte by handing the first cup to her.

Charlotte eyed her warily as she took it. "You have me suspicious, Georgie. Are you here to tell me about the engagement?"

Her friend paused as she made her own tea. "What engagement?"

"Michael's." Even saying his name in this context was painful, and her throat protested vigorously. She sipped her tea quickly in an attempt to soothe it.

"Michael?" Georgie repeated, resuming her tea making. "Michael's not engaged."

Charlotte exhaled a short breath of irritation. "Kindly don't pretend to know more of Society's tidings than I. We both know better."

Georgie sat back, stirring her tea gently, her lips starting to curve knowingly. "I was with the Greensleys last evening, and Jane said Diana was particularly interested in every Chronicles issue relating to Best Bachelors suddenly."

That was startling, and Charlotte had no words for the space of three heartbeats. "She did?"

"Everyone heard her." Georgie shrugged and took a honey biscuit from the tray. "I don't see a reason to learn about bachelors if she has an understanding, do you?"

Charlotte shook her head, unwilling to consider any of that. "But Michael plans to ask her. He went to Derbyshire on business, and one does not have to think hard to understand the exact business."

Georgie quirked a brow. "And you don't like that."

She shook her head, her heart migrating into her throat. "And I hate that with every ounce of air my lungs breathe in and out," she admitted in a watery rasp. "It makes me sick. I want to die." She looked away, the waves of emotion finding hold in her chest, choking her words.

"Well…" Georgie murmured softly, "shouldn't you tell him so? Ideally before he offers and finds himself bound in honor before he is bound by law."

Charlotte looked back at her friend after a moment, expression cold. "I don't see a single reason why that would be worth my consideration."

Georgie shrugged a shoulder. "We couldn't let Michael be a jilt, now could we?"

"Why would he be?" she demanded, tired of the discussion, tired of the hurt, and tired of the futility of it all.

"I have no doubt when Michael hears how you feel, he may respond with some encouraging words of his own." Georgie bit into her biscuit, then gestured with it. "I rather think he's been saving up encouraging words for some time, just needing your ardor to match."

No, that was not it at all. Michael had loved her once, if his words were to be believed, but that was all behind them now. He was marrying Diana, whether it happened tomorrow, next week, or in six months. It was happening, the pieces were in motion, she knew it all.

Hoping for anything else was too painful.

"He loves *her*, Georgie."

"Mmm, does he?" Georgie mused, eyes narrowing in doubtful speculation. "As I recall, he cancelled an outing with Diana just to come and see how you were. She doesn't know that, of course, but it would suggest…"

Charlotte was up in a flash, darting out of the room as her lungs burned with a fire of hope, her legs pumping as she raced up the stairs.

"I'll just eat these biscuits while I wait for you," Georgie called after her, laughter ringing through her voice.

There wasn't time to think about what she would do, when or how. All she knew was she needed to look less like death and more like life before she saw Michael again, and she had every intention of seeing him sooner rather than later.

Surely there was some event tonight. There was always something.

She laughed breathlessly as she reached behind her to fumble with the buttons at the back of her dress. She would need to speak with Jonathan before she did anything she could not get out of, but she dared not think too far yet.

All she had was hope, and it was enough to take a chance on.

Chapter Twenty-One

Opportunities are a funny business, though I have yet to find laughter accompanying them.

-*The Spinster Chronicles, 23 July 1818*

"What in the world are the Radcliffes doing here? I thought they were in Scotland."

"They were. Just arrived yesterday. No idea why they've decided to attend tonight, but Janet is delighted to have them."

Michael looked at Tyrone in bewilderment. "Why? There's still a great deal of speculation and gossip surrounding them. They'd never be permitted in Almack's and other hallowed halls."

"Are you saying my halls are not hallowed?" Lord Sterling asked with playful superiority as he came up behind them.

"Well, you're no Almack's," Michael retorted without concern, grinning at the man.

Hugh grimaced beside him. "Thank heavens. That place still haunts my dreams."

"The matrons will be delighted to hear it," his brother assured him, clamping a hand on his shoulder. "And they aren't the only couple to return to London now." He gestured to a striking couple chatting with the Spinsters.

"The Vales?" Michael exclaimed, gaping outright. "Did she not just have a child?"

Lord Sterling nodded, grinning wryly. "Indeed, but she was well enough to travel, so when I heard they had returned, we extended an invitation. Didn't think they'd accept, but there they are."

"What in the world brought them all back now? It's nearing the end of the Season at this point, hardly any events remain." Michael shook his head, taking in the additions to the Spinsters' group with disbelief.

"Two guesses," Tyrone said rather blandly. "Charlotte. Wright." He indicated the group with a lazy finger.

Blinking, Michael looked at the group again.

There she was. Radiant in a gown he had never seen before, one of pale yellow and dotted with white rosettes, additional white flowers in her hair. She smiled and laughed with her friends, just as she had done for years. Yet something about her now was all the more striking, and he needed a moment to catch his breath.

"How do you mean?" he heard Hugh ask Tyrone. "You think they needed to meet Riley before he proposes?"

Would punching the host's brother be frowned upon? Of all the idiotic suggestions…

"I think they came to be sure she was whole," Tyrone explained without violence, which was more than Michael could have done. "Miss Wright is never unwell, and yet she begged off of everything for nearly two weeks. I have no doubt they rushed to London for her sake alone."

That was a much more palatable suggestion, and Michael was pleased to consider that instead. He still had no idea what had caused Charlotte's ill health, but he supposed that was not important. What mattered was that she was here tonight, which meant she was feeling recovered enough to appear in Society again. They could start their friendship again in truth, older and wiser, both with a more proper understanding of just what it was that lay between them.

He'd be only too glad to continue as they had been before.

And he knew himself well enough now to know that he could not drive out his love for Charlotte completely. He could only bury it, live with it, and move forward in full awareness of it.

Just as he'd always done.

"Is your Miss Palmer coming tonight?" Hugh asked Michael, the question innocent, but something deeper lingered beneath it.

Michael told him the truth. "I have no idea. And she is not

mine." He shrugged a shoulder, smiling at his friends.

Tyrone made a face of consideration. "Well, well. Won't that surprise the masses? If you'll excuse me, I owe Miss Wright a waltz." He left them without any further ado.

Michael watched him go, frowning. "Why does he owe her a waltz?"

"You'd know better than me," Hugh told him with a shrug. "Has he done her a favor?"

"How would I know?" Michael scowled, shaking his head. "I don't like it."

Lord Sterling laughed to himself. "Only because he was one of the Spinsters' choices for Best Bachelor. But what do you have to worry about with Tyrone? Charlotte is entertaining Mr. Riley, is she not?"

"You are increasingly less helpful," Michael growled as he watched Charlotte interact with Tyrone, noting the amusement in her face and the laughter they shared.

"Did Riley receive an invitation?" Hugh asked his brother.

"No. Charlotte had refused due to being unwell, so I didn't bother. Then she changed her mind this morning, and I didn't see the need to invite him at this late hour."

That was some small comfort. Diana wasn't here, and Riley wasn't here. No courtships on display, no façade to uphold, and no agenda to see to. He could be him, and she could be her.

They didn't have to speak, and it would be right enough if they didn't. Perhaps they would dance, perhaps they would not. They had started over the other day, and he had no expectations of it. No, that wasn't quite right. He expected to find a friend in her, and that he would be a friend for her. He wouldn't be at her heels as he had been for so long, but he would be there in her life all the same.

Was that enough?

"Are you feeling more like throttling someone now?"

He glanced at Hugh's rather leading question. "Why? Do you need somebody throttled?"

Hugh chuckled and nodded, clapping Michael on the arm approvingly. "That is much better, Sandford. Much, much better." He continued to nod, smiling as he turned away.

"What?" Michael demanded after him, but no answer was given. He turned to Lord Sterling, the only one still standing near him.

The man looked just as confused as Michael felt. "I have no idea what's going on. Don't look to me for answers."

Michael made a face and tugged at his cravat. "I'm beginning to think I don't know, either. Is your sister here? I know I can safely dance with her without raising speculation or making anyone overly upset."

Lord Sterling laughed and gestured the way. "Yes, Alice is here. Don't tell my wife you view my sister as safe. I think she has aspirations for you both."

The idea made Michael groan, and he slowed his step. "Please, no. I cannot bear to disappoint your wife, and I don't want to give your sister hope. I don't want to do anything except get through this evening with some entertainment in life and my reputation intact. I don't want to start rumors, I don't care to stop any, I simply want to be here. I know I cannot be invisible anymore, but please don't make me important."

Lord Sterling folded his arms and gave him a thorough look. "Are you finished?"

Michael blinked once. "Yes…"

"Good. Dance with Janet first, she'll be pacified that way. Come on." He put his hand on Michael's back and steered him onwards, shaking his head in some disgruntlement.

As luck would have it, Janet was with the Spinsters conglomeration, which enabled Michael to join them in a natural way without raising speculation.

He'd thank Lord Sterling later for that, if nothing else.

He shook hands with the men, extended greetings especially to Camden Vale and Lord Radcliffe, whose courtship of Lady Edith some months past Michael had entirely missed. Both seemed particularly pleased with their lot in life, and Michael found himself strangely envious of their joy.

He caught sight of Janet and moved to her. "Lady Sterling."

Her dark eyes twinkled as she grinned. "Mr. Sandford. I'm so pleased you could attend this evening."

"As am I, my lady," he replied with a bow. "Might I have the honor of the next dance?"

Her expression brightened further still. "Why, of course! I've seen you dance a bit more this Season, and I must say you are rather good at it."

"Passable at best, my lady, I assure you." Still, he smiled at the compliment, as one was prone to do in Lady Sterling's company. "It is all due to the partners I have chosen. That is the trick. A passable dancer may appear skilled if his partner exudes excellence. I never choose anything less now."

Lady Sterling shook her head, laughing quietly. "Oh, you have learned well, Mr. Sandford. Most impressive."

Michael grinned. "I beg your pardon, my lady, but I have always been able to flatter well and with sincerity."

"You simply never did?" she suggested.

"Correct, my lady."

She nodded now, seeming all the more pleased. "Perfect." She looked at something behind him, and her smile deepened. "I do believe someone would like to speak with you, sir."

Michael turned in surprise, that surprise shifting something in his chest as Charlotte stood there, lovelier this close than she had been at a distance.

Something about her seemed stiff, hesitant, almost nervous, yet a ringlet near her left ear drew his attention, his fingers itching to touch it.

"Charlotte," he said, grateful he didn't sound out of breath or guttural as he did so.

She smiled a little, but it wavered. "Michael, would you mind terribly if I had a word? Out on the terrace, perhaps?"

He blinked at the suggestion and glanced out of the windows. "The terrace?" he repeated.

"Capital idea," Lady Sterling praised. "Privacy while in full view of us. You know the way, don't you, Charlotte?"

Charlotte smiled at her, nodding. "I do, thank you, Janet." Her eyes flicked up to Michael's, the hesitation returning. "Michael?"

He gestured for her to lead on. "Of course."

The smile flashed across her face. "Thank you. Only a quick word, back in a blink." She turned on her heel and hurried away, leaving Michael to follow in confusion.

What in the world was this?

Oh, she would die before she could get the words out of her mouth.

Back in a blink? Was she all of ten years old once more trying to convince her mother that she hadn't behaved badly?

The terrace was expansive, and it was well lit, but Charlotte would have given anything for a dark garden and a hedge between them.

Her heart pounded almost violently within her, and she pressed a fist to it in an attempt to force it into submission.

How could she confess to Michael that she loved him if she could not hear anything? Could almost see her heart beat as her pulse seemed to exist behind her eyes...

"What did you need a word in private for?" Michael laughed as he came onto the terrace with her. "Surely you have no secrets from the Spinsters."

She swallowed with difficulty, willing herself to have the strength to turn and face him. "They wouldn't think so, but this has nothing to do with them, and everything to do with you and me."

"Oh, dear," he sighed, sounding so like the friend she had known before all of this that she found herself smiling, the tension in her lessening just enough that she could turn to him now.

She exhaled slowly and forced her fingers to unhook from each other and fist at her sides instead.

There would be no turning back from this.

"You're not going to believe this, Michael," she began with a strained laugh, "and in fact, I barely believe it myself, but it is the truth, and I have to tell you now or it will not happen."

His attention was fixed on her, his eyes hooded in the dark of the night. He had stilled, seeming to barely breathe as he stood there. "You hate my mother, don't you?"

Charlotte blinked slowly, then blinked again as his words replayed in her mind. "Wait, what?"

He shook his head, exhaling slowly. "I've suspected for years, but you're finally admitting it, aren't you?"

"Erm, no?" Charlotte gave Michael an incredulous look, wondering where in the world he pulled that thought from, and how he could possibly think she would need the privacy of the terrace to tell him something like that. "I mean, she isn't my favorite person, but she's not…"

"Ah ha!" he cried, pointing at her. "I knew it."

Hell's bells, he was an idiot.

"Michael," she ground out, her patience fraying at an ever-quickening pace, "that is *not* what I wanted…"

"Mr. Sandford," Janet called merrily from the door. "It is our dance, if you've finished."

He nodded and smiled at her. "Of course, my lady. I believe we are." He winked at Charlotte, which made her stomach flip. "I won't tell."

"No, Michael, wait," she begged as he started towards the door.

He turned and laughed. "Charlotte, we can revisit this later. I'm looking forward to your thoughts."

Charlotte all but growled in frustration. "Michael! You cannot marry without knowing…"

"Marry?" he replied, snorting once. "I'm not planning to marry, Charlotte. What gave you that idea?" He gave her another strange look and returned to the ballroom.

Charlotte had extended a hand during her final attempt, and now that hand turned palm up in a strange inquiring gesture as she almost slumped where she stood, blinking rapidly. "Not ever?" she asked the night air, knowing no response would come.

It was a stupid question, and it did not matter in the least. The important thing was what had prompted it.

Michael was *not* getting married.

She laughed a breathless, almost sobbing laugh and stumbled back until she hit the railing and balustrade with her back, leaning there for a moment. He wasn't going to marry. She still had time to tell him how she felt. She was not too late.

She was not too late.

The delirium passed then, and she stared at the door to the

ballroom as though Michael still stood there, scowling and shaking her head.

Did he really think she had chosen this moment to tell him about his mother? She could have gone her entire life without caring if he knew she was not particularly fond of his mother. She would need to find another way to let him know now, and another opportunity to tell him so.

All of that fear and apprehension, all of those nerves, only to be left out here on the terrace without having told Michael anything at all.

Utterly maddening.

Charlotte shook her head and walked back into the ballroom, heading directly for her friends.

"Did you tell him?" Prue asked the moment she saw her, eyes bright.

Charlotte stared without emotion. "Tell him what?"

Edith, newly arrived and glowing in her married bliss, looked almost crestfallen now as she shook her head at Charlotte. "Och, lass…"

"What?" Charlotte asked, curious now.

"Oh, for pity's sake," Grace grumbled nearby, looking at the rest with a sour expression. "She didn't tell him."

A groan resounded from the entire group, and Charlotte looked around at them all in outright astonishment. "Tell him what?" she inquired again, her question far less flat.

"That you love him, Charlotte," Prue said, taking her hand and smiling sweetly. "We all thought you would."

She eyed her typically stammering friend in disbelief. "The fact that you can even suggest that without stammering is remarkable."

Prue giggled and squeezed the hand she held. "The thought does not make me nervous or anxious in any way. It is so right, so perfect, that it does not frighten me in the least."

Charlotte shook her head slowly. "Then perhaps you should tell him, because it frightens me out of my wits." She looked at all the rest with some resignation. "When did Emma tell you?"

"Emma?" Elinor demanded with indignation they had not seen from her since her marriage. "My sister knows? I mean, we've all suspected for years, but Emma *knows*? And she didn't say?"

"Someone warn Emma she may die tomorrow," Charlotte muttered, which Prue echoed with a nod, her cheeks coloring.

Emma dying brought on Prue's nerves, but Charlotte losing every ounce of pride and dignity over Michael did not?

How perfectly lovely.

"Emma never told us anything," Georgie assured her, leaning closer. "We just know."

Charlotte sighed heavily and put a hand to her brow. "He didn't even give me a chance to say anything, the fool. He thought I wanted to tell him... Something else. Something completely inane by comparison. I can't even..." She growled and began rambling in a stream of French for the pure chance it gave her to be freer with her words than polite company might have liked.

Georgie coughed a laugh while Prue hiccuped, and Grace hissed and waved the others off from coming closer.

A low chuckle rumbled from just to her left and behind her. "You missed a conjugation in there," Camden Vale pointed out as if that were helpful.

She glared at him over her shoulder and snarled.

He grinned and put an arm around her shoulder, pulling her in for a hug as though she were a sister. "I missed you, Charlotte."

"If only the feeling were mutual," she grumbled, shoving away from his chest, but smiling reluctantly at him. She looked out at the dance floor and watched Michael dance with Janet. "Bloody fool."

"Do you want to speak to him again tonight?" Cam asked quietly. "Francis can make that happen, you know."

Charlotte shook her head, taking a deep breath. "No, I'm rather afraid the moment is gone for now. I'll find another way to tell him."

"If he doesn't prove accommodating," Aubrey suggested as he sidled over, "let us know."

She gave him a sharp look, but was surprised to see Tony, Sebastian, Hugh, and even Lord Radcliffe standing by with the same determined expression. "What, all of you?"

Lord Radcliffe smiled, which was a rare enough sight. "Why not?"

"Heavens, you need to ask?" She gestured to the lot of them.

"All we're missing is Hensh, and I'll have a battalion."

"You called?"

Charlotte rolled her eyes dramatically and turned to see Henshaw approaching, Kitty Morton's hand tight in his. "Oh, good," Charlotte grumbled. "I feel so much better now." She eyed their hands and raised a brow at Kitty. "Kitty Morton, have you come to tell us something to explain the glow in your cheeks?"

The girl blushed further, but her beaming smile could have rivaled the sun. "Perhaps."

Izzy and Sebastian pushed forward, Izzy clasping her hands under her chin. "Well?"

Kitty and Henshaw looked at each other, smiles both tender and adoring, then Kitty looked at her brother and sister-in-law. "Lieutenant Henshaw has made me an offer of marriage, and I have accepted him."

"Thank God," Cam said without any hesitation whatsoever. "Has anyone been waiting for this as long as I have?"

Several hands raised, and Henshaw glared at each of them in turn. "Marvelous help you all were here, thank you." He looked at Charlotte with a quick grin. "I win, my dear."

She narrowed her eyes. "You are not married yet, Hensh. But you do have my profound congratulations." She smiled at them both, then stepped out of the way in order to let the others through. She sank into a nearby chair, exhaling a weary, heavy sigh.

"I know that sound all too well, my dear."

Charlotte turned her head to look at Lady Hetty, quietly sitting in her chair and surveying the room as a whole. "Why do I believe that?"

Lady Hetty's smile, rarer in sight than even Lord Radcliffe's, was almost whimsical on her wrinkled face. "I know a little something of being the last, Charlotte. I know the pain of seeing those you hold dear happy and thriving in all the ways you would wish and not having the same yourself."

In an instant, Charlotte's eyes began to water, and she bit her lip. "It seems so simple, in a way. And yet the path of it is hidden from me."

"Oh, you're well on your way; I heard them." She lifted her chin towards the group and winked at Charlotte. "A handsome man, and no mistaking it. Good catch."

Charlotte sniffled, laughing at the comment. "I haven't caught him yet. And I don't even know why I bothered wanting marriage at all. You of all people know what I would sacrifice. Perhaps this pain is proof that I shouldn't do this."

Lady Hetty thumped her walking stick against the ground hard. "Charlotte Wright, do you think I have chosen my life out of fear or surrender?"

"No…" she said at once, more out of defense than a true response. "Of course not, I simply…"

"A wealthy spinster is still a spinster, my child," Lady Hetty interrupted. "I have remained so because I never had reason enough to marry. I was like you, popular and sociable. Well sought after and the envy of several. Fortune hunters had no chance with me if I did not like them for themselves. And, as it happened, I did not with most of them. I do not regret the path my life has taken, but that does not mean it is to be envied."

Charlotte frowned at that. "Would it make me a fraud? To proclaim in our Chronicles that there are worse things than being a spinster, and then to marry?"

Lady Hetty's eyes narrowed, and she exhaled as she studied Charlotte. "Would you be marrying to avoid remaining a spinster? Or would you be marrying for love, affection, comfort, or any other sensible reason that an heiress would choose to do so of her own will?"

Charlotte's eyes immediately shifted back to the dance floor, where Michael and Janet still danced, laughing merrily together. "It would be because I love him," she admitted in a whisper. "And because I could not bear to lose him."

"Then I would say you are practicing what you preach, my dear." Lady Hetty patted her hands twice, then squeezed them. "And if that idiot boy doesn't snap you up, I invite you to come live out your days with me. I'll even leave you the house in my will. Make a spinster fortress in my name."

Charlotte laughed at the images her mind was conjuring, then turned to the older woman and pressed a fond kiss to her cheek, surprising them both. "I quite adore you, my lady, and I don't care a fig for what anybody else says about you."

Lady Hetty's eyes turned misty, and she pinched Charlotte's cheek. "Everybody else is jealous, girl, make no mistake. And if you manage to marry before that Henshaw fellow, I'll give you a barouche as a wedding present."

"Deal, my lady," Charlotte agreed with a laugh too loud for polite company, but not caring a fig for that, either.

Chapter Twenty-Two

On occasion, one must be rather decisive about things. It is the only way to bring about results. But only on occasion.

-The Spinster Chronicles, 15 November 1819

There was something about being in the Wright family home that made Michael smile no matter the occasion. It was his home away from home, and events held there might as well have been ones he hosted. He didn't mean to take up the responsibilities, but he knew the house and the people so well that he seemed to take part in the duties without intending to. Any time he saw opportunity, he acted on it.

The garden party today would be different. Mostly because he was fascinated by what Charlotte would try to do.

After their private word on the terrace, she'd tried again to speak with him alone when they were at the Ingrams' home for an afternoon of conversation and games. Unfortunately, she had tried to commandeer him during the lawn games that had started, which had not helped matters.

"Michael, there is something that I really must discuss with you as soon as possible. Would you mind walking with me?" she'd asked, her smile bright, but forced.

He'd nodded, but then Aubrey, Lord Ingram, had come and insisted that Michael come and partner him for bowls. With an apologetic shrug to Charlotte, Michael had gone along with him rather than take the private word with her.

The glare she had launched at Aubrey's back would have killed the man had anything materialized from it.

The ferocity in her eyes had started Michael thinking, and he had done little else since. What could she want to speak with him about that could not be said before company? She'd never been particularly private, though some occasions between them had held conversations he doubted she had shared with others. But those times had usually come when they were already in each other's company, and not from any structured moment alone. They'd never intentionally had moments alone; it had always happened as the natural way of things.

What was she trying to accomplish?

It didn't take long for him to get a fair idea, considering the last few weeks and the looks, conversations, and contact they'd had. He didn't dare put a name to it, having felt the wounds of disappointed hopes for years, but if he was right, Charlotte might have something vastly intriguing to tell him.

But there was no sense in making it simple for her to do so.

It was not particularly accommodating of him, but there was an inordinate amount of fun in being pursued by the woman he had pursued for years. He'd let her tell him eventually, he was not entirely cruel. He just needed to see how determined she was. There was nothing that drove Charlotte more than obstacles to her success. A driven Charlotte in this regard could be a rather grand sight.

All the better for him.

Striding out to the gardens, Michael eyed the gathering with some anticipation. All of Charlotte's friends in the Spinsters were here, or would be shortly, as well as Lord and Lady Sterling, Mr. and Mrs. Andrews, who were great friends of the Vales as well as the Radcliffes, and various other members of Society that he actually could tolerate for more than five minutes at a time. Any event hosted by the Wrights usually involved the best of Society, which made invitations difficult to come by.

Michael always had a standing invitation, and had the last week or so not happened, he might have had that revoked this time.

"My sister was looking for you," Charles Wright mentioned as he passed him to head out to the guests. "I'd make yourself scarce, she's rather in high dudgeon."

The warning made Michael laugh to himself. She'd be in even higher dudgeon once he played with her a little.

"That should not make you smile." Charles shook his head, exhaling heavily. "What are you up to?"

He shrugged easily, loving the edge of excitement he felt nipping at his heels. "I thought I might provoke your sister a little. For her own good, of course. It will be worth it."

Charles grinned the way only an older brother can. "It is always worth it to provoke Charlotte. Carry on." Chuckling, he moved out into the gardens fully, shaking his head.

Well, at least somebody else would appreciate Michael's plan.

Michael continued to survey the gathering, and suddenly locked eyes with Charlotte, who was watching him steadily from her present position under a tree.

He let himself smile at her, trying to ignore how his heart pounded the longer he stared, and waved as though this were any other time he had come to her home.

The quick flash of smile was well worth everything. She waved back, the gesture surprisingly discreet for her, which only further supported his suspicion.

He shook himself free from the sudden Charlotte-induced stupor and wandered into the gardens, taking a glass of lemonade from the table that had been set up. He nodded at Miranda, whose return to London had been much heralded, and shook his head in amusement at the sight of Henshaw and Kitty Morton, who had already found a quiet spot for themselves to speak without much by way of chaperone.

He'd suggest someone take up that role after a few minutes, but surely they deserved a few moments unobserved. Or as unobserved as they could be at a gathering like this.

A movement to his left caught his eye, and he saw Charlotte heading in his direction. He moved to a footman nearby at once. "Come get me in three minutes," he ordered through a polite smile. "Make something up."

"Sir?" the bewildered lad queried.

"Just do it. Trust me."

He didn't seem convinced, but he nodded. "Yes, sir."

"Good man." Michael nodded in return, then walked away, continuing to greet others politely. Every nerve and fiber was attuned to Charlotte and her position to him, though, and he waited almost breathlessly for her to reach him.

Then, at last, she was there.

"Michael."

He turned and smiled at Charlotte, willing himself to appear only glad to see her, not overly eager. "Charlotte. Marvelous turnout today, your mother will be pleased."

She nodded, looking around, though it was a cursory look at best. "Yes, I suppose she will be. She's in conversation with Mrs. Lambert at the present, which should worry anybody and everybody, but there are worse options."

Michael agreed with a nod. "Mrs. Lambert may raise concerns in certain ways, but at least she is safe."

"Unless she is talking of tea, and then we are all doomed." Charlotte looked up at him with a quick smile, so like their former ease he ached for it.

But they could not go back. Only forward.

Michael sipped his lemonade cautiously. Charlotte could make the first move here, if she thought to do so. If he knew her as he thought he did, she would leap at the chance.

"I've broken with Jonathan Riley."

That was not the opening he had anticipated, and he did not have to pretend at choking on his beverage. "Oh, no," he said with as much feeling as he could muster, shaking his head and adopting a sympathetic expression. "Charlotte, I am so sorry."

She lifted her chin, gloriously steady in this moment. "Don't be. I found I was wasting both of our time, and it is far better this way."

Was it, now?

Marvelous.

Michael shook his head as if in despair. "You liked him so much. You ought to take time to heal."

Charlotte's brow creased a little. "I don't need to."

He pretended not to hear and only exhaled a heavy sigh. "The loss will be painful, I know. You must be feeling it keenly; I can't imagine how you're facing any of us with that on your heart."

"What?" Charlotte bleated, utterly lost now. "No, Michael, I'm fine."

He put a hand on her arm, squeezing gently and looking at her as though she would break before his very eyes. "Don't be brave, Charlotte. It's better to mourn these things."

"Mourn what?" she demanded with an edge of irritation to her voice. "I'm the one who ended things."

"Nevertheless…"

"Mr. Sandford, there is a message for you, sir."

Perfect timing.

Michael turned to the footman with wide eyes. "A message? Of what sort?"

The footman had clearly been thinking about this, for his expression did not change. "The rider did not say, sir, only that it was urgent."

Michael sighed and gave Charlotte a pitying look. "Excuse me, will you?"

Her brow snapped down. "Michael, don't you…"

But he was already walking away, laughing to himself, the footman on his heels. "Sir, if I lose my position…"

"You won't, I promise," Michael assured him. "In fact, I'll see to it you get a bonus."

"Thank you, sir."

They rounded the stairs to return to the house, and Charlotte had watched them the entire time, her eyes narrowed now as she followed his progress.

Charlotte had discovered feelings for him. Just how deep those feelings were and what she wished to do about them remained to be seen. But it was clear that what they had been was not enough, and their individual courtships could not stand, and had not done so.

Still, it was difficult to keep from reveling in the feeling of victory that swirled about his head. He wanted to give her a signal, some hint that he knew what she was trying to do but wasn't going to carve out a time for her to do it.

Oh, why not?

He flicked a devious smile at her, and saw her jaw slacken as she gaped. He would be in for it now.

He could not wait.

Whatever game Michael was playing, she needed to end it, and end it now.

If she didn't love the man to bloody distraction, she might have given up by this point, thinking that each interruption to her attempts might be a sign she should not do so. She might have eventually considered going back to Jonathan and telling him that she had been premature in ending his expectations. That conversation had been simple enough, rather uncomplicated, all things considered, and had actually felt like a relief to have over.

They might not have been as compatible as she had hoped at the start, and certainly weren't as compatible as she and Michael would have been, but that wasn't insurmountable. She could go back to that simplicity.

If she wasn't desperate to tell Michael how she loved him, she might have even thought that today, had he not smirked like that.

But now, she had none of those thoughts. Blasted brute was intentionally drawing this out for her, and he was enjoying every moment. Did that mean he knew she loved him? Did that mean he still loved her? The possibilities were many, and her options were few.

She was not one to give up, but there was only so much she could take. The only thing she really wished to do at this moment was disappoint Michael's game, whatever it was. The trouble was that disappointing his game would also be disappointing the thing she wanted most, and she had never been particularly good at sacrificing her own wishes.

Downing her present glass of lemonade, she turned to face the nearest hedge and growled in frustration in as muted a way as she could while still being true to her feelings.

It was an odd, strained sort of sound, and her face buzzed because of it.

She rubbed at her cheek, frowning. "Hopeless," she hissed.

"Likely, but I wouldn't give up just yet."

Unaware she had been heard, Charlotte turned in surprise to see Hugh Sterling standing beside the same hedge, peering into his glass with what appeared to be a passing interest.

"Oh no?" she asked, not taking care to temper her tone. "Why not?"

"Because the man is beyond besotted still, and he won't be happy with anyone else." He shrugged and sipped his drink, not looking at her. "Up to you, though."

Charlotte blinked at his words, feeling as though her mind were skipping rocks. "He... you... he loves me?"

Hugh glanced at her slyly and nodded. "Oh, yes. He made a valiant effort not to, I'll grant him that, but it was no use."

She could barely swallow for the pressure of joy filling her. "Are you sure?" she whispered.

"Quite." He turned to face her, leaning his shoulder against the hedge and meeting her eyes head on. "I've seen the difference, Charlotte. He's yours, if you'll take him."

A breathless laugh galloped from her chest, and she grinned wildly, then tilted her head as she considered the man before her. "I don't think you're the devil incarnate after all, Hugh Sterling. What a pleasant surprise."

His smile was warm and attractive, which she would never have suspected of him. "Does that mean you think my wife has made a good match?"

Charlotte gave the man a dubious look. "Don't push your luck."

"Fair enough." He toasted her and pointed towards the house. "Off you go, then."

She winked and dashed off to the house like a shot, not caring if any of the guests or her family saw her do so. Ladylike behavior be damned, her family's reputation be tossed.

Charlotte Wright was getting the man she loved, and she was getting him now.

"Michael!" she bellowed as soon as she entered the house, slowing to a brisk walk, her strides determined. "Michael, you show yourself this minute, or else..."

"What?" he prodded, ambling towards her from the direction of the kitchen. "Or else what?"

It was a strange sensation, her heart sinking and soaring at the same time. Her irritation with him mingling with her longing for him. Her ire mingling with her affection.

What a tumultuous future could be before them.

Setting her jaw, she moved to him and grabbed his arm, yanking hard. "Come here."

"Ow!" he protested, though she swore he laughed as well. "I can walk, Charlotte."

"I don't trust you for a minute," she snapped as she continued to drag him forward. "Not a single minute, and I have had enough."

"So I see."

She ignored the note of humor in his tone and pulled him to the only ground in this house where she felt she could do this moment justice.

Her own parlor. Where endless Spinster columns had been written, plots had been hatched, and hundreds of conversations with this very man had taken place. This was her fortress, and he was her captive.

If she could get the words out.

She released his arm as they entered the room, turning to close the door firmly.

"I take it you wanted to see me," Michael said with a laugh.

She could hear him moving about the room, but she kept her face to the door just a moment longer, breathing slowly and praying she could get through this.

With a final exhale, she turned to face him, surprised to see him leaning against the back of the sofa and staring at her with a crooked smile. Waiting.

"What?" she asked, disarmed by it.

"Nothing," he replied, shrugging a shoulder. "Go on."

She hesitated, unsettled and more than a little wary. "Michael…"

He said nothing, that maddening smile remaining on his lips. His chin lowered just a touch, and a certain light in his eyes caught fire. Daring her to go on.

Oh, he was a clever wretch, and now she was just as trapped.

Perfect.

Without a single word of her practiced speech in her mind,

Charlotte opened her mouth. "I have been blind, Michael. Nearly every day of my life, I have been blind and foolish and utterly stupid. I always thought that I needed a sweeping romantic story for the ages, one that broke all constraints and sent us to our knees with longing for each other, whoever he would be, and that nothing else would do. I was waiting for that storm to find me, expecting to be knocked aside and forever changed. What I did not, and could not, expect was that something quite different lay in store for me."

Michael's smile remained, but his eyes had darkened, and his attention seemed more pronounced. More dangerous.

More intense.

"Something deeper," Charlotte went on, her entire frame pulsing in time with her heart, "and something softer. Something gradual, and ever-increasing. Something that had always been there, and always will be. Something so intertwined with everything I am and everything I hope to be that I didn't even recognize that it was there until it was..." She swallowed hard, took a deep breath, and lowered herself to her knees.

Michael's smile faded and his eyes widened, the heat still swirling there.

"But it still brings me to my knees all the same," Charlotte whispered. "And the longing I have felt these past few weeks surpasses anything I ever thought I would feel. Because I've found the love I've always sought, Michael. And it's..."

A knock at the door sounded, bringing Michael's eyes to it, and curling Charlotte's rising tide of passion into a wave of unfettered temper.

"So help me," she barked towards the door, "if there is one more interruption of this particular conversation, I will kill the interrupter with my bare hands!"

Silence met her threat, and shuffling steps retreated quickly.

Charlotte wet her lips, and returned her attention to Michael, who was now trying not to laugh and giving her an almost adoring look that made her hope.

"Get up, Charlotte."

Perhaps not.

"But..." she protested, then stopped herself and looked at the ground, gathering herself, "I need to have this moment."

"I'll give you the moment, but please, get up."

She shook her head firmly. "I need to be submissive. I need to prove my point."

"For the love of God, woman, you can prove your point standing on your own two feet, submissiveness be damned."

Charlotte looked up at him, amusement rising, his expression of exasperation utterly perfect for this moment. "You don't think it suits?"

His smile spread with glorious slowness. "I don't think it should have any part of you, and I think I know you well enough now to say so."

She shrugged, pushing to her feet, and sobering as she did so.

There was only one thing left to say, really, and perhaps she should have started with it.

Steeling herself, she met his eyes, willing her trembling fingers to still before her. "I'm in love with you, Michael," she admitted with a raw honesty that stole her own breath from her. "Only you. Forever you. And I don't know how to apologize for making you wait all this time."

Michael's chest moved on a slow exhale, and he pushed off of his perch on the sofa, coming towards her without any haste. Without a word, he slid his hands on either side of her face and touched his lips to hers, his thumbs gently stroking against her cheeks, his fingers tilting her face just enough to perfect the angle between them. Again and again, his lips took hers, molded with hers, each kiss a slow and thorough waltz between them, one that wrung every ounce of her sanity, sense, and thought from her.

She whimpered against this dismantling, delicious, fervent barrage of his lips, clinging to his waistcoat as though he were the only thing that kept her from drowning in this. She arched against him, reaching for him in the only way the moment allowed.

His kisses gentled, became feather-light and grazing. "I don't need an apology," he murmured as his lips brushed against her tender skin. "I don't *want* an apology." He exhaled shortly and kissed her again, this time lingering in a way that made her knees shake. "I want *you.*"

Charlotte sighed, curling against him and pressing her face into his chest as she trembled. "You have me. I swear on my life, you have me."

Michael chuckled and pressed his lips against her hair, wrapping his arms around her, running his fingers up and down her back in a soothing, tempting pattern. "Don't swear, my love. On your life or anyone else's. It's not necessary."

"I feel as though I've cheated you," Charlotte told him, raising her head and sliding her hands up to link behind his neck. "I've been dying for love of you for weeks, ever since I thought you went to Diana's family, and it's just…"

"When was I supposed to have done that?" he interrupted, looking down at her in surprise.

She gave him a wry look. "Were you not in Derbyshire recently? On private business?"

Realization dawned, and he laughed softly, touching his brow to hers. "Ah, the rumor mill ran along, did it? I was in Derbyshire on private business, yes. Purchasing a horse from a private breeder for Eliza's birthday."

"You made a fuss to Emma Partlowe about secretly purchasing a horse?" Charlotte retorted, too blissfully content to be as outraged as she ought to have been. "What is wrong with you? I thought I had broken my heart!"

Michael pulled back and ran his thumb along her lips, wringing a shiver from her. "Are you telling me I nearly lost my kingdom for a horse?"

Charlotte's ticklish desire abated in the face of the droll remark, and she raised a dubious brow, though her toes still curled at his attentions. "When you are through being quite pleased with yourself, I should like to finish what I was saying."

Nodding sagely, Michael raised his finger from her lips, held it in the air in a pause, then latched his hands around her again. "All right, I am finished. Please, continue."

"Idiot," she whispered fondly, unable to keep from smiling as she ran her fingers through his hair. He seemed to ripple in her hold as she did so, which made her continue the motion. "Haven't I cheated you, love? You've loved me for so long, while I have barely become aware of it."

He pulled one of her hands from his neck and kissed the palm gently, pressing it against his heart. "Never. Do you hear me? Never think I have been cheated. Never compare our experiences. Just love me."

"I do." She raised on her toes and kissed him softly, praying he might know just how much.

"Charlotte," he moaned, holding her close and touching his lips to her brow, "am I dreaming this?"

She smiled at his sweet question. "Probably."

He snickered, the sound reverberating through her. "I knew it. Do I have to wake?"

"I don't think so." She raised her head and winked at him. "I'm rather enjoying your dream."

He smiled at her, gently stroking her cheek again. "I always knew if I stayed by you, one day you'd see me."

Charlotte frowned in surprise. "What are you talking about? I always saw you."

"No, sweetheart, you didn't." He shook his head, then cupped her cheek. "I was there, but you didn't see me. I knew that, and I was fine with that. You knew I was there, knew I would be there, and that was enough. Until it wasn't. I thought if I was the last man standing, finally you would see..."

"You wanted to be the last resort?" she asked, her heart breaking at the thought.

"No. I wanted to be your only resort."

She took a breath, rubbing her thumbs along the back of his hands. "I don't understand."

He paused, wetting his lips. "I've known how I feel about you for years. I always knew that you were the one for me. I just needed you to realize that, as well. I needed you to see that you were in love with me."

Charlotte cocked her head at that. "But what if I didn't?"

Michael grinned, as only Michael could. "Then I was going to kidnap you and take you to Gretna Green."

She barked a laugh. "My family would never have forgiven you for that."

"It was your father's suggestion," he informed her with a smirk. "And your brother offered the carriage."

Her eyes narrowed. "And my mother?"

"She told me how to get in."

Charlotte shook her head, grinning at her family's antics. "When the devil was all this?"

He shrugged as his fingers slid down to toy with hers. "Five years ago, perhaps. They remind me of it annually."

That long? Her family had known that long? How had she missed it?

"But you didn't kidnap me," she pointed out as gently as possible. "You took up with Diana."

"I tried to," he corrected, bringing their joint hands up to his heart again. "Could have. Would have. Poor Diana, I would have made her a pitiful husband."

Charlotte leaned forward until their noses brushed. "You'd have been a marvelous husband to her."

He smiled sadly, kissing her once. "No, my love, I would have known every moment of the rest of my life that I had made a mistake and ruined more lives than my own." Again, very softly, he kissed her, taking great care to do so. "It's only you for me, Charlotte Geneva Wright, and a moment ago, it sounded like you said it is only me for you."

She made a derisive face and scoffed. "I didn't say that. I said I adored you to the core, that I've loved you longer than I can comprehend, deeper than I can feel, and more completely than the soul can attest. It's far more poetic than saying there is only you for me."

"It's certainly a *longer* statement..." he admitted, though his hold on her tightened.

"A good vocabulary is vital to a lady," she insisted.

"So is concision."

Charlotte huffed in disappointment. "You have no appreciation for poetry."

Michael shrugged nonchalantly. "Never have. Simplicity works best for me."

"Cretin," she grumbled, folding her arms about his neck and

attempting to bring them to a more even level. "Then try this and see if the clarity suits you: I want you. No other. Ever. Better?"

He grinned slowly and leaned closer, his lips hovering just above hers. "Much."

She closed the distance between them, then kissed the man until both of them were burning and senseless, at which time they returned to the party and made a rather long-awaited announcement that surprised absolutely no one.

Epilogue

Ah, bachelors. So many to choose from, yet so few who are worth choosing. Allow those of us who have seen a fair few, who have done our research, and who know a thing or two, to help you dear girls choose. Do choose wisely from our selection, won't you?

-*The Spinster Chronicles, 25 February 1819*

"Oh, no... Not again."

Jonathan Riley looked up from his quiet drink at the club and glanced over at the man who had spoken. There weren't many men sitting about at the moment, and the ones that were sat far enough apart that conversation wasn't required. Yet an exclamation in a mostly empty room piqued his curiosity, and he opted to go against his natural reserve.

"Something wrong?"

The dark eyes of Tyrone Demaris lifted from the news sheet he had been reading and met his. "I should bloody well say so."

Jonathan nodded. "Sorry to hear that."

Demaris snorted loudly. "You should be. It will affect you, too."

That was not what he had expected, and Jonathan reared back in his seat a little. "Me? What in the world does anything have to do with me at all?"

"Oh, a great deal, you will find, and you will find it very shortly." Demaris pushed out of his chair and strode over to him with the news sheet in his hand. He slapped it on the table in front of Jonathan, a finger jabbing at the paper. "You've made the Best Bachelors list,

Riley. My felicitations."

"What?" Jonathan demanded, glancing down at the paper.

The Spinster Chronicles.

Now he knew this had to be a lie. His courtship with Charlotte Wright had ended rather abruptly not long ago, but without any malice. She loved someone else, she'd told him, or else she'd have been perfectly happy to continue on with him, perhaps even to marriage.

That was the first time the word marriage had been used between them, but he'd have gotten there eventually.

He couldn't be upset about being released from a courtship because she loved someone else, and he respected Charlotte enough to be happy for her. He would lie if he said he was not disappointed, but he was not distraught, either.

To be perfectly frank, he'd miss the prospect of Charlotte's fortune almost as much as the pleasure of her person. He was no fortune hunter, but it was no secret that her fortune would have significantly improved his plans. He did not need to marry a fortune, but it would open several doors. More than that, he had liked Charlotte genuinely. Could have loved her.

He hadn't expected to.

He never expected love.

Still, there was no possibility that the Spinsters would have included him in their Best Bachelors article after all that.

But it was there, plain as day, and specific details of his life and prospects included with his name.

"Bloody hell," he hissed, eyes widening.

"Quite." Demaris dropped himself into a chair at the table, shaking his head. "I was in this mess last year, and it upended my whole life in Society. I was so hoping they would skip me and leave me in peace. Alas…" He sputtered, pursing his lips.

"Why did they put me in here?" Jonathan demanded, looking at Demaris as though he would know. "Why?"

"Probably pitying you for that whole jilting business," another voice in the room announced blandly.

Jonathan looked around for the source, and Demaris only laughed. "It's not jilting if there's no understanding, Deaton."

Lord Deaton lowered the book before his face and gave them both a bemused look, his fair brows rising. "Think that if you like, but he'll still be the man Charlotte Wright almost accepted."

"She didn't!" Jonathan insisted. "I never asked."

"It doesn't matter," Deaton assured him in a flat tone. "That's the point. This is how they make up for it. They're trying to shove you in front of the other misses as a good prospect, because you were good enough for one of them. Almost."

Jonathan scowled and looked down at the paper, then smiled at what he read. "You're in here too, Deaton."

The man froze, his fair eyes going round. "The hell I am."

"Justin Gray, Lord Deaton," Jonathan read aloud. "Ten thousand a year, estate in Dorset, schooled at Cambridge, no gambling debts, no scandals, and a skilled horseman." He looked up at Deaton, almost smug. "Good for you, Deaton."

Lord Deaton muttered incoherently, scowling and slouching further into his seat.

"There was someone else from Dorset, wasn't there?" Demaris looked at Jonathan inquiringly. "Or am I wrong?"

Jonathan looked down. "Let's see... Frederick Perry; Lachlan MacDougal, Baron Halsey; Edmund Asheley... Ah. Benedict Sterling. A doctor." He glanced up at Deaton. "You know him?"

Deaton smirked at the question. "I do, as it happens. He'll be so pleased."

"As we all are," Demaris said, groaning a sigh. "What a right mess. My brother will lord about this for weeks."

"Poor you," Deaton told him without any hint of concern.

Demaris glared at him before looking up at the ceiling. "What do you think possessed the Spinsters, capital S needed now that all of them are married, to throw a bunch of bachelors to the wolves?"

"Boredom," Deaton suggested, flicking through his book. "Spite. Entertainment."

Jonathan rolled their eyes. "I doubt any of that. It's probably just indulging what everybody presumed they would do from the beginning, which was make matches they approved of."

Deaton looked at him wryly. "You know that Charlotte Wright is the one who puts this out, right?"

"Charlotte Sandford, thank you very much," Demaris pointed out, wagging his finger in the air. "I was there, I saw it happen."

"Shut up, Demaris," Deaton said simply.

Demaris chuckled at that and saluted the man. "Aye, sir."

Lord Deaton snapped his book shut and sat forward in his chair. "I don't like this. I don't like any of it, and I'd prefer that my life, my prospects, and my interests remain my own business. I am sure the rest of you feel the same. So, what do we do about it?"

"Do?" Jonathan repeated. "What do you mean?"

Deaton gestured as if it were obvious. "Do, Riley. We need to do something to combat this. Or end it. Something."

"Gents, I'm having a thought…"

Jonathan and Deaton looked over at Demaris, his slow words both worrying and encouraging.

He grinned at them both, folding his arms. "I'm having a very, very interesting thought."

Coming Soon

Fortune
FAVORS THE
Sparrow

Agents of the Convent
Book One

by

REBECCA CONNOLLY

Also from Phase Publishing

Tiffany Dominguez:
The Eidolon

Emily Daniels:
Devlin's Daughter

Lucia's Lament

A Song for a Soldier

Grace Donovan:
Saint's Ride

Laura Beers:
Saving Shadow

A Peculiar Courtship

To Love a Spy

Ferrell Hornsby:
If We're Breathing, We're Serving